Blind Beauty
K. M. Peyton

To the memory of dear Wise Words,
his human friends,
and Philippa in Ireland

Scholastic Children's Books
An imprint of Scholastic Ltd
Euston House, 24 Eversholt Street
London, NW1 1DB, UK
Registered office: Westfield Road, Southam, Warwickshire, CV47 0RA
SCHOLASTIC and associated logos are trademarks and/or registered
trademarks of Scholastic Inc.

First published in the UK by Scholastic Ltd, 1999
This edition published in the UK by Scholastic Ltd, 2011

Text copyright © K M Peyton, 1999

The right of K M Peyton to be identified as the author
of this work has been asserted by her.

ISBN 978 1 407 12430 8

Printed in the UK by CPI Bookmarque, Croydon, Surrey.
Papers used by Scholastic Children's Books are made
from wood grown in sustainable forests.

1 3 5 7 9 10 8 6 4 2

www.scholastic.co.uk/zone

Blind Beauty

Contents

Part One

Part Two

Part One

1

Shiner

The foal was born without eyes. Just empty sockets.

When Declan cleared the membrane and saw what had happened he let out a wail which so startled the mare that she staggered to get up.

Declan leapt to her head.

"My poor old baby! Lie still, you stupid old cow! What have you done, you stupid girl?"

"It's because she's so old. Twenty-three! I told you it would kill her," said his wife Myra. "This is worse. Worse than killing her. I'll ring the veterinary."

"What for?"

"To lay it to sleep, of course."

"No. You'll not do that."

"What do you mean, no?"

"Give us time. There's no hurry. Let the mare settle."

"It's best at once. For the mare."

"Not for me though," Declan said. "It's not best for me. Don't ring yet."

Word soon went round that crazy Declan insisted on keeping his blind foal. It was a filly and he wanted to keep the mare's famous bloodline going, his last chance to make a fortune. They all thought he was mad.

He had inherited the mare from an uncle, when the mare was twenty years old and had been barren for three years. She was going to be put down. Declan had tried for three more years to get her into foal and had at last succeeded. Now this!

When he had made the mare and foal comfortable and got the foal suckling, he went indoors and cried. He was only twenty-one, after all. His wife Myra was twenty and their little girl, Tessa, four years old. Tessa came and sat on his knee.

"Daddy crying," she said in amazement. She traced the tears flowing copiously out of his bright blue eyes with a pudgy, dirty finger. She was used to laughter, anger, gloom and inebriation, but not grief.

"Why?"

"Daddy's new baby's got no eyes. That's why he's crying."

"My teddy bear got no eyes."

"He's got you to look after him."

"I'll look after Daddy's baby too."

"You do that," said Daddy. "You look after my baby for me."

Tessa was used to horses, seeing legs alongside and bellies overhead like great brown clouds. Declan looked after horses for Mr O'Shea. Only the old brown mare was his own. She had bred twelve good winners and no duds and was much respected. She was called Betty but her real name was Moonshine Fields.

Tessa called the blind foal Shiner. She looked after her, as promised.

When the foal was lying down Tessa went and laid beside her. She could put her fat fist into the eye sockets, it fitted exactly. The foal seemed to like the warm feel of it, and lay still. If she was a cat she would have purred. Not having any eyes did not seem to affect her much. She didn't bump into things. "She's got another sense, to make up for it. In her whiskers," Declan said. "See how she holds her head. And her ears stand up like a hare's. Nature knows what she's about."

Nature decreed that Tessa and Shiner bonded. Tessa could do anything with Shiner, yet with other people Shiner turned away. Tessa could fetch her in from the field. She went out with a halter and Shiner put her head low so that Tessa could put it on. She stood patiently while Tessa got one ear caught up, or the rope twisted, or put it on back to front. Then she would follow the child's stumbling footsteps back to the farm, trusting the way.

Sometimes it was a long way. The horses' field ran down to the shore a mile from the house. When the mares and their foals were sated with grazing they would go and pick along the sandy beach to explore the seawrack and driftwood, the old plastic bottles and flotsam that had washed in from the Atlantic. A wide river came inland there, winding past the farm. Herons stood patiently on the edge of the mud when the tide went out, and the gulls wheeled and bickered overhead when the fishing-boats came in. To Tessa it was a sea of grass which she could barely see over, and a blue heaven. She could smell the seashore, tell the direction of the river by the tonk-tonk of the boat

5

engines and the screams of the gulls. Shiner would come to her, sensing her golden head moving through the grass. Taller and taller Shiner grew on the good grass, but her eyeless head nosed ever more gently at Tessa, a flutter of welcome moving in her nostrils.

She was a bay with no white on her. She was a fine filly, they all said, shaking their heads. The old mare, Moonshine Fields, died that winter, and Declan was proud that he had kept the filly because, blind or not, she was going to breed him valuable foals.

He had no money to pay for a good sire. He spent his money on betting and drink and Tessa grew up with the noise of bitter argument accompanying her home life. She spent all her time with Shiner because Shiner loved her and she loved Shiner. There was little love at home. She would lie in the stable with Shiner in the straw and listen to the Irish rain beating on the tin roof. She would lay her head on Shiner's flank and feel secure and loved.

"The child's more horse than human," they said.

"I love you, Shiner," Tessa said.

But one day, after more noise than usual, Myra came storming into the stable and wrenched Tessa from Shiner's side.

"We're going," she said. "I can't stand any more."

"Going where?"

"We're going to my auntie in Liverpool, that's where."

Tessa never saw Shiner again. She cried herself sick and in Liverpool grew thin and angry. At school she would not speak.

The auntie Mabel was kind, but Tessa did not respond. She would sit staring out of the window, silent, seeing nothing. Auntie Mabel and Myra took her to watch the Grand National but when she saw the horses she cried, and that night she cried herself to sleep.

But later her mother came to her and said, "We've come into a bit of luck, Tessa-girl. Keep your fingers crossed for me. You could well have horses again."

Myra had been working as a barmaid and met a man called Maurice. Maurice took Myra out in his Mercedes and Tessa came too.

"Call me Uncle Maurice," he said to Tessa.

Tessa looked up and met the eyes of the man who had his arm round her mother. She stared. The eyes had a peculiar grip, piercing and cruel. It was instant hate on both sides.

Tessa sat in front because she got sick in cars, and Uncle Maurice turned his head sideways over Tessa to take notice of her mother. He smelled like a woman, Tessa noticed, nothing like her father. Her father smelled of horses and leather and sweat.

A hedgehog was crossing the road in front of them. Uncle Maurice altered course very slightly to run it over. Tessa cried out. She jumped round in her seat and saw it, squashed, through the back window.

"You pig! You pig!" she cried out.

"Tessa!" Myra was shocked. She hadn't seen. Declan would never do a thing like that.

But Uncle Maurice only laughed.

2
Shiner's Foal

*S*hiner walked round and round her box, stopping every so often to paw the ground. The straw was all over the place.

Declan leaned over the door talking to her all the time.

"You don't know what's happening to you, do you, my darling? Well, it's no different if you've got eyes to see or if you haven't. None of you mares knows what's happening the first time you foal – why should you? There's none of these classes for you, that tell you all about it – not like there is for the ladies. You're on your own in this, my darling, but your Declan won't leave you, don't you worry. You'll be all right."

On and on he talked, to soothe her with his familiar voice. It didn't matter about the words being rubbish. The tone was what mattered. Although Tessa had been gone three years, she was the one who could have calmed Shiner. She was the one who should have been doing this, little as she was. Well, not so little now. She would be eight by now, quite a young lady. There had been magic between her and the filly. That bitch Myra had never told him where she was, not since Liverpool. Not that he wanted to see Myra again, not ever again.

"But my little Tessa, my little golden girl, I'd give everything I have to see her again, even you, Shiner. Well, perhaps. I'm not sure about that, Shiner, because what else have I got in this life save you, my darling, and you are my really own, my Shiner, my dear mare, my sweetheart."

It took a long time. A dreadful time. She couldn't see the foal and didn't know what it was, and when it was delivered she got up and rampaged round her box, dripping sweat and whinnying. Declan had to lie over the foal and protect it and got badly kicked for his pains. Seizing an opportunity, he managed to gather it up bodily and get it into a corner. He stood in front of it and fended Shiner off with slaps whenever she crashed near. There was no chance of giving it a suckle, poor little devil. And from what he could see of it in the dark – he couldn't reach his torch and they had never had the electricity – it was a strange, pale little thing with ears like a donkey's. It wasn't big and strong. It was weak, but it wasn't wimpy, trying to demand its suckle and getting knocked for six for its pains. And trying again.

"God help us!" prayed Declan.

The sweat poured off his back like it poured off the mare's. It was two o'clock in the morning and he was on his own with no one to help him. What a fool he was not to have persuaded Paddy down to see it out with him! He hadn't guessed at this happening. He had thought it would be easy like it nearly always was, and if it wasn't he was near enough to a phone for the veterinary. But there was no leaving the stable, not now.

It was a long night. Gradually, as dawn came, Shiner began to calm down, but she wouldn't accept the foal's suckling. She stood shivering and kicking. When at last young Liam came into the yard to get his car to go to work Declan was able to shout out, and Liam fetched a rug and rang Paddy to come down quick, and when Paddy came he held the mare while Declan got the foal to suckle. At last! Declan was flaked out.

But later, when the sun came up, he was able to put mare and foal in the little field Shiner knew, and she fell to grazing as if she had been starved a week. The foal galloped and fell over. Got up, bucked and reared and fell over again. Declan leaned over the gate, watching.

He was relieved it was all over, and should have felt proud and pleased. But the foal! It was all wrong – puny, ugly, long in the back, washy-coloured. The only good thing about it was that it was a colt. But a poor consolation for his dreams. Declan felt like crying. Shiner was all he had, and her foals were to be his fortune. But this – this would be laughed out of any sale-ring.

It tried to gallop and went down again. Luckily the grass was thick and the ground soft with rain. By the shape of it, you wondered it could think of galloping at all. It wasn't having any success. But still it tried.

The only thing you could say about the foal – it had guts.

Declan tried hard to console himself with this thought as he turned away wearily to find himself some breakfast.

3
Tessa Goes Home

*T*essa sat in the train and watched the countryside flicking past, seeing nothing, not even where to jump the hedges and fences if you were on a horse. Maurice had refused to send the car for her.

"If your school can't put up with you, we're in no hurry to see you down here."

Myra had never learned to drive, of course, even though there were three cars in the garage. She had learned other things – how to be smart, for example, in all its senses – but not how to handle a car, nor her daughter. They had sent Tessa away to boarding school at the age of eight, to try and "give themselves a chance", as they put it. She had been sent home by two of the schools, and now by the third. Excluded, they said. This time for smoking. "Everyone smokes at twelve," Tessa said carelessly. "Insolence and general unpleasantness," the headmistress added. "We have to consider the other girls." Tessa was sorry to lose the other girls, the ones the school thought she was corrupting. There were three of them – the first time in her life she had made any friends. She knew now that she wouldn't see them again.

Who would she see?

Maurice had a son of eighteen called Greevy (or Gravy, or Greasy, to Tessa) but he was as foul as his father. Luckily he too was away at boarding school and not underfoot often. Her best friends were Betty the cleaning girl and George the gardener. George was old and deaf, and Betty stupid. Betty had taught Tessa to smoke in the cupboard under the stairs. But Mrs Tims the housekeeper had found them. Mrs Tims was horrible, but didn't report the news because she knew Betty would be dismissed and she would be lucky to get another cleaning girl within six months. Nobody much wanted to work at Goldlands.

Tessa hated Goldlands. She hated Maurice and she hated Myra now that Maurice had made her smart. Besides hating Maurice she was frightened of him and thought Myra was too. She was frightened of going home and frightened of what was going to happen to her. But when Tessa was frightened she stuck her chin out and faced it head on. She would kill Maurice! She thought of ways of doing it as the train chattered on its way: a carving knife (too messy); pushing him in front of his racehorses on the gallops (nice, as long as the horses weren't hurt); running him over in the drive (she had taught herself to drive the smallest of the three cars when everybody was out). Maurice kept the keys hanging in the kitchen, and never knew. She had practised all round the drives and lawns, and George had kept mum and mowed over her tyre-marks afterwards.

She could poison him perhaps – put cyanide in his whisky, save it was hard to buy (she had tried the first time she came on

12

holiday from boarding school), or perhaps slowly with arsenic, like poisoners in Agatha Christie. She would like him to suffer first, and know with his dying breath that it was she who had killed him. She would like to see a look of craven defeat in his staring eyes. He had strange eyes, a way of looking that went right through you. Tessa, who could insolently hold the gaze of school teachers longer than they could endure, could not hold Maurice's gaze. It made her go funny. Sick. She knew that her mother had married him for his money. But he certainly hadn't made her happy, Tessa could tell. She had been much happier with Declan, when they hadn't been fighting. In between the fighting there had been lots of laughter. Tessa hadn't heard her mother laugh for a long time now.

So going home was not anything to look forward to. Cruelly, just as after four years she had got to quite like boarding school, she was now thrown out of it. The other times she had been pleased. But this time she wasn't. She couldn't see any future for herself at all. Even going back to Declan, which was her dream, was now impossible, for Declan had moved on and no one knew where he was.

If Tessa had been the crying sort, she would have cried. But self-pity was not one of Tessa's habits. She clawed herself out of trouble as best she could and tossed past failures aside. If she had to live at horrible Goldlands, so be it. But she would find her own way to win.

To her surprise, Myra had come to meet her, sitting in the car with George. Myra hugged her and kissed her and said in the same breath, "Oh Tessa, what have you done, getting yourself thrown out again? We'll never get you into another school now!"

"I don't mind."

"You're only twelve. It's not like you can leave!"

"If nobody'll have me, I've no choice, have I? I don't mind."

"Well, you wouldn't." Myra's voice trembled. "I can tell you someone who does."

Tessa didn't answer. She was even more angry now, seeing the woman that had once been her cheerful feckless mother tied up in a tight skirt and satin blouse and her hair all highlighted, with the lines of worry (or fear?) on her face growing deeper by the month. What was Maurice doing to her?

"Why don't you leave him?"

"What do you mean?"

"You look so miserable. Not like you did once."

Myra looked shocked. "Do I? Leave him? Don't be so silly! What a thing to say!"

Maurice had made her stupid too. He was always doing her down, sapping her confidence. Once she had overflowed with confidence. One thing Tessa knew, Maurice wasn't going to change *her*.

She felt sick, heading for Goldlands. It was May and the hedges were bright with flowers, the white hawthorn blossom just beginning to break. After a shower of rain, its pungent scent filled the lanes. Over the downs a blue-black cloud lay as if to part the shining grass from the blue sky above. White cumulus sailed along before the wind, high and ever-changing. Weather delighted Tessa, even rain and snow. There were times, if you were really down, you could get put right by enjoying the weather: the wind and the wildness – know that there was life beyond your own bad spot. She seemed to have had a lot of bad spots in her life.

"Is he home?"

"No. Not till tonight. He's gone racing."

Myra had always loved racing.

"Why didn't you go?"

"He didn't ask me, darling. Besides, you were coming."

But Tessa knew he never took her. And if he had asked her, Myra would have gone, whether Tessa was coming or not. Tessa was used to knowing things that were never actually said.

"I don't know why he goes; it never seems to make him happy," Tessa said. She could still remember whooping times with Declan at the races, when he had tossed her in the air with joy when the right horse won. Maurice always seemed to have a face like thunder when he went racing.

"He has to win," Myra said. "He races not because he loves the horses, but to win. To make money."

"How boring," Tessa said in her put-down way.

Myra tossed her coiffed head in annoyance but said nothing. Perhaps she too remembered what fun it had been with Declan.

Maurice made a lot of money and liked it to be noticed. His cars had swanky number-plates and were white with red leather interiors, and had tinted windows as if he were a pop star. And Goldlands . . . Tessa looked with loathing as the car left the lane and turned in at the electronic entrance gates. Such grandeur! A golden stone wall replaced the cheerful hedge, as expensive a wall as ever was built – for what? Tessa wondered. To impress the neighbours? The driveway went over a slight rise, with mown grass on either side, and over the rise one came upon the front of a large, brash modern house. Behind the house the land fell away into a wide valley, and the view from the back was magnificent – of rolling downs and woods. Tessa knew that Maurice had bought the land from a bankrupt farmer, and owned the whole valley. Much of the farmland was tenanted out and Maurice had no power to evict his tenants, but how much they welcomed their new owner Tessa did not know. From Betty's gossip, she knew that they thought him ignorant of farming and they feared for their good relations. Maurice Morrison-Pleydell was a developer and thought of land in terms of golf-courses, supermarket sites and holiday complexes – not a happy omen for the men whose lives were in his land. The former landowner had been an old farmer whose family had owned the place since Tudor times. He had rashly speculated and lost all he owned in the Lloyds disaster. His home, known as the Home Farm, lay abandoned behind a screen of trees some half a mile from Goldlands, the barns and milking parlours now deserted and the house empty. Maurice left it empty – "I don't want neighbours as close as that" – and didn't care about the lovely old house rotting away. He didn't like old buildings.

Tessa's only consolation at Goldlands was playing in the old buildings, because they had the homely run-down feel of her old Irish home. She had asked for a pony to keep there, but Maurice had refused. Who was going to look after it when she was at school? Myra offered gladly but Maurice said he didn't want his wife mucking out and smelling of manure.

"George could do it," Tessa said. "He wouldn't mind."

"I pay George to do the garden and drive the car, not to play about with pets."

"It would be something for her to do, dear. It's lonely up here for a child."

"She can use her bike if she wants to get around. What's wrong with a bike?"

"It's not like a pony. It's got no heart. Like you," Tessa muttered under her breath.

"What did you say?"

"I said a bike's got no heart," Tessa said loudly in the stupid-didn't-you-hear-me-first-time? voice that got her into trouble at school.

"Don't you use that tone of voice to me." Low and menacing.

"What tone of voice?" Careless and insolent.

"You know very well what I mean. Get out of my sight. Go."

"But she's eating her dinner!" Myra wailed.

"Go," said Maurice, and she went. She slammed the door hard. If Maurice called her back she didn't hear.

Once she said, "If you hit me I'll go to the police."

He said, "You go to the police and they will call in the social services. I'd think again if I were you."

But he didn't hit her. She knew he would like to sometimes. She would like to hit him, beat him with tight fists, smash his face until he cried out. He was so cool. He never lost his temper. Just looked at her.

Who was he anyway? she wondered. He didn't have a pigeon-hole she could slot him into. Very rich, but not well-educated, as far as she could tell. His friends gave no clue – all sorts – racing men, lawyers, land agents, grocers, golfers . . . they came for dinner parties sometimes with their hard-faced wives. Caterers would come in to do the cooking. Myra would do herself up to the nines and drink a lot so that she was happy and vivacious, but Tessa knew that she wasn't happy underneath. It was all a sham. She was nervous of them and had to put on a front. She had never had to put on a front with old Paddy and Liam and Declan's mate Harry and his crazy wife Sheila, who had all shrieked with laughter in the kitchen. If it wasn't a party, Maurice didn't seem to have any friends. Nobody ever dropped in for a chat. He never brought just a couple home, for fun, or a man friend for a drink like Declan used to. All the people who came to dinner parties were to do with his making money.

"Try not to annoy him, Tessa," Myra said despairingly as the car swept up the drive. "It won't do you any good."

But she enjoyed annoying him. It was one of her few pleasures in life.

18

"He'll be back for supper. It's all right now."

Tessa noted that Myra used "all right" for Maurice not being there. It came to her lips quite naturally. They both felt the same. Tessa was tempted to cry out, "Oh Mum, it's awful – you too!", put her head on her mother's smart bosom and cry her eyes out, but she had learned long ago not to give way to such weak feelings.

They got out of the car and George unloaded all her boarding school paraphernalia in two trunks.

"You can throw all that away, George," Tessa said with a grin. "I won't want it any more."

Tessa travelled light and had nothing she treasured amongst the clothes and rubbish.

Myra said, "Don't be ridiculous! Bring the stuff in, George. Really, Tessa!"

Tessa ran up to her room. It was enormous and had a wonderful view over the valley. Apart from that it was like a hotel room, tastefully furnished (by an interior designer from London), with pictures on the walls chosen by the designer. Tessa had printed nothing of herself on it at all. She had a den in one of the stables at the home farm, and her few dear possessions lived there – one of Moonshine Fields' shoes, her photos of Shiner, a jersey of Declan's she liked to wear – it was unravelling and came down to her knees, and an old book about the Grand National.

In her bedroom she flung herself on the bed and picked up the remote control for her television. She switched on a stupid

19

programme. She felt dead inside. She supposed she was frightened, but even that feeling was dull. She had learnt to block being frightened, having been lectured so many times at school. What could they do, after all? She had no idea what was going to happen next. At the moment she didn't care.

They didn't eat until Maurice came home, and she was starving. After a bit she went downstairs – a grand, stupid staircase that took up half the house, but was very impressive when you came in at the front door. She went into the kitchen where Mrs Tims was preparing the dinner. Mrs Tims was a sour old stick – nobody nice ever stayed.

She said, "You've done it again, then? Got yourself *expelled.*" She hissed the word.

"Excluded," Tessa corrected her. She went to the biscuit tin and helped herself. "What's for supper?"

"You'll see soon enough."

The kitchen was like a clinic, shining white and horribly clean. The floor was of white marble. Mrs Tims, an elderly and rather untidy person herself, looked out of place in the grandeur. She let it down quite badly. Tessa thought of remarking on this, but decided otherwise. She opened a cupboard, took out a bottle of cooking sherry, and fetched a glass.

"Don't you touch that, my girl!"

Tessa poured it out and drank it. It tasted horrible but felt nice. She wished she had a cigarette. She knew Mrs Tims couldn't stop her. Mrs Tims just set her face and pretended not to know.

"It's all right. I'm not going to get drunk."

"I don't know where you're heading for, my girl, but I can tell you one thing – it's trouble."

"I'm not your girl, thank God. And I don't mind trouble."

"You've got the devil in you, that's for sure."

"Better than boring old Jesus."

"That's a dreadful thing to say! That's shocking, that is."

Tess sighed heavily (rudely) and departed. She went into the living room – a vast, characterless place with balloon-like armchairs upholstered in cream dralon. Her mother was painting her nails, having spread out *The Sun* in case she dropped a spot. The furniture would be much improved with red spots, Tessa thought.

"I'm starving. How long have we got to wait?"

"Not long, probably; he's only got to come from Newbury."

"I hope he won, that's all."

But even when he won he only set his lips, no doubt wishing he had put on a bigger bet. Betting was a mug's game, Declan always said. If you won you wished you'd put on more, and if you lost you wished you hadn't put on any at all. It hadn't stopped him wasting his money, all the same.

"Don't play him up, Tessa. Just keep your head down. You know how it is."

"Yes, yes, yes. Just like you."

Myra bit her lip and did not reply. Tessa did not feel sorry for her, but despised her for what she had got herself into.

They heard the sound of a car on the gravel, the door

21

slamming, the key turning in the front door. Myra jumped up and the nail varnish bottle shot up in the air. Tessa lunged forward and caught it just in time. Myra went white.

"Oh Tessa, oh my God!" she moaned.

"Mum! Don't!" For a moment Tessa was anguished. As if it mattered! Her mother had turned into a stupid dummy.

"Don't bait him, Tessa, just don't."

Tessa was tempted again to give her mother a hug and say, "Of course I won't," to put her at ease, but it was no longer in her nature. It would have been a lie in any case.

The door opened and the two of them stood hastily to attention like children at school. Tessa felt the comparison and scowled. Sometimes her courage failed her.

"I see our delinquent daughter is back," Maurice greeted them.

The obvious reply – "I'm not your daughter" – sprang to Tessa's lips but she swallowed it back for her mother's sake.

"Did you have a good day, dear?" Myra gibbered.

"Not particularly. Sometimes I wonder about Raleigh's competence."

Raleigh was her stepfather's racehorse trainer. His stable was quite near, just over the downs opposite, and the horses could be seen at exercise in the valley early in the morning. It was a very smart stable, the most expensive in the land. (Of course.)

"Oh dear."

Myra knew everything about racing, but dared not venture the obvious opinion – that racing was a capricious sport and it didn't do to lay blame. She guessed that Maurice must be an extremely unpopular owner. Trainers liked owners who took the rough with the smooth, who praised and encouraged, and lost sportingly.

"No one has a better reputation," she said. "What more can you do?"

"What indeed?" said Maurice sarcastically.

"I'll tell Mrs Tims to serve the dinner."

Myra departed.

Maurice turned his gaze to Tessa and raked her up and down as if she were the disappointing horse. Straight to the knacker's! she thought. But it wasn't a joke. It was like being flayed alive.

"So? The bad penny's back again? You're getting to the end of the line, Tessa, aren't you? Pushing your luck?"

"What luck?" she said, trembling. "With you for a stepfather?"

"Believe me, you'll know it when the luck fails."

He turned his back and marched out of the room.

Tessa felt rage shake her. She wanted to spit at him. The pig! Luck! What luck had ever come her way? Losing her real father, getting him in exchange? Being given a home in his foul mansion? She'd be happier living on the street!

Well, perhaps she would. Run away. She tossed her head defiantly. But even to her, this time, it did seem like the end of the line.

Over dinner she said nothing. She watched him overtly: his

grubby lips taking in the food, the grooves running down from his squidgy nose like drains, widening and closing to the grinding of his yellow teeth. Reptilian eyes, flicking up and down, missing nothing. Thinning black (dyed?) hair trained over the scalp and held with something sticky that smelled of . . . ugh! Tessa shivered. Jasmine – or was it drains again? Everything about him repelled her. Drains, that was a good name for him. Full of foul matter.

"Greevy will be home at the weekend," he said to Myra. "I was talking to Raleigh this afternoon about the possibility of Greevy working there. As assistant trainer," he added, before Myra could think of mucking out.

Myra's eyebrows shot up in surprise, but all she said was, "How nice."

"He doesn't know anything," Tessa said.

"Assistant trainers learn," Maurice said heavily.

Tessa guessed that Raleigh was not in a position to turn down Maurice's suggestion. Maurice had six horses in training with him and two of them were very good ones. No trainer could bear to lose good horses – and Maurice, for sure, would take his horses away and send them to another trainer if Raleigh offended him. Putting up with Greevy would be the lesser of two evils. Poor Mr Raleigh! He was quite a nice man and clever with difficult owners like Maurice.

"We've also got to decide what to do with you, madam. You needn't think you're going to lie on your bed and listen to pop music all day."

"Like Greevy," Tessa said.

Greevy was thick and had no interests in life beyond music and fast cars. But at eighteen he had already lost his driving licence.

"You're twelve. You've got to have an education, I suppose, but God knows who'll take you on now. There must be a sin-bin somewhere where kids like you can be dumped. I'll have to ask around."

A sin-bin . . . Tessa thought that sounded interesting. Her spirits rose a fraction.

But at the thought of Greevy coming home in two days' time they sank again. Running away was the only option left if no sin-bin was forthcoming, and where on earth was there to run to?

4

"Feed the brute and treat it nicely"

*M*aurice had no luck with his sin-bin. The nearest was forty miles away, with no vacancies. Because Maurice was so annoyed at this failure Tessa was pleased, although she had been quite optimistic about her future in a sin-bin.

Perhaps getting the disgusting Greevy installed at Down Valley racing stables gave him ideas, for he said, "Good hard work might do you no harm. Burn off some of that temper. You won't have to go to school again until next September and between now and then you might as well get your butt off a chair and do something for your keep. On a farm perhaps."

Tessa curled her lip. Who was going to employ a twelve-year-old tractor driver? There were no children's jobs on farms any more, only high-tech stuff. He didn't know anything about farming, in spite of owning half a dozen.

Greevy was used to getting on under the wing of his rich father. He seemed to consider it his right. Maurice had bought his school a new playing field when Greevy once got into the sort of trouble that Tessa was kicked out for, and nothing more was said. Tessa had fantasized at times about Greevy being nice and their having good times together, and every time he came home she hopefully looked for signs of improvement in him, but each time her hopes were cruelly dashed.

"Jeez, you going to be underfoot all the time?" he remarked when he arrived home and heard of her "exclusion".

Tessa did not deign to reply.

She supposed there was very little chance of Greevy improving with age. He was spoilt rotten by his father but – unlike his father – he was quite good-looking. Tall and dark and gangly, he might one day be elegant in an actorish sort of way. He could turn on charm if he wanted something, but it wasn't the real thing. For now, he was really boring.

Myra said, "His mother, Maurice's first wife, died of cancer."

"A happy release," Tessa said.

"I wish you wouldn't say things like that! She was a dancer. Really pretty. I've seen photos of her."

"Maybe he treated her better than he treats you. You shouldn't stand for it, Ma. The way he talks to you."

"I don't want for anything, do I?"

Myra was hopeless, Tessa thought. Want for anything? Only affection, respect, kindness, a laugh or two . . . you name it. But Tessa didn't follow it up.

She could not bear the atmosphere in the house, the vapid, ugly spaces inhabited by people who were all miserable, stranded miles away from jolly Tescos and Marks and Spencers and McDonalds, from people who laughed and loved each other in their tacky semi-detacheds. This grand place was characterless and grim, like a prison. It *was* a prison.

She went out the back way and walked across the lawn and stood staring out over the valley. There was a deep stone ha-ha which stopped the cows coming in, and standing on the edge of it she had a view of grassland sweeping away below her to the chalk stream that swirled rapidly down the bottom. Large tracts of woodland covered the far side, interspersed with fields of corn that were beginning to yellow for summer. It was a tourist's vista, like out of an AA book.

She sat on the ha-ha, swinging her legs. If she ran away, where would she run to? Oh Declan! But even if she found him, he might not want her any more. He had never chased after her when she left, after all. She was too young to rent a flat, even if she had the money, and if she lived on the street she was bound to be picked up as under age. She passed for sixteen in the dark, but wouldn't in the cold light of day. If she really annoyed Maurice, he would hand her over to the social services as being out of control, and she would end up in care. Her past history would not stand her in good stead. She couldn't see any alternative – she would stay and get gloomy like Myra, and pretend she didn't want for anything. A nice house, good food. . .

"Oh Christ! I can't!" she screamed out loud.

She launched herself off the ha-ha and fell in a heap in the grass ditch, nearly breaking her ankles. Pity it wasn't her neck! She lay and sobbed where no one could see her. Or hear her.

She didn't care. She hadn't cried since she was little, but now it didn't matter. There was no one.

"Have you hurt yourself?"

Startled, Tessa turned her head and saw a horse's legs and the underneath of a bay horse's belly. It was just like when she was little in the fields at home, looking up at the broodmare, Shiner. It shook her into silence.

She scowled.

"No!"

She scrambled up to prove it and stood back to the wall.

The bay thoroughbred was carrying a young man. The horse was spooky and nervous, but the man sat with the quiet authority of a very good rider.

"Just making sure. No offence," he said, and the horse moved away. The young man didn't look back. Thank heaven for that! Tessa thought. His lack of curiosity was brilliant.

Having given in to tears, been discovered, and thought of nothing constructive for her future, Tessa went back to the house in a bad temper.

At supper she cheeked Maurice and was banished to her room. She watched television until two o'clock in the morning.

The next morning Maurice stormed in, ordered her to get up – because she was starting a job.

"What job?"

Maurice didn't reply.

She went down to breakfast and said again, "What job?'

Greevy jeered and said, "Dad's thought of a great idea. You work for these people and however bad you are and however much they loathe you they can't give you the sack because Dad owns their place and all their land. They fall out with him and they've had it."

This was actually not true but Tessa was not to know it. He might own their place but tenants' rights were powerful.

"Bit like you at Raleigh's then," she retorted. "If Raleigh falls out over you he'll lose your dad's horses."

"Yeah, well, I'm going to a proper place. You're going to a dung-heap."

Maurice said, "Go and get in the car. George will run you there. I've made the arrangements. Nine till six, six days a week."

"Where? Where's this job?"

"A farm down the valley. It's called Sparrows Wyck."

"What have I got to do?"

"Whatever they tell you. They've got horses, cows . . . God knows. Just behave yourself, keep out of my hair, till the Education lot find another place for you in September."

"What hair ?" Tessa retorted.

"Hop it. Get your jacket. George is waiting." Maurice's colourless eyes glittered.

Tessa was furious. If she had found a job for herself she might have been quite pleased, but to have been tossed into one like this, at Maurice's command, outraged her. If he thought she was going to toe the line he could think again.

She fetched her dirty anorak and slouched out to the car.

Sparrows Wyck was two miles away down the valley she had been staring at the day before. Two miles across the fields but four miles round by the road. Today it was raining slightly and a soft mist lay over the bottom of the valley.

"People been there all their lives," George said. "Very close family. They don't take kindly to strangers."

He turned the shining white car into a narrow, pot-holed lane.

"Hope I'm not going to do this drive every day."

"Don't worry, you won't. I'm not staying."

"No. Can't think what they'll find for you to do in a set-up like theirs. The old man must've bribed them to take you. The woman runs the house – worse than Mrs Tims, she is. Mouth like a rat-trap. And the outside work – it's not for a shrimp of a girl like you. The boys do that."

"What boys?" Tessa showed slightly more interest.

"Boys to me, love. Old men to you – gone twenty, thirty, for sure. The sons of the house."

"Huh!"

Tessa shrugged down into her seat, watching the windscreen wipers clearing a vision of high hedges and fields of thick grass. The buildings when they came to them were like Declan's in Ireland – a yard of decrepit stables with patched roofs and chewed half-doors, a row on either side. A gate shut the yard off from the lane. At the top were hay sheds, now nearly empty.

"I'll put you down here then," George said, obviously not keen to meet anyone. "Your father said you're to walk home."

"He's not my father," Tessa snapped.

"Lordy, you've both got the same temper," George said mildly.

Tessa wanted to say sorry, but the word was impossible for her. She screwed herself out of the car and slammed the door. George backed away and disappeared round a bend in the lane.

There was no one around. Most of the stables were empty. Four were occupied by thoroughbred-looking horses contentedly eating hay. The only sound was of their quiet munching and the running of the rain in the gutters.

"What a dump!" thought Tessa.

She wandered up and found a door at the back of the haybarn that opened into another yard. More stables, tractor sheds and a house. The house was old and forlorn, humped against the rain, a curl of old-fashioned smoke blowing from its chimney. After Goldlands this was another world. Tessa, although she liked old places, was angry at being dumped in this scene of dereliction. She thought of Greevy smarming it in the pristine yards at Mr Raleigh's, where it was all polished shoes and uniform sweatshirts. The contrast made her prickle with rage. She would get herself the sack as soon as possible.

Gritting her teeth, she crossed over to the house and knocked on the back door. She could not escape the fact that she was nervous, even frightened. But the feeling was all too familiar. There was a porch full of dirty gumboots and dirtier jackets and a cardboard box that looked as if a dog slept in it. As no one answered she went in and knocked on the inner door. Through the glass panel she could see several people sitting round a table eating breakfast.

Her throat felt dry. A man turned round and shouted something. She opened the door and went in. They all stopped eating and stared at her. Tessa had never felt so small in her life.

There were three men and two women. No one said anything. They just stared. It was quite plain they didn't want her here.

"I –" But Tessa found she could not speak. All the spunk was knocked out of her.

They started eating again and resumed the conversation she had interrupted. As if she wasn't there. One of the women, who looked fiftyish, answered George's description with a "mouth like a rat-trap". (And eyes like flint, Tessa would have added, the way they appraised her.) The younger woman, a hunky, black-haired twenty-something, gave her a dubious look and dropped her eyes again to her bacon and eggs, as did one of the younger men. The oldest man carried on eating without even looking at her, but the other man gave her a wink and made the faintest gesture with his head to an empty chair that was half pulled up to the table. A brindle-coloured lurcher lay under the table at his feet.

He was the man she had seen on the horse the day before.

Tessa thought, Damn them all, and marched firmly to the chair and sat down. She could play the same game too. Ask no

33

questions. They all ignored her and continued eating and talking. The talk was of milking parlours, getting rid of rats, and schooling horses. The appetites were large and copious mugs of tea were being emptied. The man on the horse fetched another mug from the dresser and poured tea which he pushed in Tessa's direction. The others glared at him. Tessa was beginning to enjoy herself, seeing a situation here worthy of her talents. She wasn't going to stay, whatever happened, not with this load of country cretins. She could give them worse treatment than they could give her. She was better practised.

When they had finished they all got up save the older woman and went out, shrugging into anoraks and boots. The door slammed, the rain dripped outside the window from a broken gutter, a cock crowed from somewhere. Tessa went on sitting.

The woman said sharply, "What's your name?"

"Tessa."

"Your father said——"

"He's not my father. I'm Tessa Blackthorn. Not Morrison." The woman shrugged.

"Clear these pots away and get outside. They'll give you a job."

"Good," said Tessa.

She went out, ignoring the pots. There was a milking parlour behind the house and the cows were filing out into the fields. The smell was of home, a long time ago. But she wasn't going to fall for that kind of sentiment. They hated her, she could see, and that suited her.

She went back to the stable yard where the woman was wheeling a barrow towards the occupied stables. Tessa stood watching her, offering nothing.

The woman opened one of the doors and went in to the horse. She tied it up and started mucking out.

Tessa leaned against the door.

After a few forkfuls the woman said, "What's your name?"

"Tessa."

"Did your father run you down here? It's quite a walk."

"He's not my father. He's my stepfather."

"Hmm." A few more deft flicks with the fork and she said, "My name's Gilly, by the way. I work here. I'm not family."

Was she perhaps saying that she, unlike the others, had no personal interest in Tessa's employment? If she was, Tessa chose to ignore it. She wasn't impressed with Gilly's looks, but did recognize the expertise with which she handled her work. Gilly ordered her to empty the barrow on the muck heap which was a muddy walk away behind the stables. But when she had done it, Gilly came with her the second time and said, "You've got to learn. Even a muck heap. There's a proper way. Square, straight sides, no sliding down like a pyramid. You build up the sides. Like this."

Tessa glowered. She learned how to make a muck heap. She learned how to muck out, how to tie a quick-release knot, how to sweep a yard. How to wash grooming brushes. She asked no questions, did sulkily what she was ordered to, no more. She knew how to make people hate her. Maurice wanted her in this job, and she would do her best to get the sack. Gilly's early overtures soon changed to cross commands.

"I'm stuck with you because the others don't want you here, you know that, don't you? So don't make my life a misery. You should be at school anyway. You're no use in this yard."

"I don't care."

Gilly rolled her eyes and said nothing.

Tessa held out. She was used to pitting herself against the opposition. It made life more interesting. If they had liked her and made her welcome she might have succumbed, because the actual work was at least more interesting than staying at home watching television all day. But the more unlikeable she made herself the more she felt she held the upper hand. Maurice wanted her here. She would force them to sack her.

She got to understand the politics of the place. Sparrows Wyck was a small dairy and arable farm run by the eldest son, Peter, and his mother, Matty Fellowes. They were tenants of Maurice who owned the place. Although Peter ran the farm with the help of a cowman, his main ambition was to train racehorses – not flat racers, but horses over the jumps – the winter game. He hoped this would make them some money, but so far they had had little success. They took in about a dozen horses for training in the winter, but at present most of these were out at grass or back home with their owners for their summer holidays. It was as small a racing stable as they came, in complete contrast to the huge and successful yard where Greevy worked.

Jimmy, the younger son, was the horseman of the family and schooled the jumpers for Peter and problem horses for anyone who sent them to him. He also took horses to break in. He didn't interfere much with the racing side. He was his own man, very quiet in his manner, and kept largely to himself, with his lurcher Walter for companion. His brother Peter was excitable and given easily to both rage and laughter. The third man, Arthur, gnarled and elderly, worked in the stables with the racehorses. He was some sort of a relation, said little, and came up from the village. The mother, Matty, was impassive and rock-like and kept to her household duties, not interfering. As well as running the home, she did the paperwork for both the farm and the racing department, and ran a poultry business as well. She only ever left home once a week to go to the supermarket. Tessa found her hard to fathom, not enjoying the scrutiny of her pale green eyes. Her natural expression was stern, but the "mouth like a rat-trap" was not in fact as severe as George's description implied. Tessa sometimes thought she saw the suggestion of a smile, but so enigmatic it was hard to tell. Tessa hated her the most, because she could not be sure of the effect she was making on her. It was fairly plain that the others found her a pain, although Jimmy quite often, in his quiet way, gave her the chance to make amends by offering a dry comment or a smile. Not that she would take him up on it. But she liked watching him riding in the manège and lurked there quite often, behind the stables, when he was schooling one of his problem horses. He was so quiet and still on a difficult horse, so utterly in command, that she was fascinated. She wished she could ride. It would be a good way to thumb her nose at people on the ground, show them she was something.

Gilly rode well too, although she was the wrong shape, too beefy for a woman. But she handled horses with total command, even Jimmy's stroppiest, which Tessa was tartly ordered not to go near.

"Can't have the boss's daughter trampled to death; that would never do. Daddy might be down to complain."

"He's not Daddy. I hate him."

"You're not alone."

But even in this Tessa could not bring herself to be an ally.

"Trouble is, there's not enough for you to do around here in the summer. Not until the jumpers start coming in at the end of July. By September there'll a dozen, as well as Jimmy's. Plenty of work, but you'll be back at school by then."

Will I hell, Tessa thought. Nobody would take her. Myra had tried everywhere.

She used to time her arrival (she walked across the fields) with the end of breakfast. No one had invited her to breakfast. She knew it was because they disliked her. But one morning when she got there, there had been an emergency with some cows getting out on to the road, and breakfast was half an hour late. She went in and sat down uninvited. She helped herself to a mug of tea. No one said anything.

Peter was sounding off about a new owner who was sending him a horse to train. It was now well into July and soon the horses would be coming back. This new one belonged to – according to Peter – a senile coal merchant.

"He's never had a horse before. He wants to win the Grand National, like the old guy that owned Red Rum. So he went to the sales and bought one, just like that. He said no one bid for it and he was sorry for it so he bid and got it. I ask you! What are we getting?"

The others all laughed.

"As long as he pays –"

"We don't want to be a laughing stock, all the same."

"It'll never get on the course if it's as bad as it sounds. Someone'll have to let him down gently."

"We'll be fair with him," Peter said. "But I tell you, he's barmy. I talked to him on the phone. Nutty as a fruitcake. Sending the horse tomorrow."

"What on earth's Sarah going to say? She'll be back next week. She's always trying to get you to say no to dumbos," Gilly said to Peter.

"She'll have to take it. We need the money," Peter said tartly.

Jimmy said, "We need a reputation more. You get a reputation and the money comes."

Tessa had heard of Sarah before – the head lad apparently, who left in the spring when the horses stopped racing and worked elsewhere for three months. Gilly said she was "a tartar". Tessa was quite looking forward to meeting her.

When they were going out, Tessa heard Peter say to Gilly, "Give the damned horse to Tessa to look after. Two no-hopers. They'll suit each other."

Tessa pretended not to hear. She didn't think of herself as a no-hoper, rather as someone who was doing her own thing regardless. But she could see it wouldn't suit them to see it that way.

Gilly said, "Getting a horse might improve you. Nobody gives you work because you're so snotty about taking orders. Face like a thunderstorm. Easier to ignore you. I suppose that's what you want."

True, but Tessa didn't answer.

"Even if the horse is a no-no, the owner pays for it to be treated like a star. You'll have to get that into your thick head."

In spite of herself, Tessa felt a faint interest in "her" horse. The next day she waited impatiently for the horsebox to arrive. Gilly made her put a straw bed down in one of the empty, disinfected looseboxes, and put hay ready and a water bucket. Three other horses had already come back from grass. They were impressive glossy animals. Gilly and Arthur took charge of them. Apparently they were ready to start work again, to get fit over two or three months and start running in

November. This meant lots of slow exercise to get their muscles hard, until they were ready to canter, and then run for their lives. Tessa leaned over the half-doors studying them, admiring their impressive appearance. Even if they weren't Gold Cup winners, they looked like it.

"Pity you can't ride," Gilly remarked. "There's a lot of riding to be done between us, this time of year."

Tessa would not let on that she wished she could. She tossed her head impatiently to indicate riding was for the mentally impaired. Gilly sighed. There was a limit to her patience.

"Sweep the yard," she snapped.

It was big yard with uneven concrete, and a pig to sweep. All Tessa was fit for, Gilly decided.

Tessa's horse arrived in the early afternoon.

With the other three, Tessa stared in dismay at the dismal animal that stumbled down the ramp. Peter and Jimmy frowned, then laughed.

"The Grand National, he said," Peter snorted. "God save us!"

"You have to laugh, or you'd cry," Jimmy said.

The horse was very tall, long-backed, gaunt and ribby with a dull hide the colour of faded conkers. It had an amiable face, an ugly white blaze, and long, wagging ears. Its pale-coloured mane and tail looked as if goats had been at them. It was as unlike the three other arrivals as a horse could possibly be.

"No wonder no one bid for it," Peter said.

To cap it all, following on its heels, unhaltered, came a small piebald Shetland.

The driver said, "That one's free. They won't go anywhere without each other, so I was told. Put it in the same box they said."

"Cripes, I don't believe this," Peter said.

Jimmy grinned. "Just the job for our Tessa."

They gave her the head-collar rope.

Tessa felt humiliated beyond words. It was all a great joke, with them enjoying taking it out on her. They were all laughing.

"The man's a maniac. It'll never see a racecourse, this one, let alone Aintree."

"You'll have to tell him," Jimmy said. "It's not fair to take his money."

"Put him in his box, Tessa," Peter said. "We'll have to let the old man down gently. I told you – he's an idiot."

"Mind the horse doesn't tread on you. You'll never walk again," Jimmy said.

The horse followed Tessa through the open door. The piebald pony trotted in behind.

The driver said, "The pony's called Lucky."

"Got the horse's passport?" Peter asked.

"They never gave it me. Horse is called Buffoon, that's all I know."

"We want the passport. Tell 'em when you get back. Or I'll give them a ring."

The driver closed up the ramp and departed and the others peered in over the door, still unbelieving.

"I'll tell you one thing," Jimmy said, "this one will do nothing for our reputation."

"No. But meanwhile, he's paid the first month in advance. That's rare enough. We feed the brute and treat him nicely. After that. . . " Peter shrugged, laughed. "I thought I'd seen everything! Just goes to show. . . "

They all wandered away, chortling. Tessa took off the horse's headcollar, choking back tears of disappointment, now there was no one to see. They'd made a fool of her, and so had the horse.

"You pig," she said viciously.

The horse turned its ugly head and regarded her kindly. Then it went to the haynet and snatched a mouthful. What it dropped on the floor the little pony hoovered up. What a pair! The pony seemed to underline the ridiculousness of her charge.

Tessa tried to tell herself that nothing was any different, but she could not fool herself into believing that she hadn't cared tuppence about what stupid horse she was getting. A little part of her had felt interested, keen even. It had thought she might get – by chance – the best one in the stable. Then she remembered she wanted to get the sack. Or did she? She didn't know what she wanted. She laid her head against the great gaunt flank and cried. Nobody would see. Nobody cared. Not even the stupid horse. It turned its ugly head to look at her. With hay sticking out of its mouth it looked more like a yokel than ever. Whoever christened it Buffoon had the right idea.

"I hate you!" Tessa cried and thumped its belly.

It gave a surprised snort and a sad look, and shifted away slightly.

"You make me sick!"

Tessa cried and was ashamed. It was getting to be a habit. She hated this place and she hated home and she longed for the sin-bin which was too full of other sinners to take her in. There were other people like her out there – if only she could be with them!

Jimmy's lurcher Walter came trotting across the yard. Tessa opened the loosebox door and called him in. He came in his friendly way – he was only a year old. He cheered Tessa up. She stopped crying. She would have loved to have a dog but Maurice wouldn't let her. Not even a cat. Too many hairs on the carpet. Walter covered her wet face with wetter licks, and actually made her laugh. Then Gilly looked over the door and bawled her out.

"For God's sake, get the dog out of there! He's not allowed in the boxes! You wait till Sarah comes back – I'm warning you, we've been easy on you, the way things are. But she won't be – Mr Mucky Morrison's daughter or not – you'll get stick if you don't mend your ways."

"I'm not his daughter!" But Tessa liked the name – Mucky Morrison. It suited him.

"Whose daughter are you then, if it's not a rude question?"

"Declan Blackthorn's."

"And who's he when he's at home?"

Tessa didn't answer. What could she say? A feckless Irishman who fathered her when he was hardly out of school, who disappeared when needed?

Gilly's face softened a fraction. She couldn't fathom Tessa, who went out of her way to be so obnoxious, but Gilly thought of her in the same way as she was used to considering a problem horse. There was a key to Tessa's behaviour, somewhere. Problem horses were nearly always the fault of *somebody*, somewhere along the line. Gilly thought the same was true of Tessa. Having Mucky Morrison for a stepfather was a fairly obvious reason for her hate-everybody attitude, for starters. And who knew what had happened before that? Gilly knew that Tessa would never confide her troubles, even if she recognized them herself. Gilly didn't mind playing her along, but Sarah was another matter.

"You'll have to mind Sarah. Just a friendly warning."

"Huh!" grunted Tessa. "Why's she any different?

"You'll see. Meanwhile, get to work — your new horse could do with a bath. And then you can learn to groom — properly. I'll show you. It's hard work, to do it properly."

Buffoon was tied up in the yard by the drain. Gilly unreeled the hose.

"His mate can have a spruce-up too. Tie the pony up."

It was hot and Buffoon enjoyed the cold hose. His friend

Lucky kicked and reared against his head-collar, but Gilly only laughed and smothered him with soap bubbles. He positively sparkled when she had finished, and Buffoon's dusty coat was much improved.

"He can look his best, however modest his best might be," Gilly said.

She squirted a jet at Walter, who fled.

"I bet I'll be the mug that has to ride this one. Jimmy and Sarah won't be seen dead on him. Unless you learn. . ."

"I don't want to!"

One of the smart ones, perhaps . . . Tessa had her pride.

When she got home that evening she had to listen to Maurice and Greevy gloating over a new horse, Crowsnest, bought that same day out of a flat-racing yard at Newmarket. It was a winning stayer, and Maurice had "snapped it up", outbidding a well-known owner who also kept his horses with Raleigh. Raleigh was "over the moon" to get it in his yard. Greevy was assured of his job, however inadequate an assistant trainer he was turning out to be. Listening to them, Tessa had no inclination to mention her yard's forlorn new horse. She sat in stubborn silence.

Myra was wittering on about her lack of success in finding Tessa a school place.

"It looks as if you'll have to be taught at home. They send someone."

"Poor bloody teacher, stuck with her," Greevy said.

"Why don't you grow up, Greevy?" Tessa enquired. "For an adult you sound like someone out of primary school."

Greevy glowered. With a boil on his neck, he got worse by the day.

"Oh, you two, stop it," Myra sighed. She was scared of telling Maurice that the education department said he would have to pay for Tessa's private tutor. If he could afford boarding school he could afford the tutoring, they had informed her. They weren't to know that he had been happy to pay boarding school fees to get Tessa out of his way, not for anything to do with education. He would be less than happy to pay out if she were still to be underfoot.

"I don't want an education anyway," Tessa said. "I know all I need to know."

"Now who's talking rubbish?" Geevy jeered. "Peabrain. You wouldn't last a minute at Raleigh's."

"Nor you at Mr Fellowes'."

"Well, we all know why you're still there."

"And the same applies to you."

With this unedifying gridlock the conversation came to an end.

Tessa went up to her room and turned on the television. It was a relief from the real world.

The next day, when she was sweeping the yard, the lorry-driver who had brought Buffoon drove in in a Land Rover and handed her a slim, stiff-backed book.

"That horse's passport. Buffoon. Your guv'nor will want it. OK?"

"Yeah, I'll give it him."

The man drove off. Tessa idly leafed through the papers. It was headed "Document of description for the identification of foals, yearlings, racehorses, broodmares and stallions". After several pages of boring rules in both English and French she came to a drawing. Under the drawing was a box headed, "Name of Dam". And in the box was written in ink "Shiner".

5

"I will be good!"

It was no good pretending any more that she didn't care. Knowing that Buffoon was Shiner's child changed Tessa's life.

She told nobody, not even Myra.

It was August, dry and dusty, and as she hurried to the stables in the morning she knew that, for the first time in her life, there was something she desperately wanted — to stay at the stable and look after Buffoon, the despised, useless new horse. He was a sin-bin candidate, like herself. Not wanted. They belonged together. Fate had delivered him to her. It was more than coincidence. She would die for him. To her, now, he was beautiful.

As she hurried along, leaving a trail of dew through the downland grass, she knew she was being ridiculous. Hysterical even. But she couldn't help it. She had never in her life had anything to look forward to, never had an ambition, save the perennial wish to get away from her situation. Now her burning wish was to stay where she was. But she was only supposed to work at the stables until the end of the month, when — somehow — she was bound for an education. Even now Myra was trying yet another school, an ill-thought-of comprehensive, the last resort. Tessa knew they didn't want her at Sparrows Wyck, she had made herself too grouchy and unwilling. Gilly had already told her that Sarah would give her short shrift . . . Her mind tumbled over all the obstacles to her new, burning wish.

She prayed aloud, "I will be good! I will be good! If only I can stay. . ."

But how could she become a real stable girl, when she was only twelve?

Desperate anxiety hastened her steps. For the first time she arrived early, while they were still at breakfast. The horses were still finishing their small early morning feeds. Tessa went in to Buffoon and threw her arms round his neck. He turned to her with gentle surprise. Lucky butted her for a titbit, too small to reach Buffoon's feed in the manger. This is where I belong, Tessa knew, against all logic. She buried her face in Buffoon's moth-eaten mane.

"You are mine," she said. "My beauty. I shall never be parted from you."

Even as she said it, she knew she was crazy. It wasn't true and never could be but she would die first before she changed her mind.

When Gilly came out Buffoon was mucked out and Tessa was grooming with her sleeves rolled up.

"Hey, what's bitten you?" she said.

Tessa did not deign to reply.

In the tack-room, Buffoon's gear was polished and shining, standing out from the rest of the grubby tack. Soon his grooming brushes were washed and laid out in the sun to dry. Nobody said anything, but they all noticed.

When the horses went out on exercise, Gilly rode Buffoon, and Tessa watched them go with light in her eyes. She turned Lucky out into the small paddock behind the stables and he settled to grazing, knowing that his friend would be back in a couple of hours. Tessa tidied the loosebox, swept the yard, and went to the manège when Jimmy was just coming out with a young horse. Jimmy was the only one Tessa liked.

She hung around while he untacked the horse, and took the gear back to the tack-room for him. When she returned, he was washing the horse down with the hose. Walter leapt around, dodging the jet of water. Tessa knew that when Jimmy had finished he would put the horse away, sit on the hay bales and roll a cigarette. Over his head was an ancient notice that said "No Smoking". Tessa sat on a hay bale, waiting.

"Hi," he said, quite amicably.

He sat down and got out the cigarette papers, pulled one out.

"I want to learn to ride," Tessa said.

Jimmy got out the tobacco and picked out a meagre ration of shreds.

"I want to ride Buffoon."

Jimmy didn't say anything. Tessa then remembered Gilly saying once that Jimmy never gave lessons. Well, what else could she do but ask? No one else would teach her. She sat staring at the ground, waiting.

Jimmy lit his cigarette and took a pull. He had a weather-beaten face and hair that grew close and curling to his head. His eyes were very blue and direct. Tessa supposed she liked him best because he never criticized, never said much at all, just did his own thing. He had a kind way of looking, with a slight smile. Peter his brother was much more excitable and short-tempered, and had made his dislike of Tessa quite plain. Unlike Jimmy.

At last Jimmy said, "Change of heart, eh?"

"Yes."

Jimmy stared into space for a bit, inhaled on his scrappy cigarette and eventually said, "This afternoon, if you like. Half an hour. See how you go."

Tessa bit her lip, holding back an impulse to leap up and hug him.

"Yes," she said.

The stables were quiet in the afternoon after the midday feed. Gilly went home for a couple of hours, Peter went off to his office, or the cows, old Arthur went to sleep. Tessa was there waiting long before Jimmy came. She thought he had forgotten, her heart was pounding. But he came soundlessly round the corner of the barn, saw her and smiled.

He used one of his young horses, a thoroughbred, but put it on a lunge-rein in the manège. When Tessa got up, it all came back to her, the sight of the long neck ahead and the perky ears, the slab of shoulder working smoothly, the gleaming coat sliding over bone and muscle. Declan had thrown her up on lots of horses once, old ones and young ones, and the familiarity soothed her. She knew she would be good.

"You're a natural," Jimmy said.

By the end of the half-hour she was rising to the trot with only a few misses.

"I can't teach anyway," Jimmy said. "It's up to you. But I'll give you half an hour in the afternoons until you're safe to be let out. Buffoon's no trouble, only getting him to move. You won't have to know much to ride him."

"I love him." She didn't know why she said it.

Jimmy said, "I've noticed." He didn't smile. "Don't make it hard for yourself. I doubt he'll stay long."

Tessa thought, if he goes I'll follow him. Wherever. She didn't care. Jimmy saw her sharp chin lift. What an odd girl she was!

A woman came round the corner of the barn, lean as the lurcher, a mass of dark red hair knotted roughly back, purple-blue eyes like lasers taking in the scene.

"Blooming riding-school is it now?" she jeered at Jimmy. "I thought you never gave lessons?"

Jimmy just smiled. He introduced her. "This is Sarah, Tessa. Our head lad. Not 'lass' – more than our lives are worth if you call her that."

Sarah gave a bark of a laugh.

"Hullo, Tessa. Pleased to meet you. You're honoured, being taught by this one. He never teaches."

"Yes." Tessa did not disagree. She slipped to the ground.

"You're Mucky Morrison's daughter, I understand?"

"No, I'm not! I'm Declan Blackthorn's daughter."

"Oh, Declan's? I never knew he had one."

Tessa looked up, stricken. "You know him?"

"I met him at Goresbridge once. Last year, I think it was. He tried to sell me a useless horse."

She turned to Jimmy and started to talk to him, and Tessa was left to take the horse she had been riding back to its box. She felt as if someone had hit her, hard. But why was it such a surprise? Ireland wasn't a large country and all the horse people milled around meeting each other all over the place. If she really wanted to, she could no doubt trace her father. But why on earth would he be glad to see her? Tessa shrugged unhappily. He certainly had never tried to trace her. Even so the mention of him, so casually from Sarah, was a shock.

Sarah was a bit of a shock too, although Tessa had been warned.

When she looked in at Buffoon, she said, "What a dog they've given you! Poor Tessa! I'm not surprised Gilly and Arthur didn't want him. What madman thinks this is a racehorse?"

Tessa did not say anything, biting back a rude reply. She saw that Sarah was someone to be careful with. Something in the set of her head, the light in her eye . . . she was tall and quick and would have been beautiful but for the almost male strength in her face. Imperious. Headmistress material, Tessa thought – the sort she preferred not to come up against. Magistrate's bench . . . a shiver ran through Tessa. Everything mattered now, and she must not alienate Sarah, whatever she said about Buffoon. Life was suddenly very challenging.

"He's a good horse," she said stubbornly. "I know he is."

Sarah grinned.

"One thing about racing, it's full of surprises. Who knows? I won't argue with you. Time will tell. Talking about surprises, how did you get Jimmy to give you a lesson?"

"I asked him."

"The British team has asked him, to no avail. What is it about you?"

Tessa had no reply. A surge of gratitude ran through her – almost love – for Jimmy. It shook her. She wasn't used to these sort of emotions. They confused her utterly. She was only used to hating, resisting.

Sarah said, kindly, "When you go back to school, you can come in the evenings, and weekends, if you like. Wisbey will have Buffoon next week, when he comes back. You can help him in your spare time. He's a nice lad."

"Wisbey?"

"He works in a holiday camp in the summer. Comes back in September. Like me. There's no work here in the summer, then come autumn it's all go."

Tessa could not believe it – was it all going to be snatched away from her? Somehow she had convinced herself there would be no school for her, just a tutor for an hour or two whom she could easily ditch with her usual tactics.

Wisbey? She hated Wisbey. Like poison.

"I want to do Buffoon," she said stubbornly.

Sarah gave her a sharp look. She said, "We can all *want*."

So what did *she* want? Tessa wondered viciously. She had everything, as far as Tessa could see: a good job (the boss), looks (if she took the trouble, which she obviously didn't), her own life. She lived in her own caravan, which arrived the same day and was parked up by the milking parlour.

Tessa went back and sat in the straw in Buffoon's stable, watching him doze, his head in the corner. Lucky came up and shoved at her for titbits, and she stroked his soft nose. She knew she was still, basically, unwanted, not necessary, unloved. They were all quite happy to see her depart, would not give her another thought. It was how she had made it.

But Jimmy, who would not teach the British team, had said he would give her half an hour every day. It was something to hold on to. The only thing. While she was still free.

"And you, Buffoon. My beauty! You've got to love me best. You've got to!"

The tears were welling up again. She was furious with herself. Buffoon lifted his manky tail and blew out a gust of wind.

When she got home that evening Myra was waiting for her, all smiles.

"Guess what, Tessa? That school – Mancroft – they say

there's a place for you. In spite of everything they'll take you. Isn't that wonderful? A fresh start; I know you'll try this time! It's not far away and you'll make friends. You've got to go and see the headmistress on Wednesday."

She put her arm round Tessa's shoulders.

"Maurice will be so pleased."

6

Riding Buffoon

*T*he school was on the edge of a large town, flanked by an industrial estate. The headmistress, Mrs Alston, was not unlike Sarah, but older and uglier. She had a rectangular face, a stern jaw, and curly grey hair that looked slightly out of place, too perky for the expression it surrounded. She had the same aura about her of being quite ready to put the frighteners on – cross me at your peril. She had been recently brought in to "turn the school around". It was a school that parents didn't want their children to go to.

Myra was obviously frightened to death of her before she started, but Tessa just did her usual thing – stared and said nothing. No one could get to her on this front, she was too experienced. To make it feel better, she thought of Jimmy and his lessons. He had said he would give her half an hour in the evenings, even if she had to go to school. It was all she had to hold on to. Wisbey was arriving two days before term started. Tessa wasn't even listening as Myra bumbled on.

Until she was aware, at last, of a silence.

"So, Tessa, how do you feel about coming here?"

Tessa just stared.

Mrs Alston stared back.

"Say something, Tessa. Don't be so rude!" Myra wailed.

Tessa shrugged.

Mrs Alston's eyes narrowed.

Tessa knew then that Mrs Alston saw her as a challenge. Mrs Alston's mind worked the same way as Tessa's. Tessa felt a little nip of interest. She would enjoy working out her next expulsion. A quick one. But not to overstep the mark, not to become a "young offender". Tricky. A challenge.

Tessa could not help smiling.

Mrs Alston smiled too.

"Good. We'll see you on Wednesday then. Thank you, Mrs Morrison-Pleydell."

"Is that all?" Myra was flummoxed.

"I've seen all I need." Her voice was grim.

A secretary showed them out and all the way back in the car Myra berated Tessa for her lack of co-operation, her manners, her *attitude*.

"It'll get you nowhere in this life, Tessa! I can't make you out. I don't understand you! There's a fresh start waiting there, and you won't even listen. You'll end up in one of those young offender places or whatever they're called, and then you'll be sorry! Locked in."

"I want to stay as I am."

"Well, there's a law about getting educated. I can't change the law, can I? There's some things in this life you've just got to do."

Yes, thought Tessa, look after Buffoon. Her chin went out. Myra, recognizing the expression, sighed heavily.

Tessa went back to Sparrows Wyck for her lesson.

"They're taking you on, are they?" Jimmy asked.

"I won't be there for long," Tessa said. "I want to be here."

Jimmy took a drag on his spindly cigarette and said, "Be careful, Tessa."

"I've never wanted anything before." Why did she say this to Jimmy, she wondered, even as she said it? These were things one didn't say. But Jimmy only smiled.

He said, "The horse might not stay for long."

"He will if he's good."

"If he's good, yes." Another puff, another smile. "Tell you what, I reckon you could ride him out in the morning. You're good enough. Gilly says he's quiet as a lamb."

Tessa felt as if her heart were swelling inside her so that she would burst. This was the first time ever that she was getting her heart's desire. It knocked her speechless. She was afraid she was going to burst into tears, and jumped up and ran away.

Jimmy finished his cigarette thoughtfully, and shook his head.

It wasn't anything anyone was going to remember, save Tessa.

The first ride went out at eight, and the second one at half-past ten. Tessa was there at six, grooming Buffoon. She had to get a stool from the tack-room to do him properly, for she was small and slight for her twelve years. When he was shining clean, she picked out his hooves and oiled them, and combed out his mane and tail so that every strand was separate. His winter coat was coming through in a slightly darker shade, although he was still the washy chestnut that most horsey people disliked. But – "They come good all shapes, colours and sizes, if you're lucky," Jimmy said.

Tessa could feel her insides skipping with excitement. She had never experienced such a wonderful feeling. Yet nobody in the yard thought anything of it, only that it could be useful if Tessa was good enough to ride out – save them some work.

Sarah, Gilly and Arthur rode the three best horses, Gossamer, White Smoke and the one they all called God Almighty. His real name was Gaelic and unpronounceable, but sounded roughly like God Almighty, so God Almighty he was. He was nothing to look at, a gaunt, large-framed bay with piggy eyes, but he stayed for ever and was a good jumper, and had won several races on small tracks. Gossamer, another bay, was young and beautiful and promising, bought out of flat-racing, and White Smoke was, in spite of his name, a rather plain dark grey with a pleasant nature but not a great deal of talent. Sarah rode God Almighty, Gilly rode Gossamer and Arthur rode White Smoke. Jimmy came out and legged Tessa up on to Buffoon and adjusted the stirrups for her. The others rode racing style, short, but Jimmy gave her midway length.

Did he guess how she felt? He looked at her, and she, so high, had to look down to see his smile of encouragement. She was trembling like a leaf.

"You're fine," he said. "Nothing to worry about. Enjoy it."

He slapped Buffoon's rump. Buffoon stretched out his neck

and yawned. The lurcher Walter followed Jimmy as he took Lucky out into the paddock, and the small string moved out of the yard the back way, on to the track across the downs. Tessa had walked it so often that she knew every dip and rise, every clump of knapweed or flash of yellow vetch, yet now she saw it as if her eyes had been shut all her life, shining and sparkling with early morning dew, framed by the long red ears ahead of her. Buffoon walked slowly but his stride was so long that he had no trouble keeping up with the others. Gilly, alongside on Gossamer, grinned and said, "One thing, he's a good walker."

Tessa could not stop her smiles breaking out. Gilly noticed, and laughed.

"You're a nut, Tessa," she said.

And Tessa smiled back. Gilly nearly fell off her horse.

It was only a walking and trotting morning, no cantering, so Peter hadn't bothered to come out with them. When work started on the gallops, he would drive out in his battered old Land Rover to watch and assess progress. The gallops lay on the side of the valley opposite Goldlands, and were used by Raleigh's horses at times, although he had smarter ones above his own yard over the ridge of the hill. Now, as they rode down the slope towards the ford across the river, Tessa saw a string of horses on the far hillside coming towards them. Cruising along in front was Raleigh's Discovery.

"Old smarty pants," Gilly said disparagingly.

Sarah said, "I'd give my right arm to have a horse that would make him sit up and take notice. He's so flaming patronizing. And that smarmy little creep of an assistant he's taken on —"

"Hush, that's Tessa's stepbrother," Gilly said, and laughed.

Tessa felt her cheeks burning.

"I hate him," she said.

But even the thought of Greevy could not douse her happiness. The feel of Buffoon beneath her, like a great tank, brought back all her baby memories of Shiner and being tossed up on to yearlings' backs by the laughing Declan — she felt she was back in touch again, with Buffoon come to her by a special design of the Almighty. The long red neck in front of her, topped by its moth-eaten mane, nodded lazily towards the ford where a heron stood watching. Unafraid until the last minute, it rose up suddenly on its great spread of wings, trailing its legs through the reeds. Gossamer and White Smoke, who would both shy violently at a plastic bag, passed without a tremor, only pausing to paw in the water as usual. Sarah and Gilly legged them on, not wanting to get soaked. Buffoon followed unconcerned, and Tessa had a sudden vision of him as a foal at Shiner's side trailing along the Atlantic beach amongst the seaweed and the old plastic rubbish, then darting forward to gallop over the small dying waves on the golden sand as once Shiner had done, even without sight. What had Shiner made of the ocean, unseeing? Tessa remembered how she had wondered about it, even then.

The horses started a long trot up the track out of the valley. Tessa found Buffoon's stride longer than any of Jimmy's horses, and bumped several times, trying to get the rhythm. Buffoon dropped back because Tessa was not able to collect him and press him on, and his natural laziness took over. The others waited for her at the top, grinning at her red face, full of concentration.

"You've got to be really strong to collect him," Gilly said sympathetically. "He just falls apart left to himself."

"At least he doesn't mind being at the back, that's something," Sarah said. Apparently if God Almighty was at the back, he let out a series of bucks to show his displeasure. "As long as he minds when he's racing . . . that's when it matters."

But Buffoon was so laid back, why should he exert himself to win a race? The thought went idly through Tessa's head, and caused a spasm of fear. Oh God, she was pinning her whole future on something so fragile it was scarcely there! It didn't bear thinking about. Her future at Mancroft loomed, real and dreadful, as good as death. Tears welled up in Tessa's eyes, but as she was still at the back, nobody saw.

As they came out on to the wide track along the top of the down they passed the Raleigh string collecting to start work on the gallops. Raleigh was out of the car, giving orders, Greevy at his side. They looked up and Raleigh called out "Good morning" to Sarah.

Tessa hoped Greevy wouldn't recognize her, but she could see that he did by the way his mouth fell open. She straightened up in the saddle, looking ahead, and they went on past the string. There were about twenty horses, all gleaming expensive beasts, the best in the country. The riders were the usual motley lot of both sexes. One pimply boy, farthest from Raleigh, called out to Tessa, "Got 'im from the circus, did you?" and there was a gust of laughter. Gilly half pulled up to wait for Tessa, sympathetic. But Tessa's eyes were stony again, still sparkling with tears.

Gilly didn't say anything.

It was the beginning of September and the air was crisp and dry, the sky pale, a skylark or two soaring. The distances were hazy, violet, half rubbed out in the autumn warmth which was bringing out a rime of sweat on the horses' necks. Tessa sniffed it in, the smell of the day with all its cartwheeling emotions – she found it hard to come to terms with . . . half dread, half ecstasy. But Buffoon . . . he was everything. Was she mad?

After a long trot along the ridge and round the end of the valley they came down slowly along the side of the river through the cow pasture, cooling the horses off in the shade of the willows. Buffoon snatched at the leaves, stopped to rub a fly off his leg, lagged behind. Tessa rode him dreamily, the dread banished, joy triumphant.

"How did you go?" Jimmy asked her.

"It was wonderful. Perfect."

Sarah said, "She did well."

"Praise indeed!" Jimmy murmured. "Perhaps you should have your lessons on Buffoon."

But Peter forbade it. "The owner's paying us to train a racehorse, not run a riding-school."

65

"It's harder to ride a lazy horse than a hot one."

"Wisbey will take over on Monday. It's no good giving her ideas."

Tessa glowered. She hated Wisbey. Monday was the day she started school.

As she walked home in the evening her mind was churning. The glory of riding Buffoon was overlaid by the dreadful, imminent future. Her mother was all smiles since the school place had been confirmed.

"A fresh start! You must make the most of it, Tessa. I'm sure it will be all right this time. You'll make nice friends at school, and then you've got the stable for your hobby to play around in, in your spare time! Everything will go well, I'm sure."

Tessa was equally sure it would not. Her hobby! She could make no rejoinder that was civil. As she scowled across the supper table Greevy grinned and said, "What on earth was that nag you were riding this morning? It's never going to see a racecourse, surely?"

Tessa could not bear it. Hating herself, she got up and ran out of the room. Flinging herself down on her bed she vowed she hated them all: her mother, Greevy, his father, *Wisbey*, Peter, Sarah . . . not Jimmy. Only Jimmy escaped.

"I will – I *will* –" she wailed into the muffling pillow, kicking the wall so hard that the smart wallpaper was left with black marks.

Will what? (Become happy and lovely watching Buffoon

win the Grand National, no less. . .) She was on a hiding to nothing. Despair engulfed her. Her wracking sobs echoed round the characterless bedroom as the autumn light faded outside, but the house was so big nobody was going to hear her. Nobody cared anyway. Tessa howled.

7

A Dangerous Girl

*T*hey hated Tessa at school. The teachers handled her like a red-hot brick, knowing her reputation, not wanting a confrontation. Mostly this meant avoiding her, ignoring her — trying to sum her up.

She gave them little to go on. She would not speak to anybody. Her work was purposefully dreadful, if performed at all. The teachers let it go, making no remarks. They were nervous of her tight, scowling face with its piercing grey-green eyes which stared insolently. They could not work her out.

Tessa knew the usefulness of silence. You gave yourself away if you spoke. Her fellow pupils were wary of her at first, but after a few days the bolder ones attempted contact. Some attempted friendship, the stronger ones a challenge. Tessa did not want friendship but she relished a challenge. She recognized bullies when she met them, and looked for one. It did not take long.

There was a girl called Jackie, very large and strong, with an aggressive personality. She had a gaggle of hangers-on and they preyed on smaller timid girls, and made their lives a misery. Tessa suspected they extorted money. Jackie had a father who met her occasionally from school, and was the prototype – large, strong and bossy, the sort who would abuse teachers if they reprimanded his daughter. In her various schools Tesssa had met all these sorts before and knew the way they operated. To gain her own liberation she would have to take someone down with her, and it might as well be someone who deserved it, in her opinion. She chose Jackie.

Being small for her age was a bonus. Also the fact that she was delivered to school by a chauffeur (George) in a smart car. This was toffee-nosed in the extreme and tempted Jackie into her first derogatory remark.

"School bus not good enough for you, eh? Us rough lot?"

Tessa looked up at her, satisfied with what she saw: a stupid face, vicious, jealous eyes. Jackie had the build of a coal-heaver, but none of the amiability of many overlarge people. She was very greedy, and bullied for bars of chocolate out of lunchboxes, and crisps and biscuits, as well as pocket money. "Or else –" Her build stood her in good stead, like a bouncer. Nobody stood up to her, not even the teachers, because of her father. Tessa, noting all this, felt an old surge of excitement. This was what she was good at. She bided a day or two, until the time was ripe.

At lunchtime in the dining room the pupils with lunchboxes sat at one end, screaming and squabbling and flinging bits of food. Tessa sat alone. She had a lunchbox and a second covered plate. She watched Jackie do her usual swiping of the best bits of other people's lunch and waited until her turn came. Jackie never missed her out, because she had no friends to protect her.

"What's in there then?"

For once Tessa replied. "Want to see?"

"Yeah, I might like it."

Tessa had chosen well. She whipped off the cover, picked up the dish and splodged a thick custard trifle square into Jackie's face. It was full of cream and jam, one of Mrs Tims' best, and Tessa ground it well in, and up into the girl's greasy hair for good measure, leaving the foil dish sitting askew on the top of her head.

Uproar ensued – glee and wild shrieking from the oppressed, and immediate retaliation from Jackie's gang. Tessa was prepared for this too. As they came at her, she turned and snatched a knife out of her schoolbag – another of Mrs Tims' useful accessories – and faced the oncomers with it raised and ready.

They stopped in their tracks, gasping. This brand of violence was something altogether different, far more shocking than the trifle. The uproar turned suddenly to silence. A white-faced teacher teetered on the edge of the crowd.

"Tessa, dear, is that wise?" she bleated into the hush.

Tessa shrugged. She was enjoying herself for once, but the object of her action was achieved. She had no need of any more. Jackie's father would see to the rest.

Which was how it turned out.

"I have no alternative but to suspend you," Mrs Alston said to her sadly. "I suspect you did it entirely for that reason."

"I wasn't going to use the knife, only stop them doing me over. I knew what would happen when I sloshed Jackie."

Mrs Alston was far too astute for her comfort. For all her grim demeanour, she was someone Tessa wanted to think kindly of her. A bit like Jimmy. She could not fathom why. Most people she totally despised.

"I know Jackie's a bully – I shall sort that out. But it wasn't the bullying, was it? You want to leave?"

"Yes."

"Why?"

Tessa did not reply. She wanted to tell her, but couldn't.

"You have such a strong character. You ought to channel that strength into something worthwhile."

Tessa wanted to cry out, Yes! Yes! I am, that's why! But she did not know how to make contact. There was nothing Mrs Alston could do for her, save let her go.

She went. Her mother cried. Maurice locked her in her room for a couple of days, while he remembered, then he went away and Tessa was back at Sparrows Wyck the same day. She ran all the way, sobbing for breath, for happiness, for fear . . . *Wisbey* – Wisbey had her job! She would kill him! Her breath made clouds on the cold autumn air, the grass was crisp underfoot. The chestnut trees in front of the farm were weeping great swags of brown leaves and conkers bright as horses' hides. The freedom gave her wings.

The horses had been ridden out. A boy was unsaddling Buffoon in the yard, a bounding Walter getting in his way. Gilly and Sarah were rubbing down Gossamer and God Almighty. Walter leapt up at Tessa, frenzied with joy at seeing her again.

Tessa pushed him away, flung her arms round Buffoon's neck and buried her burning face in his mane.

"Gerroff my horse!" Wisbey cried. "Who's this maniac?"

Tessa could hear the others laughing. Walter leapt up again. Wisbey shouted at him. But Buffoon nuzzled Tessa's face.

"He remembers me! He knows me!" she whispered. She turned glowing eyes out of the lovely smell and tickle of Buffoon's neck, and saw Wisbey's outraged red face. He hit her with his body brush on the side of her head, knocking her backwards. She fell over the water bucket and Walter leapt on her prone figure, covering her face with wet licks.

Sarah tried to keep order, but couldn't stop laughing.

"You two idiots! Behave like human beings, for God's sake! Wisbey, this is Tessa – you've heard of her. You have to make allowances – she's mad. Tessa, shake hands with Wisbey. He looks after Buffoon beautifully. You should be pleased."

"Buffoon is mine!"

"How come you're not at school?"

"I've been suspended. I can't go."

Tessa got up and faced Wisbey warily. He scowled at her. He was an untidy youth with spots and reddish hair like a brush, a scalping in decline. He was built like a small tank, his eyes were like guns.

"Yeah, I've heard of her," he admitted. "Didn't believe it."

"I'm back," Tessa said. "I can do Buffoon again."

Sarah said, "It's not as easy as that. We'll talk about it."

"He's mine."

"Actually he belongs to a Mr Claude Cressington, Tessa, and he is in the charge of our guv'nor, Mr Peter Fellowes. It's not for you to say, I'm afraid. Wisbey might let you muck him out, mind you."

Sarah's voice made it plain she was not to be argued with. She saw Tessa's expression and added, "Later, Tessa. Not now. You can clean his tack."

In the tack-room Tessa tried to keep her counsel when the others came in and put the kettle on. She remembered she did not show anything, but things were getting out of hand lately. They tried to make her say why she had been thrown out of school again but she would not be drawn. Jimmy came in while this conversation was going on and looked at her and said, "Her way of coming back here, I reckon. Eh, Tessa?"

She would not admit it, even to Jimmy.

"Going to keep up your lessons – the ones that matter?"

"Oh yes! Yes please!"

"Good."

Tessa could not remember feeling so happy as she did at that moment, not since Declan and Shiner. She *loved* Jimmy – like Buffoon . . . it was all too much for her. She had to go out. She could not cope.

"What did she do, to get thrown out again?" Jimmy asked the tack-room.

Gilly, who knew all the local gossip, said, "She drew a knife on Jackie Barstow."

Wisbey's eyes widened.

"A knife! Blimey! You didn't say she was dangerous! Only mad."

"She's dangerous if she doesn't get what she wants," Sarah said.

Jimmy said to Sarah, "Give her Buffoon. She's got nothing else in this life."

"But to be so besotted – it's dangerous – what will she do when he goes?"

"For now. She'll grow up eventually."

"Yeah, go on," said Gilly. "Wisbey doesn't want him – remember what he said when he saw him? Bloody cab-horse, he said. He only likes him now because he's so easy to do. Give him something worthy of his talents!"

Sarah said, "He can have God Almighty."

"You're joking?" Wisbey was uncertain.

"No, I mean it. He'll give you something to think about."

Wisbey's eyes shone. "I thought he was yours?"

"I'm Head Lad, remember. I don't 'do' horses."

"You could have fooled me," Gilly said.

They all laughed.

So Tessa got her wish, Wisbey got his heart's desire in God Almighty and Sarah took over a new horse called Catbells.

There were now fifteen horses in the stable, a few new ones and the ones that had been having a summer holiday. The others did three each and Tessa was given Buffoon and a gelding everyone called the Littlun, because he was scarcely fifteen and a half hands high. He was ponyish in his ways, quick and agile, and quite different to ride from the ponderous Buffoon. In fact, as Tessa's expertise grew, she enjoyed her exercise on the Littlun because he wasn't such hard work as Buffoon, he was so eager and keen to go. For all his hard food and new fitness, Buffoon was still like a double-decker bus, slowing down at every opportunity.

The others all ribbed Tessa over Buffoon, but she learned to take it. She did not answer back, but her silences were no longer what Gilly had described as "evil". Inside she smiled to herself. Nothing could budge her trust in him.

To her, he was a great horse.

Peter got worried because he was employing a twelve-year-old child and could get taken to court. Tessa refused to be paid, so said there was no problem.

"You won't be able to stay – it's only temporary, until you get yourself an education," Peter said, to allay his own fears.

But Tessa said, "I will stay."

She knew now that there was no school that would take her, not after the knife. Jackie's father tried to involve the police over the knife, but Mrs Alston refused to co-operate with them. It was an in-house situation, she said. If Mr Barstow didn't like it he could withdraw Jackie. She arranged for Tessa to have private tuition at home. As this was only a few hours a week, and in the afternoons, it did not interfere with Tessa's stable life. The tutor was a hardened, retired battleaxe, of which sex Tessa found it hard to determine, but as Tessa was so happy with the way her plans had succeeded she worked with a will and made no trouble. So much so that the battleaxe told Mrs Alston that she ought to be reinstated, there was nothing wrong with her attitude.

"There will be, if she comes back," Mrs Alston said. "What does she do in her spare time, I'd like to know?"

"I don't know, but she smells of manure."

"Strange. Leave her be," said Mrs Alston.

"She's a clever girl."

"I know that."

And Mrs Alston laughed.

A Great Gallop

$\mathcal{T}$he walking and trotting days were now changing into canter and work. Peter would start racing his horses at the end of October and they needed to be fit and strong. They had to be tried out on the gallops to test their stamina and speed.

Peter said, "Is Tessa ready to ride real work?"

"Oh, she'll come to no harm on that bus Buffoon," they all said. "Humour the girl."

Tessa was used to cantering Buffoon. It felt like being on a garden swing, backwards and forwards, flump, flump, the long red ears wagging at the end of the long scruffy neck. However many oats disappeared into his belly, Buffoon was always gaunt, his hip-bones sticking out like an advertisement for a horse charity. Tessa called him her beauty. They all laughed. Greevy was incredulous that Peter kept such a nag in his stables. Tessa could not rebut his criticism, as it was the same she heard every day – only kindlier and jokier – in her own yard. But nothing budged her devotion. Only with Greevy, it hurt. Maurice owned the Raleigh stable star, the horse called Crowsnest. It was black as a winter night and as strikingly handsome as Buffoon was ugly. He was a horse everyone turned to admire. Even Tessa could not help catching her breath when he came towards them up the gallops, the silk-smooth coat rippling over shoulders that worked like pistons, raking out over the autumn turf. The racing press hyped him and earmarked him for the Champion Hurdle, the great race in March at the Cheltenham Festival. This is the meeting when the best meet the best, after the winter's jousting.

Greevy was confident.

"You wait. He's a winner. Dad's going to make a pile."

The first prize was in six figures.

"You'll be there one day, Buffoon," Tessa said to the horse as she groomed him. "You'll beat that Crowsnest, I know you will."

Not in the Champion Hurdle, perhaps – Tessa thought big: more like the Gold Cup or the Grand National.

There was no one to listen to her rubbish, only the amiable horse who flicked a long ear back at her. Tessa knew he trusted her now. She trusted him too. She always talked to him, although she still said little outside his box.

When Peter said she could ride him in his first real gallop, she was not afraid.

"Of course not," she said scornfully, when he suggested she might prefer Wisbey or Gilly to take him.

"You've got to roust him up – I want to see what he can do. He can go with God Almighty and Gossamer, the three of you, and I want you to try and stay with them. He won't, of course, but do your best."

"God, he's slow," Wisbey grumbled. "He'll only just have started when we've finished."

It was a wet, mizzling day, not cold. They rode out in a line, hunched into anoraks. Peter had gone ahead in his Land Rover to the top of the gallops. He had taken care to time it so that there were no Raleigh horses about. One did not want the serious tests to be remarked by rival stables. Tessa tried to keep Buffoon alongside God Almighty, where Wisbey sat with his smug, superior expression, secure in his faith that he rode the best. God Almighty had won some good races, and was expected to win more. He was the only half-decent horse in the stables.

"I'll see you right," he said to Tessa. "Just track me. Don't be afraid."

He was trying to be encouraging.

Tessa thought patronizing.

She did not reply. Her face was set and determined as she pulled up at the bottom of the gallop. They lined up together under Sarah's fierce eye, the three of them, with Gilly on Gossamer.

"You go like it's a race, Tessa – go for it. See what the old boy can do. When I drop my hand."

There was no wait, they were away. Tessa saw God Almighty and Gossamer galvanize ahead of her, their great muscly hind-quarters powering them up into the rain, throwing gouts of mud back into her face. Buffoon launched himself like a ship into a head sea, wanting to please, following his friends. Tessa fought for her balance, pulled herself up with a handful of mane and crouched low over the mountainous withers. Her ship was under way. But in no great hurry. The gap between him and his friends widened.

"Buffoon, show them, you idiot! You're Shiner's boy, not a cab-horse. Do it for me, Buffoon, go!"

An ear twitched back. She knew his mind – what, go? Why? I'm happy here. . .

"Buffoon – go! Show them! Show them! I *know* you can!"

She was batty, and knew it, feeling the adrenalin running, the rain in her face, the great warm smell of the horse in her nostrils, the sound of hooves on the downland turf. Mud splattered her. The jockeys in front were always clean, she remembered, clean and smiling. . . *I want to be in front.* . .

Slowly, slowly, the message communicated.

The hill steepened. Buffoon's stride lengthened, the stride he didn't know he'd got. Nobody had told him, before now, what he was for. All that good food and built-up muscle . . . why? The idea of it trickled into him as he felt the mad little ant on his back communicating messages of glory.

And Tessa knew he understood. Whatever else he wasn't, her horse was intelligent. Nobody had ever doubted that. Perhaps too clever to be a good racehorse, they said in the yard. (After all, no one could make a horse try if he didn't want to, not even the best jockey in the world. And why should he? All that effort and pain and only the whip for reward, to go even faster. Clever horses said, Not me, sonny boy.) But Buffoon liked to please, and Tessa was his special mate, and now he found his legs were doing extraordinary things, eating up the ground, raking out farther than ever before, and the other horses' tails were in his face suddenly, and they were holding him up.

As Tessa went past she had a glimpse of Wisbey's face and heard his shout shredded on the wind — rude, anxious expletives. She knew God Almighty was flat out, for they were breasting the last furlong where Peter waited beside his Land Rover, and at the top they must pull up.

But by the time they passed the Land Rover Buffoon was five lengths clear and still travelling. Tessa just sat there, all her strength drained away holding on to that power. She was like a rag, crying, and still powering on.

"Buffy, please!"

Her full weight on his mouth meant nothing to him. But her anxiety seemed to suggest something . . . what, he wasn't sure of. . . He was so enjoying it, his heart bursting with the feel of his own power, but the message on top had changed. He could feel something negative up there, he wasn't pleasing her any more.

Kindly, he dropped the bit. The fizz went out of him and he came back to a hard canter, blowing out great snorting breaths into the rain. Tessa couldn't see for mud and rain and tears . . . tears of what? Fright, perhaps, but more a hysterical jubilation at what had happened. He *can* do it! was exploding in her brain! After all they said . . . *cab-horse* . . . my darling beautiful Buffoon!

She wiped her face hastily. She was miles away from the

81

others and had to walk back, it seemed for ever. Would Peter be angry? She didn't know what to expect, feeling limp now as a woollen toy, her knees trembling. Buffoon stretched out his neck, shaking his long ears, quiet as a child's first pony. The rain and sweat shone like oil on his great shoulders. Tessa could feel the rain creeping down her neck.

The other three were walking their horses round in a circle to cool off. Steam rose from them so that they looked like a small laundry in action. Sarah had ridden up slowly and sat on Catbells talking to Peter. As Tessa came up they raised their eyes and stared.

Tessa pulled up.

"I'm sorry, I couldn't help it."

Sarah burst out laughing.

"Sorry?"

Peter came up smiling, and put his hand on the steaming neck.

"It was a great gallop, Tessa. Knocked us for six. He's never shown anything, after all, never really taken up the bridle before, lazy sod that he is." He laughed. "What did you say to him?"

Tessa grinned. "He's the best. I told him he was."

"You're the only one that thought it. Now we're all impressed. Good work, you rode well."

If only he knew! Tessa thought. She was shaking with post-shock and the glory of it. She joined the other two and they expressed their amazement. And respect, Tessa sensed.

Gilly said, "It was fantastic! What a stride! I couldn't believe it when you whistled past. And I was flat out."

Wisbey said, "She was bolting. At least we were in control."

Was she bolting? Tessa had no idea.

Gilly said to Tessa, "He would say that – typical man. Doesn't like to be beaten." And to Wisbey, "She stopped him, didn't she? If she was bolting she'd be over the next hill by now."

Sarah came back to join them and they walked back down the valley. Sarah told them not to mention the incident to anyone.

"Especially to Greevy, Tessa. Not a word. We don't want them to know about it."

The attitude in the yard towards Buffoon had changed, Tessa sensed. Nobody was going to call him a cab-horse any more. Tessa's devotion was no longer a big joke. If you had a good horse a bit of devotion was allowed, to be expected. Wisbey was devoted to God Almighty, and resented the fact that Buffoon had passed him as if he were standing still.

He made a lot of excuses. "I still had something in reserve, stands to reason."

"I could have gone for ever," Tessa said, remembering the feel.

When he heard all this, Jimmy said, "We'd better see if he can jump before we get too excited."

He said to Tessa, "He's so ungainly, he might have trouble." But Sarah said, "Not with Jimmy to teach him."

Nobody said if Tessa would continue to ride work on Buffoon. She did not ask. Just prayed. When she got home for her afternoon lessons – only twice a week fortunately – she fell asleep across the table.

"I didn't know I was that boring," the Battleaxe said glumly, giving her a shake. "Are you all right, dear?"

Her body ached all over and her head was still whirling. She tried to pull herself together.

That night at supper, Greevy said to her, "Big chestnut horse in your string – is that a new one?"

"A new one?"

"Can go a bit, I hear. Who is it?"

Tessa was shaken. Jimmy had told her long ago that there were no secrets in the racehorse valley. But how did Greevy know? There had been no one in sight.

"Catbells?" she lied. Catbells was a chestnut, but lean and small, nothing like Buffoon.

Greevy looked puzzled.

Maurice said, "There's nothing in that stable that can go a bit, lad. What are you talking about? Tessa's only keeping out of mischief down there. She's not learning anything."

He was lighting a cigar, which he always did over coffee.

"That Jimmy Fellowes – he's wasted in that dump," Greevy said. "He knows his job all right. Anyone could learn from him. He ought to be a jockey."

"He's too heavy," Tessa said.

She had heard this conversation in the yard. They all said

Jimmy should be a jockey, but Jimmy only laughed and said, "I like my food, thank you." Nearly all jockeys had to waste, to get light enough to take the rides, and many of them looked pale and wrinkled before their time. Jimmy said he was too lazy to be a jockey, and that was true. He worked in an apparently leisurely fashion, although for long hours. His work was slow and patient, suiting his temperament. Jockeys had to get up at dawn to ride work, travel to lots of different stables to try out horses and all over the country every day to racetracks. Jimmy hardly ever left the yard.

"He doesn't want to be a jockey," Tessa said.

"Raleigh would give him a job any day of the week," Greevy said.

"He's a fool. No ambition," Maurice said.

Maurice's smugness infuriated Tessa, but she knew better than to rise to the bait.

"The best, only the best is good enough. I pay for it, I expect it." Maurice blew a cloud of smoke across the table.

Tessa wanted to scream. She knew Crowsnest had cost over a hundred thousand pounds (Maurice had sold a golf course). The senile Mr Cressington had given one thousand five hundred pounds for Buffoon, the price of a superannuated riding-school hack. Yet Tessa knew — *knew* now — that Buffoon was worth ten of Crowsnest.

When she said this in the yard the next day they all laughed at her.

"Steady on, Tess! One gallop's not added ninety-nine

thousand pounds to his value! Give us a chance! And Crowsnest's already won a packet on the flat."

She told them that Greevy had heard of the famous gallop. She hadn't said a word about it.

Peter shrugged and said, "I think the birds spread gossip in this valley. Nothing goes unnoticed. The only person I saw was a woman out with her dog and a girl on a pony."

"Spies!"

"We'll keep him in the home field to teach him jumping, not use the jumps up the valley. Not yet, anyway."

The experienced horses were ready to race and the new ones like Buffoon and Catbells and Gossamer would race over hurdles as soon as they learned the game. It did not take long to teach them, even at Jimmy's ordered pace. Once they learned to jump telegraph poles on the ground, then logs, then a pile of brush, Jimmy sent them side by side with a horse who knew all about it. In company the excitement of the game got to them and they all flew over real hurdles without any trouble.

"It's just practice now they've learned to like it, not be frightened. They need to know how to lengthen or shorten a stride as the jump comes up, to get it right. That comes with experience. We want a good jockey now, to ride for the yard."

Apparently they had never had a really good jockey before. Really good jockeys were snapped up by the yards with the star horses, like Raleigh's.

"Do girls get to be jump jockeys?" Tessa asked.

"Yes. A few. But they don't get many rides."

"Why not?"

"Most trainers don't think they're strong enough."

Tessa understood this, realizing how Buffoon's gallop had drained her energy. She hadn't jumped, or ridden a finish, or done anything save hang on, yet she had been exhausted. Buffoon hadn't been asked to do another strong gallop since that day, but he had done fast canters and Tessa hadn't lost her ride. She had gained confidence quickly and he had never carted her. He was an essentially kind horse.

"I'd like to ride Buffoon in a race." She could say this now to Jimmy, although she wouldn't have said it in front of the others.

He didn't deride her, although he smiled his slow, kind smile.

"You have to get a licence first. But if you really want it . . . well, you've got the talent. You need to get stronger. And then you'll have to charm Mr Cressington to let you ride – that won't be easy! All owners want the best jockeys, stands to reason, after all they've paid out in training fees. Don't bank on it, Tessa."

They had never set eyes yet on Mr Cressington, Buffoon's owner. Peter said he rang up sometimes to enquire when the horse was going to race.

"Any day you like," Jimmy said. "He's ready."

"He says he'll come. It was his ninety-third birthday this week. I hope he lasts long enough."

"What's he like?" Tessa asked.

"I've never met him, only talked to him on the phone," Peter said.

It rarely occurred to Tessa that she didn't own Buffoon. The person who actually owned him was the last person who had anything to do with his life, she now realized. Yet he had the power to take him away, or sell him. A shiver went through her. Her mind was still struggling to come to terms with the fact that she had decided to become a jockey. Jimmy had only said it was difficult, not impossible. That was enough for her. She was twelve, and had plenty of time to learn. Get strong. Be the best!

And now Peter said Buffoon would race next week. Expect nothing, he said.

But Tessa expected everything. Of course.

9

The First Race

*W*isbey was detailed to take Buffoon to his first race.

Tessa was outraged.

"He's my horse! It's my job!"

"Tessa, you're only twelve. You look it. We'll all be run in if you do this job in public. I'll lose my licence."

Peter was sharp.

Seeing Tessa's face, he said more kindly, "You can come, if you like. Pretend you're my niece or something. But no interfering. Not a word."

"Look after Lucky," Wisbey jibed. "Lead him round the paddock."

Buffoon hated being away from Lucky. He only accepted it when he was out at exercise, but at home he would kick his door down if Lucky was taken away from him. Peter had tried to wean him off the pony, but to no avail.

"Better than a sheep or a goat," Sarah said.

They had all seen other trainers with the same problem. It wasn't uncommon.

Tessa tried not to show how screwed up she was. She travelled in the front seat of the horse box with Wisbey and Peter, who drove. The journey wasn't far, the meeting insignificant, Buffoon's race a minor Novice Hurdle with bottom prize-money. Their jockey was an old pro, due to retire.

"Just give him a good time, we're not expecting anything," Peter said to him.

Tessa was, and found it difficult to keep calm as Wisbey led Buffoon out of the paddock. Her heart was racing like a Formula One engine and the race hadn't even started. Buffoon was bottom of the betting at fifty-to-one.

Mr Cressington said he would put a tenner on.

He was a frail old boy pushed in a wheelchair by a seventy-year-old daughter whose face was heavily lined with a permanent frown.

"Don't know what the stupid old fool is thinking of," she said to Peter in a fierce whisper. "Getting into this game at his age! I ask you!"

Peter tried to think of something polite to say and failed. He smiled and shrugged.

Tessa felt out of her depth. When the horses had gone down to the start Wisbey came back and she latched on to him gratefully. Peter had gone off to the Members' stand with his owners but Wisbey was in a bunch with the other grooms – most of whom, Tessa noticed, were in the same state as she was. Even Wisbey now was quite tizzed up.

"He won't do anything, not first time," he said. "That old jockey doesn't try. He just takes the money, keeps safe."

"I thought they all tried!"

Wisbey laughed.

"You want a young jockey, who wants to make his name. Not a crazy one, but an intelligent one. There's a few, real horsemen. . ."

"Who?"

The horses were coming down past the stands, cantering to the start. Tessa couldn't keep her eyes off Buffoon who loped along in the rear, looking at the stands and the crowd with surprised eyes. She saw that he really was ungainly compared with the rest, his legs seeming to go in all directions. Ahead of him another chestnut, as if to make a comparison, floated over the ground in perfect balance, everything about him exuding class.

Wisbey nodded knowledgeably. "That one – on Aurora – that's your jockey, one of the best."

Aurora was at Raleigh's stable. His lad stood next to Tessa, shaking like a leaf. Tessa thought, I'm not the only one. Even Wisbey was excited, even for Buffoon, she could see.

As if he saw that she noticed, Wisbey said, "When it's mine – when God Almighty runs – I shan't be able to watch!"

So, she wasn't the only potty one then! Tessa felt she was in congenial company for the first time in her life, watching the motley collection of lads and lasses she was with. They were all involved, she could see, even the quiet ones who gave themselves away by their very silence. She had to be a quiet one. She was only twelve, she should be at school. She stood next to Wisbey, cold as ice, trembling.

"That old man, Mr Cressington," Wisbey said, "he'll die of excitement, I shouldn't wonder. And that rat-faced old hag'll have Buffoon sold for cats' meat sooner than you can turn round."

"Don't say that!" She spat the words out, hating him.

But he laughed, his bristle-brush hair sticking up on end in the cold wind that whistled down the course. Everyone looked frozen.

But it was Aurora's lad who was shouting, red-faced with joy, at the end of the race. Tessa couldn't even see Buffoon, her eyes stinging with tears, because he wasn't there. The horses came past, pulling up, in a fever of sweat and flying mud, and Wisbey and Tessa ran the other way, down the course, to find their horse. Long after all the others had finished, he cantered home, his long pale legs dark with mud, his eyes all surprised at the milling crowd, looking everywhere. He wasn't in the least put out, hardly sweating. He pulled up and whinnied in a thoroughly unprofessional manner.

"He wants that bloody pony," Wisbey said grimly.

The jockey slid down, rolled his eyes, and threw the reins at Wisbey.

Peter came hurrying up.

"Well, we weren't expecting anything," he said to the jockey.

The jockey laughed. "I'll be off before your owner joins us – leave the explanations to you. He enjoyed it, like you said, but at his own pace. I tried, Mr Fellowes, honest, but there's nothing there. He's as bad as he looks."

Wisbey led Buffoon away, giving Tessa a kick on the ankle as he went to stop her launching herself in fury at the amiable jockey. Peter had to turn and greet the Cressingtons, trundling towards him, and Tessa, with one glance at the rat-faced woman, turned and ran after Wisbey.

Wisbey had to pull Buffoon up to let the triumphant Aurora go past on his way to the winner's enclosure, and Tessa looked up at the successful jockey. People were reaching up to shake his hand, everyone wreathed in smiles. His lad was red-faced with joy. The jockey was trying to look nonchalant, but Tessa could see that he was bursting with triumph. He wasn't much older than Wisbey by the look of him, although it was hard to discern his features beneath the layer of mud. But Aurora was stressed out, head down, flanks heaving, his nostrils red-filled flaring pits. Tessa was shocked.

She stumbled after Wisbey, her emotions played out. Buffoon's raking stride pulled the lad along and she had to run. But Buffoon looked cool and happy, nothing like Aurora. Was that what winning meant, trying that hard? Oh, how she loved Buffoon!

In the stable yard Buffoon whinnied to Lucky who was standing with his nose sticking up over the stable door – it was too high for him to see over. He gave an excited reply and the two greeted each other like long lost friends. An official came along and asked for Tessa's identity card – she hadn't got one and was ordered out. It was starting to rain. Tessa wandered across the grass, soaked and miserable, her mind in a turmoil, trying to come to terms with the gulf between winning and losing. It was what racing was all about. She was going to have readjust her ideas, after today.

Going home in the horsebox Peter said, "Funny thing is, we know he's got it in him. We saw it. In spite of what he looks like, he's got a real engine. And that's the nub of it, when it comes down to winning. A good engine and a great heart."

"He's got a great heart!" Tessa said.

"According to you he's got a halo and wings as well."

"You told the jockey not to try!"

"Steady on, Tessa! I told him to give the horse a good time. He knew what I meant . Not put him off racing for life, in his first race. Not get him bumped, scared, hurt. They've got seven – eight – years ahead of them, these young horses, if they keep sound and right in the head. There's no hurry."

"Jeez, if you think you're going to win every time you've got a tough time ahead of you, Tess," Wisbey said.

"And remember, Cressington didn't get him so cheap for no reason. He's not the sort of horse a trainer would buy. So it's a bonus if we get anything at all, even finishing. He finished, I give him that."

Now Tessa was totally committed to work, and given to speaking – too much sometimes – Peter was showing his kinder face. Her passion for her horse worried him.

"He'll be sold, like as not, if that Cressington daughter's got anything to do with it, and Tessa will fall apart," he said to the others in the morning.

"If he's for sale, those parents of hers ought to buy him for her. It's the horse that's transformed her – remember what she was like when she first came?" Gilly was serious.

"Yeah. But that stepfather of hers'll do her no favours. He's not just mean – he's got a cruel streak," Sarah said. "Remember that horse – what was it called? – Shenandoah something –"

"Shenandoah Star," Jimmy said.

"That's it. He bought it for a packet, put a lot of money on it to win, and it didn't. He lost a fortune. And he told the trainer to punish it – shut it up without food and water for a week!"

"That was when Turner trained for him. Turner refused, didn't he? Naturally –"

"And Morrison took the horse away and had it shot. A man who can do that is not just cruel. He's not right in the head."

"Yeah, I remember that. And his other horses were taken out of Turner's yard and sent to Raleigh. I don't think Raleigh knew that story when he took them on. It came out later, when the knacker-lad gossiped."

"Well, let's hope old Buffoon learns the job. We'll give him every chance. Get a decent jockey next time."

"Get Tessa to ride him!"

"She made him run all right. That's true."

"The girl's got a talent," Jimmy said.

"Pity she's not a lad," Peter said.

"Ah, we can't all be so privileged. . ." Sarah muttered.

Tessa never gave Jimmy a chance to skive off giving her a

riding lesson. She was there every afternoon (except lesson days) on whatever horse Jimmy said. She would ride all day if she had the chance. At home she did press-ups in her bedroom, and she pinched a pair of weights from Greevy to lift. Weedy Greevy's attempts to improve his physique only lasted a week or two. She got all his cast-off equipment and worked on it religiously. She didn't grow much, but she thought she could see her muscles rippling in the bath. And her confidence on the horses grew all the time. She even learned to master the stroppy ones now.

Because she was doing what she wanted she did not bate Maurice any more, although she hated him no less. Wisbey told her the story of Shenandoah Star. Thank God he didn't own Buffoon! She remembered the hedgehog. She thought her mother was getting more like the doomed hedgehog every day, brought down by Maurice. He squashed her without killing her, breaking her spirit, seeming to enjoy the cruelty. But Tessa knew she could do nothing about it, because her mother didn't seem to recognize what was happening.

But she would put it right, as soon as she was free. When she was eighteen and free by law she would change things at Goldlands. She did not know how, but she knew she would. Whatever she really wanted, she got. She was going to be a jockey, and she was going to be strong, and her body would match her fierce mind. She thought about nothing else: her ambition, and her horse.

"How old do you have to be to get a jockey's licence?" she asked Jimmy.

"Sixteen."

Four years!

"Don't you want to be a jockey?" she asked Wisbey.

"No fear!"

"Why not?"

"I'm not stupid," he said.

Tessa thought he was. She remembered the jockey on Aurora, her glimpse of his muddy, glowing face. She found out his name. Tom Bryant.

"Next time Buffoon runs, can Tom Bryant ride him?" she asked Peter.

"We can *ask* him, but he's nearly always booked. I doubt he'd want to ride Buffoon."

"You can *ask* him," Tessa said.

"Cor, you take liberties, telling the guv'nor who to book!" Wisbey said.

But Peter, given food for thought, said to Tessa, "We'll try him again, with you on board. See if you can make him run like you did before. I'll use my stop-watch. And if he shows us anything again, I'll try and get him a decent rider for his next race."

"You must do it, Buffoon!" Tessa whispered to him as she groomed him in the morning. "It really matters — you must show them!"

She was trembling as they came to the start of the gallop at the bottom of the valley. Wisbey on God Almighty had a look on his face that meant he wasn't going to be beaten this time, and Sarah was holding in Catbells' exuberance with some difficulty. Buffoon meanwhile scratched his nose on his foreleg and yawned. Tessa hauled him in frantically.

Sarah turned and shouted, "Are you ready?" and sprung Catbells into action.

Tom Bryant! Tessa thought and slammed her heels into Buffoon's sides. He jumped up, startled, and saw the other horses flying away from him up the hill. Peter's Land Rover was a green spot in the far distance.

When it had happened before it had been a great surprise, but now Tessa was expecting it, it was far harder. Being a race jockey was quite different from just being a rider. Buffoon, so laid back, took time to change into fast mode, and the active Catbells was almost out of sight when Tessa at last managed to convey to her horse that he must run for his life. She felt him starting to take an interest, finding the power that he hardly knew he possessed – had so rarely been asked for – finding it and enjoying it, the ears pricking up into the wind with enjoyment. Tessa lifted her head and squinted up ahead, and saw Wisbey turn in his saddle to see where she was. She laughed. Yes, he could do it!

Save, as Peter pointed out, the race was just about over when Buffoon got into gear. He passed first God Almighty and then Catbells when they had already passed Peter's Land Rover. Wisbey said he was already pulling up when Tessa went past. Tessa didn't believe him. Catbells was pulling up for lack of puff, but Buffoon didn't pull up until he was over the hill and looking down into the next valley, on to the sprawling complex of Raleigh's splendid premises. Tessa couldn't make him stop, although she denied she was being bolted with.

"He takes a long time to stop," she said.

"And start," they said.

But Peter said he would try for Tom Bryant, or someone more ambitious than his last jockey.

10
Maurice's Dinner Party

*M*aurice had asked "a few people to dinner".

"Ugh!" said Tessa.

"Listen, darling, it's racing people. You might be interested. Mr Raleigh's coming, and two of his other owners, and I think his jockey."

"Not Tom Bryant?"

"Mmm, I think so. Greevy asked him."

Tessa was stunned. Usually she ate in the kitchen on dinner party days. It was bad enough in the dining-room when it was just family, but dinner parties were her idea of hell, listening to Maurice's fat friends talking about money for hour after hour. She never said a word, save to correct anyone who thought she was Maurice's daughter. "*Step*daughter," she would say icily. "My father is Declan Blackthorn." She loved to say his name: Declan Blackthorn. Maurice hated that, she knew. She could feel his eyes on her, hating. She liked it. Nobody spoke to her after that, as a rule.

But Tom Bryant . . . in her very dining-room!

"Yes," she said. "Count me in."

"Wear a decent dress and don't rile Maurice, to please me."

Myra knew more about horses than Maurice and a lot about

racing with her Irish past, but Tessa knew she wouldn't say much. She was always nervous in company, waiting for the put-down which Maurice invariably delivered in front of his friends. He was pleased to introduce her as his wife, as she looked flashily attractive when she dressed herself up, but when she had had a few drinks and started to flirt and enjoy herself, he got angry with her. These days she remembered, and her nervousness was increasing. Her hands shook when she lifted her wine glass. Tessa noticed all this, and it fuelled her hatred of Maurice. Myra, who had once gone to great lengths to keep her figure, no longer had to watch what she ate. Without trying she was thin, almost haggard.

"Tom Bryant's coming to dinner," Tessa crowed in the tack-room.

Sarah looked worried.

"Not a word, Tessa – not a word about Buffoon! Don't go spouting your gab to Tom Bryant, of all people."

"But we want him to ride!"

"Yes, and he'll be asked, when the time's right – if that day should ever come – by Mr Fellowes, not a twelve-year-old child."

Tessa was scorched by Sarah's laser-purple eyes. Everyone flinched when Sarah was annoyed.

"No gossip at all!" she snapped. Then, in a resigned voice, "Not that we've any secrets here. No great talent to keep under wraps." Then, with more interest, "No reason why you shouldn't listen to their gossip, mind you, and report back."

All the same, Tessa was excited by the thought of meeting Tom Bryant and studying him as to his suitability to ride Buffoon.

She spent a long time in the bathroom washing her hair and making sure there was no stable smell left about her. Apart from her hands and her short, broken nails, she thought she looked very elegant in a dark velvet dress that Myra had bought for her in London. She did not lack smart clothes, but hardly ever wore them. The imported dinner-party cooks seemed to be doing a good job, judging by the smell coming from the kitchen, and Maurice seemed to be in one of his rare good moods. Tessa thought her mother looked stunning in a black, beaded dress – perhaps her new slimness was becoming, after all – and a good deal of make-up brightened the usual wan complexion. After a couple of whiskies her old sparkle came back, and Tessa could quite see why Maurice had wanted to marry her. She remembered clearly the woman her mother had once been, bursting with high spirits, provocative and with a furious temper. The shadow of her old self was back, as she got up to welcome the guests at the front door.

Tessa held back, and for once did not contradict the assumption that she was Maurice's daughter.

James Raleigh was, close to, a large, handsome man with a strong presence. Tessa could imagine everyone jumping to attention in his yard, as they all jumped to Sarah at Sparrows Wyck. He had a sharp-faced, extremely beautiful wife called Diana who was well known in the eventing world, but rather more reserved in her manner than her husband. Tessa got the impression that she was attending in the line of duty – in fact, as the evening got under way, she realized that all the guests were there for a purpose: a big sale of horses in training was coming up and Maurice was planning to buy. He wanted advice. As well as the Raleighs there was an Irish couple who seemed to have a lot of know-how about the horses on offer, and Tom Bryant's father who was a well-known bloodstock agent. Tom Bryant was there more as a companion to his father than in his jockey capacity, Tessa deduced, for he was put at the bottom of the dinner table next to her, and – like her – did not speak unless he was spoken to.

Tessa was bubbling with curiosity and excitement but had to keep all her faculties well under control. She could see that Tom Bryant was not in the same league as the older people, in spite of the fact that, when they had spent their thousands on buying and training the horses, he was the one on whom it all depended to make the expenditure worthwhile. What a responsibility! thought Tessa. Especially when the owner was someone as rapacious and ungenerous as her stepfather.

"He's not really my father, he's my stepfather," she said to Tom Bryant when the others were all talking.

Tom said, "Lucky for you."

"I hate him."

Tom grinned. Tessa realized that he wasn't all that much older than she was – eighteen, perhaps – and was lean and hard as whipcord, and extremely good-looking in spite of a bent nose and a scar across one eyebrow. He was well spoken and obviously well educated, and had come to prominence in point-to-point racing very quickly: he was the present whizz-kid jockey. Jimmy said jockeys could go down as quickly as they came up and said that Tom Bryant's rise to fame was well deserved, but dangerous. "Once you're up there, there's only one other place to go, and that's down. He's very young to take that sort of responsibility." Tessa studied him to see if the responsibility rested heavily upon him, but he seemed quite careless of it to her, more bored and impatient with his companions than respectful, glancing at his watch occasionally. He yawned several times.

Tessa was tongue-tied, not knowing what to say to him. But her mother, lifting her glass of wine to her lips, called gaily across the table, "Tessa goes down to Sparrows Wyck to ride, Tom. I expect you've seen her on the gallops."

"That string of hacks! We've seen them," Greevy said.

Tessa scowled at him. She had been hoping, lately, that Greevy was improving under Mr Raleigh's influence, away from his father, but every time she thought this he ruined it by his sneering and doing-down. If they didn't hate each other so they would get on, having a lot in common. He looked very presentable, she had to admit, in his formal party suit, his spots going through a good phase at the moment. She supposed he was jealous of glamorous, successful Tom. Anyone would be.

"Mr Fellowes' horses?" Tom asked.

Tessa said, "Yes. Jimmy gives me lessons."

"Jimmy Fellowes? You should be good then."

Tessa wanted to say, "Yes, I am," but didn't think it would be right.

"I want to be a jockey," she said.

Greevy laughed and Tom said, "You're mad. It's really tough for a girl. Even taught by Jimmy Fellowes. Trainers don't like 'em."

"I know."

"Who do you ride? There's only one good horse down there, the one with the Gaelic name."

"God Almighty. That's Wisbey's."

"And a new one."

"Buffoon?" Tessa couldn't help herself, her face lighting up.

"No. Catbells – that was good on the flat."

Raleigh, catching the conversation, asked her across the table, "Who's the chestnut job we've heard rumours about? That's a new one, I understand."

Tessa panicked, remembering Sarah's eyes.

"I – I don't know –"

"You said a new one – Buffoon, was it?"

"No! Not Buffoon! He's useless!"

Tessa nearly choked, saying this in front of Tom Bryant. She wanted to die, betraying her darling.

But Maurice said, "It's rubbish, Sparrows Wyck, a load of no-hopers. The girl just amuses herself."

Raleigh said quietly, "They know their job, just haven't had the luck."

"You make your own luck," Maurice said confidently.

"Up to a point. But in racing —" Raleigh shrugged. "Ask a jockey." He looked across at Tom and smiled.

They went back to talking about the horses for sale, and Tessa, in spite of Sarah, whispered to Tom, "Buffoon isn't useless. I had to say that. But he isn't. Remember that. But you mustn't say."

Tom looked at her pointedly. He had wonderful very blue eyes.

"You mean, if I remember, it might be lucky for me?" Although he was teasing her, Tessa thought there was a serious meaning to his question. It was the way he looked at her, sharply, asking.

"Yes," she said. "Yes." Then, remembering Sarah, "But you mustn't say anything! Promise?"

"Promise," he said. And laughed.

At the top of the table they were talking about the Grand National.

"I want a National type," Maurice was dictating. "Long distance, tough. Heart. It doesn't matter about the looks."

"You can't tell heart from looking," the Irishman said. "Only by doing."

"I want to win the Grand National." Maurice made it sound like an order, fired at his minions.

"Don't we all?" said Tom.

He spoke quietly, meaning it for Tessa, but it plopped into a sudden silence and everyone heard it plainly. Tom blushed as Maurice turned angry eyes on him.

"What's wrong with that, young man? Do you think I'm foolish?"

"No, sir, not at all."

"When I have the horse, you might want to ride it. Remember that."

"Yes, sir."

Tessa saw that Raleigh was amused, trying not to show it. Maurice didn't talk like an ordinary human being, she thought. It was all brow-beating stuff, *telling* everybody. Maurice never listened. He had all the expertise round the table, but asked no questions, just told them.

Myra, now full of confidence in the company she enjoyed, turned to Maurice and said, "He's a star, darling. By the time you have your horse, you might have to beg him, on bended knee."

Even Tessa could see that this was an extremely silly thing to say to Maurice. She could tell by the look on his face that he was going to say something terrible to Myra, and she couldn't bear it. She shot out her hand and knocked Tom's full glass of red wine into his lap, and shrieked.

Myra shrieked too. "The carpet! Oh, Tessa!"

Tessa dropped on the floor with her napkin, mopping frantically, and everyone got up and looked helpless.

"Salt — you put salt on red wine to take out the stain," said

Diana Raleigh, and Tom dropped down on his knees beside Tessa with the salt-cellar.

"I did it on purpose, to stop him," Tessa whispered.

"Stop him what?"

But they were surrounded by feet and helpers and Tessa had to retreat. Salt was fetched from the kitchen and ladled on the stain. The party resumed. The sale catalogue was discussed, scribbled on, the plates cleared away by the hired maids. Six of the best horses in the sale had been marked and the optimum price scribbled in.

"He's some spender, your father," Tom whispered to Tessa.

"*Step*father."

"Sorry. Hope he's good at choosing winners."

Tessa could see that Raleigh was really pleased at the prospect of having these good horses in his stables, and was being charming to Myra at his side, and buttering up Maurice. Maurice was loving it, seeing his power over these people. Myra, responding to Raleigh's charm, was bound for disaster, Tessa could see, and there was nothing she could do about it. She had a vivid memory of seeing her mother, after too much to drink, sitting on the lap of Declan's best friend and kissing him heartily, and Declan tipping the chair over so that they all fell on the floor, after which a great punch-up ensued. She could remember her mother laughing and shrieking and joining in, and herself crying in her high chair and nobody taking any notice. She remembered it now, seeing Myra turn to Raleigh, eyelashes aflutter, and saying,

"Perhaps I could have a horse run in my name if you would train it for me? I'm sure Maurice would love that, don't you think so?"

Tessa saw alarm bells registering in Raleigh's brain, as he laughed awkwardly.

Maurice came to his rescue by saying brutally to Myra, "Don't make such a fool of yourself, Myra." And to Raleigh, with a laugh, "Her education lets her down, I'm afraid. It's like the horses – you choose them by their looks, but they let you down in public."

It was incredibly rude and Raleigh, to his eternal credit in Tessa's eyes, recovered from his embarrassment, turned to Myra and said, "I would be pleased to train a horse in your name, certainly, should the opportunity arise." And gave her a sympathetic smile.

But the damage was done and Tessa saw Myra shrivel up, tears coming into her eyes. Her happiness was drenched, her ego flattened. She put down her glass and stared at her plate, her face drained and ugly. Diana Raleigh changed the subject to give her a break, and the difficult moment passed, but there was now a coolness in the atmosphere and the party broke up early.

Bryant, the bloodstock agent, would bid for the horses.

Bryant the jockey whispered to Tessa as he left, "Buffoon, you said. That's the one?"

"Yes."

*

Six weeks later, Tom Bryant saw a large ugly chestnut horse pass his own tiring mount in the last hundred yards of a hurdle race at Newbury, heard its number called the winner and looked up its name.

"Buffoon."

So the little girl was right. He remembered her shining eyes, her plea for secrecy, and laughed out loud.

11
Tom's Question

*B*uffoon pulled down a mouthful of hay from the rack and munched steadily. Lucky waited at his shoulder for the chunks he dropped, and snuffled them up out of the deep straw. He had already eaten his ration, dropped on the floor.

It was three years since his first race. He was seven now. His ant-like carer was fifteen, but no one would have guessed.

She had to stand on a chair to fold back Buffoon's rugs for grooming. She had grown, but was still small and slight. She was never going to have to waste to make the weight in her chosen profession, unlike most jockeys. Tom Bryant, tall by nature, had a hard time keeping down to ten and a half stone, and often looked gaunt and pale.

"Only another year to go, Buffoon, and I can get my licence." She talked incessantly to the horse. The others laughed at her, but Tessa knew Buffoon liked her company. It was only for her that he pricked his ears and softly whinnied over the half-door as she went past, even when it wasn't feeding time.

"You love me, don't you, Buffoon? You and me, we're a pair. Perhaps I will ride you in a race one day, you never know your luck. Although not while Tom wants the ride, I dare say.

I'll never be as good as Tom, it's just not possible. Save you know me, you run for me, don't you? I always knew you'd make it, and all the others laughed, and we'll show beastly Maurice, we'll grind him into the mud, Buffoon, we'll make him sick. Him and his hundred thousand horse – and Tom likes you better, Buffoon. Tom wants to ride you, he says so, but he's got to ride beastly Maurice's horse. . ."

She chuntered away and Buffoon twitched back one long red ear to take in her voice, which he recognized amongst all others. Although Wisbey was his lad at racetracks, Tessa was always there, always waiting for him when he came back (she now had a stable pass with her security photo on it, and didn't get thrown out as she once had), waiting with Lucky beside her to tell him what a good boy he'd been. When he had battled his great heart out and come from behind to grind down the quick boys out front, listening to the crowds' cheers . . . how Tessa wept and screamed amongst the other lads as her horse came home . . . he knew all this as Tessa's voice droned on in the stable. Up on her chair she strapped his gleaming hide with all the vigour of her stringy arms. She was thin but rippled with hard muscle, not an ounce of softness anywhere. "Like cuddling barbed wire," as Wisbey said in the tack-room, having tried a pass or two. They all laughed. "She's not taking to you when Tom Bryant's about," they said.

Or Jimmy, Sarah thought, but didn't say.

Slight as she was, Tessa had learned to groom with the best, throwing all her strength behind her brushes, so that Buffoon, in spite of still being the ugliest horse in racing, was never criticized for his appearance. His great gaunt frame was covered with a coat so bright that every hair seemed to sparkle; his pale legs were immaculate, his stringy tail plaited impeccably. Fully mature he was now seventeen hands high, but his legs still seemed to go in all directions and his wide-blazed face was still considered more appropriate to the circus than the paddock. He was well named. Had Declan christened him? Tessa suspected he had, and was always waiting for the day when he would turn up at the racecourse to claim credit for breeding this strange horse. But he never did.

Mr Cressington should be well-pleased with his buy. "Freakish," Peter said, shaking his head in disbelief when Buffoon came home in front. The longer the distance, the more likely he was to win. It took him over a mile to get his legs sorted out.

"You old fool," Tessa whispered to him, slamming her brush down over the bone of his mountainous withers. "Peter says you're a Grand National horse, did you know that, you old fool? The longest, hardest race in the book. That's where we're going next year, we're going to win the Grand National, and Mr Cressington will leap out of his wheelchair and dance all the way to the bank."

The old daughter had changed her tune since Buffoon had won a few races and she had pocketed the change left over from his training fees. She didn't talk about selling him any more. Tessa was mightily relieved. Sometimes she dreamed that Buffoon would win the Grand National and Mr Cressington in gratitude would leave her the horse in his will, and drop dead.

"Tom is coming to work you this morning, dear Buffoon. He likes you, he likes you! He wants to ride you in a race. He wants you to be *his* horse. Tom – the best, the greatest – *his* ride –"

"Jeez, you're a real nutcase, Tessa Blackthorn."

Wisbey, in passing, had stopped to listen to her chunter.

"It's God Almighty he wants to ride, you know that. Tom Bryant thinks our little stable is worth taking notice of, because of God Almighty."

"Because of Buffoon!"

"Perhaps he likes them both." Wisbey knew it was useless arguing with Tessa. "But he can only ride them when he hasn't got to ride for his own stable. And how often is that? We're lucky to get him tomorrow."

God Almighty was running at Newbury the next day and Tom was free to ride him. There were other jockeys, of course, but Tom was the magic name of the moment, acknowledged as the best.

"He's a horseman," Jimmy said. "More than you can say for some."

Tom was to meet them up on the gallops. Tessa tacked up Buffoon, and put Lucky out in his paddock as usual. Lucky turned and stuck his head over the gate and whinnied a fond farewell. Buffoon turned his long neck and whickered in return.

"You gump," said Tessa, leading him up to the mounting block. "What would you do without him, you old idiot? You'd go bananas, wouldn't you?"

She felt perfectly at home on the big horse now, and had no trouble in keeping him up with the rest of the string, although he was still lazy at exercise. Nobody disputed that she was an ace rider, although they all said she would never make it as a jockey.

"Tell me one girl who has?" Peter challenged her.

"Mrs Henderson was ninth in the Grand National and she was *old*. Charlotte Brew on her own horse got to the twenty-seventh fence. . . Lorna Vincent and Gee Armytage—"

"Yes. But *lasted*, year after year with winners every week, like the big boys—"

"Me. I will."

They all jeered. It was a cold, sunny day in February and they rode up the valley in a gang as usual. The last of the frost crunched underfoot in the bottom by the river and the reeds serried stiffly in white coats, standing to attention. Buffoon blundered into a fallen branch and nearly had Tessa off over his shoulder.

"Clumsy beast," she chided him. "Look where you're going!"

Tom's smart MG was parked up at the top beside Peter's clapped out Land Rover. The MG had Tom's name and sponsor on the side – not very good for when he was doing a tonne in the outside lane, late for a race. They trotted the horses steadily up the long hill; they were all super-fit and went easily, pulling as the gradient steepened. They pulled up beside the trainer and jockey.

Tessa grinned at Tom. She hero-worshipped him and was wildly jealous of the girls that came and went in his life, and had no compunction in telling him so. He didn't brush her off, he wasn't big-headed like some of the successful ones. He respected her for her guts and for her riding and he never patronized her.

They had to swap horses, first Wisbey for Tom to ride God Almighty, then Tessa for Buffoon. After fast work, Tom schooled both horses over a line of jumps beside the gallops. He had never ridden God Almighty before, and Buffoon only once, because of his commitments to Raleigh. God Almighty had won his three last races in a row, and was the favourite for tomorrow's race. He was a strapping great horse and a bold front runner, and very kind at home. He was the stable star and they all loved him for it. And for himself. Wisbey glowed with pride and pleasure when Tom slipped off and said, "He feels great."

When he rode Buffoon, Tessa could see how Tom had to work at riding him, legging him into the jumps, because Buffoon thought it was a waste of time, working at home.

Peter said to Tom, "Don't let it worry you. After a mile or so he starts to get going. You've got to keep him up with the pace at the beginning, but eventually he'll start motoring and then you can sit up there laughing. He stays for ever and can jump a house. He's clumsy because of the way he's built, but he's clever with it – keeps himself out of trouble with his brains."

"Sounds like he could be a National horse," Tom said.

Peter laughed nervously. "Yes. I keep thinking that – next year, perhaps. But you know how it is . . . God Almighty is the best I've ever had. And Buffoon . . . possibly. Maybe our luck is turning. It goes like that, doesn't it?"

Tom nodded and laughed. "It's your turn perhaps."

Tessa was waiting to ride back, holding Buffoon. Tom came over to give her a leg-up.

"He's not such a clown," he said.

He hesitated, and then said, "Have you ever had his sight checked?"

"What do you mean?" Tessa looked down at him in terror. "Why do you ask?"

"Just something in his way of going, makes me ask. My imagination probably. I've ridden one-eyed horses, half-blind horses – they seem to find their way around. I just wondered. . ."

"No! There's nothing! I would have noticed."

Tessa smiled, covering up panic. Shiner, she was thinking, Shiner! Nobody knew about Shiner, the dam. There was nothing in Buffoon's papers to say his dam was blind.

"Are you coming to Newbury tomorrow?" Tom asked.

"I'd like to see God Almighty run. If Peter lets me, I'll come—"

Tom drove away and Tessa rode home with the string. The shock of Tom's words was a bolt to her heart. Her hands were clammy and trembling on the reins, but not with cold. When they got down to the river and rode through the ford, the water up to the horses' knees, she saw the fallen branch that Buffoon had stumbled against on the way down, and she tried to think whether what they always thought of as his clumsiness was anything to do with his sight. But she dared not think it! No way was she going to say anything to Peter. Tom was an idiot, imagining things!

Peter said there was room for her in the lorry if she wanted to go to Newbury. All being well they would be back by evening stables, and it wasn't her day for the Battleaxe. Tessa latched on to this day out to keep her mind off Tom's remark. She could enjoy the excitement and panic of watching one of the stable's horses win without suffering the terror she endured when it was her own Buffoon. Wisbey could do the suffering. He was just as potty on God Almighty as she was on Buffoon, and their rival jealousy was one of the ongoing jokes of the tack-room. Very few of the lads (or lasses) remained totally cool when their horse was running, Tessa had noticed. She was not out of place, gnawing her fingernails and screaming, in that small gang of spectators waiting with their armfuls of rugs and lead-reins. They all knew their horses far better than their owners did, and in many cases loved them as dearly as Tessa loved Buffoon.

Unlike Maurice.

"Your dear stepfather must be the most unpopular owner in the game," Sarah remarked, reading the racing paper over coffee in the tack-room when they got back. "It says here that Tom Bryant is riding God Almighty for Peter Fellowes in the big race tomorrow and – quote – 'Mr Morrison-Pleydell is angry that the jockey isn't riding his forty-to-one chance, Almond River, at Market Rasen.' She laughed. "Only our Maurice would expect the top jockey to give up a big chance like that at Newbury just to partner a no-hoper at Market Rasen."

Tessa heard plenty about it over dinner that night.

"I pay over the odds at Raleigh's to have the services of the best jockey! I have a right to Bryant's rides."

Even Greevy was obliged to point out: "Dad, you know Almond River's a dud. Tom's got a career, after all. All owners let their jockeys go for a big chance elsewhere if it's offered – even if they don't like it."

"I'm not 'all' owners! It's people like me that keep the lot of them in work and they know it. I've made my feelings known to Raleigh."

I'll bet you have, Tessa thought smugly. She guessed that some of Maurice's rage was because Tom was preferring her dud stable to his. She was really enjoying Maurice's frustration. For all his huge expenditure, his horses were not being very successful. The gorgeous Crowsnest had broken down with tendon trouble and his very expensive buy at the sales, San Lucar, bred to be a long-distance horse, had so far proved disappointing.

He had also lost money on a golf course transaction, having bought the land at great cost and failed to get planning permission. He thought money could buy everything, even planning permission, but was finding otherwise.

Tessa was pleased, and slightly surprised, that Greevy had stood up for Tom riding God Almighty. She studied him across the table. It was true that rubbing shoulders with the nice people at Raleigh's was making him into a nicer person. It wasn't her imagination. At twenty-one he had started to think for himself, and perhaps he now realized, like everyone else, that his father was a rat. He had filled out and his spots had cleared up and he was – surprise, surprise! thought Tessa suddenly – quite good-looking in his quiet, dark way.

"I've a good mind to move my horses from Raleigh's," Maurice said. "I don't think he'd like that."

Tessa thought he'd be mightily relieved. She heard a lot about good and bad owners at Sparrows Wyck. Trainers liked owners who shut up and let them get on with the job, who were supportive when things went wrong and grateful when they went right. And kept out of the way. Maurice was none of those things. Most of the Sparrows Wyck owners were friendly people who wanted a bit of good sport, win or lose, a jolly day out. They didn't bet much, which took the pressure off. Maurice betted heavily on his horses, one of the reasons Tom didn't like riding for him.

"Too much at stake. Very often the horse gets too hard a race. No thought for the future."

Greevy looked concerned at his father's remark and said, "I shouldn't do that, Dad."

"Frightened you'll lose your job, eh?"

Greevy said, "Who says I would? It's going all right."

Even Tom had said Greevy wasn't bad, Tessa remembered.

Myra said nothing as usual, frightened of putting her foot in it. Her eyes went from one speaker to the other. Yet she knew twice as much as either of them. Being brought up with the game right from the beginning made an instinct for it. Tessa suspected she had it too, why it had gone well for her at Sparrows Wyck.

She went to bed in a disturbed state, anxious for the stable's big day tomorrow, and unable to get out of her mind Tom's remark about Buffoon's sight. Nobody knew about Shiner except her. She would not mention a word to Peter. But the idea that Tom had dropped into her head was nightmarish, and she knew it would not go away.

12

A Light Goes Out

God Almighty marched into the paddock at Wisbey's shoulder and looked all round at the crowd with his long ears pricked and his eyes alight. He looked magnificent and Tessa could see the pride on Wisbey's face as he overheard the spectators' appreciative comments. It was a cold clear day, a good day for racing, and Tessa could feel herself responding to the friendly atmosphere of the crowd, all out to enjoy seeing great horses run. God Almighty was favourite, but it was a good field. He had talented horses to beat.

Tessa could sense Peter's enjoyment at being in the big league for once, with the top jockey riding his horse. He had had years building up his string, working in the wilderness, but now his luck had changed. One good horse could make a stable. Today was Peter's day. He stood in the middle of the paddock with the horse's owners, trying to stop his excitement showing. Tessa leaned over the rail, knowing that Buffoon was going to be this good in the next year or so, savouring the pleasures ahead.

The jockeys came into the paddock, a bunch of bright colours like a flock of tropical birds against the winter hues surrounding them. Tessa had eyes only for Tom, resplendent in orange and turquoise, politely shaking hands with the two nice farmer owners whose horse was their pride and joy. Peter gave him a leg-up, Wisbey stripped off his rugs, and led the horse on his circuit of the paddock. Tessa ran to meet them as they came out.

"Good luck, Tom!"

Tom grinned down at her.

"Wait till it's that orange elephant of yours."

But Tessa only laughed.

"Just get the practice in!"

She had never seen Tom laughing when he rode out on her stepfather's horses. Maurice gave his jockeys instructions, although Tom had told Tessa they took no notice of them but said, "Yes, sir", politely, to earn their bread. They did what the trainer said, or what seemed best by their own judgement. Raleigh trusted Tom, as did Peter.

Wisbey let his horse go on the course and Tom stood up in his stirrups as God Almighty took hold and bucketed away down the turf. Wisbey watched him go, then turned with Tessa to take his place with the rest of the lads. Having the favourite, Wisbey seemed to have grown in stature, almost swaggering. His red hair stood as ferociously on end as ever, clashing horribly with the jacket that matched the owners' colours. (They had given it him as a Christmas present, much to the amusement of the yard, but he wore it proudly.)

"He's never looked better, eh?" he said as the horses came back, cantering to the start. The big bay moved beautifully, tucking in his nose to Tom's light hands on his mouth. He was real class; Tessa knew that Buffoon would never be admired in the same way, but held no animosity. God Almighty was to Wisbey what Buffoon was to her. She understood the feeling. It wasn't about looks, but about character and courage. Both horses had it, far more than most.

The race was three miles and on the first circuit they came by in a bunch, twelve of them, travelling quite fast. Tom was well up, galloping on the inside, enjoying himself. Tessa knew how it was – close to – quite different from seeing it on television. The picture never got over the sense of reckless power that emanated from the field approaching a big fence; it didn't give you the smell of fear, the look in the horses' eyes, the vibration of the pounding turf, the crack of flying brushwood and snorting breath . . . all the things that made Tessa's heart pound with the joy of it, and wanting to be a part of it, in spite of what they said about *girls*. To be there, close to, was the next best thing. But then they had passed by and were going out into the country, and the noise and the tension faded. Out in the country, Tom said the jockeys chatted and swore and even agreed to split the prize money if it was going to be a close-run thing between two or three. Tom said there was nothing in life to compare with riding a great horse in a good race to win.

"He loves it!" Wisbey rejoiced. "Did you see how he looked, cocking his ears at the fence? And going for a big one – flying –"

Wisbey jumped from foot to foot, his cheeks red with excitement.

Tessa never knew what caused the frisson of fear that went through her then. It was what Myra used to say – "a goose walking on her grave". She looked at Wisbey, sick, but he was laughing.

"Come on, my son! You're going to do it!"

On the far side God Almighty lay up in front with a horse on either side of him. But whereas the other two jockeys were scrubbing along, working hard, Tom was sitting quite still, cruising.

God Almighty's stride was perfect for the jump. He lengthened a fraction, pricked his ears and took off. The horse on the outside of him, slightly ahead, for some unknown reason jumped right across God Almighty's landing place, pecked and fell. God Almighty tried to avoid him in mid-air, twisted and fell heavily, turning a complete somersault. Another horse behind failed to avoid the tangle and fell too. The other horses streamed past on either side, dodging or jumping over the strewn bodies, crashing into each other, but surviving, while the three fallen horses struggled to their feet. Two of them immediately galloped on after their fellows, but the third, attempting to follow, only made a few strides and pulled up. He tried again, two strides, and then stood still.

Wisbey let out a strangled cry. He ran down the slope, shoving through the crowd and fled like a hunted rabbit along the fence, looking for a way through. Tessa stood frozen, watching. None of them had binoculars in their bunch, and she couldn't see.

"It's God Almighty, isn't it?" she asked the nearest lad.

"Aye. Not too good by the look of it."

None of them cared about the jockeys. Jockeys survived. Jockeys didn't get put down. But the horses. . .

And Tessa ran too, crying now.

The crowd roared, the horses came past the winning post, but Tessa saw nothing, tumbling out on to the scored turf and across it, running fast. Perhaps only a tendon . . . not a fracture. Dear God, not a fracture! It was miles across the centre of the course. Two or three cars were converging, an ambulance, and the white, low-slung body of the horse ambulance. But Tessa could run as fast, spurred by fear.

The horse was standing, trying to jig about, but only on three legs. The off fore hung, misshapen in a horrible way below the knee. A small group of spectators had converged and Tom was holding God Almighty. Steam rose in a cloud from the horse, who gleamed in the winter sunlight as if he were posing for his portrait, ears pricked, eyes shining. Tom was distraught, wanting to be out of it. When he saw Wisbey he flung him the reins and started to ungirth his saddle. Tears gleamed in his eyes, he didn't say anything. When Peter came up he just shook his head, put his saddle over his arm and turned away.

"Oh Christ," said Peter.

It was all finished. The horse was shot and the great light faded from his eyes and his bright, steaming body kicked and quivered on the turf. The little group of fencemen and hangers-on stood silent. Wisbey knelt down beside the horse's head and cradled it in his arms, sobbing, until Peter came and touched his shoulder and said, "Leave it, lad. It's over for him now."

Tessa stood and stared, shaking. She was numb, seeing it, never having known death before. Not like that, in the middle of brilliance, the light going out like the sun falling from the sky without warning. So fast the passage from life to death, she could not cope with it. Like Wisbey.

Peter stood hunched, looking suddenly like an old man, all his hopes and future blown away. The vet chatted to him, knowing there was nothing to comfort, but words blurred the scene – condolences, head-shaking, sympathy. Everyone was moved. Peter went off to seek his owners.

A car had whisked Tom off for the next race. The show went on. Another car took Peter and Wisbey and Tessa back, Wisbey having to be escorted bodily away from his horse. There was nothing to take home save buckets and rugs, bridle and headcollar . . . an empty, echoing horsebox. All the other lads were quiet and embarrassed, guessing how it felt, but unable to put sympathy into words, just showing it in their manner. The crowd, too, was quieter than at the usual finish, many of them sad for the way the best horse had been beaten. Tessa overheard their comments, but kindness made no difference. She knew it could just as well have been Buffoon, or could be in the future. She knew just how Wisbey felt. For all that he was a man, and gone twenty, he cried on the way home, and Tessa put her arms round him in the front seat, while Peter drove stonily, silently, the short journey home.

"Well, it happens, we all know that," Sarah said miserably. "It's not them that suffer though – it's us that can't bear it."

"Our best horse. . ." Gilly said. "If only –"

"But even the duds. . . It's the same, even if it's a duffer," Sarah said shortly. "I've never got used to it, and I don't think I ever will. I only know that it's a great game, they're doing what they're bred for and what they love doing. When they go like that, it's fast, no suffering."

No suffering? Tessa thought. She watched Wisbey get his bike out to cycle home, a wan, puff-faced boy. There was nothing to be said, but everyone knew how he felt – how they felt themselves, but worse, because God Almighty was his horse. The owners didn't really come into it, although Peter said they were "sick", and the old man cried.

Tessa walked home over the dark down, along her usual well-worn path. She was used to the darkness and the glitter of the winter stars over the black hummock of the horizon, the smell of the river below her and the crunching of the cold grass underfoot, but she wasn't used to feeling beaten, as she did tonight. The crass security lights of precious Goldlands stunned the night ahead of her; she never felt less like facing

Maurice and po-faced Greevy. Just when their luck was turning . . . now Maurice could gloat: she guessed exactly how he would look, sitting himself down at the dinner table with a smirky look of pity on his face. . . "Bad luck on your stable today" – and knowing that he was *pleased*. The love of a good horse didn't come into it with Maurice.

What he actually said was, "I bet your owners were sick. They must have had a good bet – he was a cert, after all, with Bryant up – and then to lose it all like that."

Tessa said, "They don't bet. They didn't have any money on. The old man cried."

She kept her eyes on her dinner, feeling herself tremble. Something was happening to her, which she couldn't control. She was aware of the whole room, as if it were waiting, all soft lamps and deep carpets, the click of Myra's knife and fork, Greevy's tactful silence . . . give him that, he didn't gloat. The thick, rich dinner of stewed steak and dumplings on her plate made her gorge rise.

Maurice laughed and said, "I don't know why some people go in for racing. What is it for, if you have a horse like that, and don't bet?"

Tessa thought she was going to be sick. But, instead of being sick, she voided her wild feelings by snatching up the table cloth, lifting it and shooting everything on the table into Maurice's lap – including her dinner, not to mention Myra's and Greevy's. It was like the custard tart in Jackie's face – brilliant, a release of pressure that made her sane again. Seeing

129

Maurice covered in thick gravy, hot steak and pureed potatoes, screaming as his lower body got burnt by the contents of the gravy-dish, was marvellous.

She got up from her chair and ran out of the room before he should kill her.

13

To Be a Jockey

"Is it true, that you attacked your father with a steak and kidney pudding and he had to go to hospital for burns? That's what everyone is saying."

Tessa didn't want to talk about it, even to Tom Bryant.

"He's not my father," she said.

"I'd love to have seen it," Tom said. "You've made yourself the most popular person in racing. You could get a job with Raleigh any day."

"I don't want a job with Raleigh."

It was hard to get much out of Tessa suddenly. She had lapsed into her silent ways. Maurice had ordered her out of his house, and she had gone back to Sparrows Wyck, for there was no other place she knew. Sarah had taken her into her caravan, and that was where she lived, until she was "sorted out". The social services people were on the trail, Myra was hysterical with fear she was going to get taken away.

Tessa kept thinking it might have been Buffoon. She could not get it out of her head: the way the light went out of the horse's eyes. She felt the light had gone out of her own, with these things that were happening to her. Tom saying . . . about Buffoon's sight. She asked him again about it, but he said, "Oh, forget it, my imagination." She watched Buffoon all the time, for signs, but only saw his clumsiness. Was his clumsiness inherent, or a sign of bad sight? She could not speak of it.

And the social services people. . .

Sarah said, "They'll take you away from here over my dead body."

Sarah's toughness extended to protect Tessa. Nobody said anything, but Tessa was not so preoccupied that she did not sense the closing of ranks around her, to save her from punishment. Maurice was saying she should be put away. . .

"Put her down," said Tom Bryant. "That would suit him nicely." And they all laughed.

The Battleaxe came to Sarah's caravan to continue the lessons. Sarah sat in the bedroom end, smoking and reading the *Racing Post*. The Battleaxe didn't seem to mind. She said Tessa was to sit for her GCSEs in the summer, and she expected her to do well.

"You've a very good brain."

"I'm going to be a jockey."

"I should think you need a lot of brain to be a good jockey."

"Not exams though."

"Exams are always very good to have, whatever. Jockey or not."

Tessa liked the Battleaxe. The Battleaxe never lectured her, just accepted – even the attack on Maurice. She said Mrs Alston had laughed when she heard, then remembered that she was a magistrate. They both thought a steak and kidney pudding was preferable to a knife.

When she had gone Sarah would emerge to make a cup of tea. She drank a lot of tea. Jimmy used to come in and they would sit drinking cups of tea and rolling cigarettes and talking, and Tessa would sit curled up in the corner, listening, watching, not saying anything. She preferred this way of living, but was terrified it was going to be stopped by Maurice's conniving with the authorities.

"Why should they change anything?" Sarah asked. "We're all happy now, even Maurice, getting you out of his hair."

"He hates me. He wants to put me away. He can too – till I'm eighteen."

"Rubbish! Not if you behave yourself. Anyway, it's sixteen, surely? And that won't be long."

"Eighteen."

"Oh well. Keep your head down till then. Keep out of his way," Jimmy said.

Sarah said, "We all know Peter's long-term plan is to run Buffoon in the Grand National. Mr Cressington's potty for it – before he dies, he says. But that's also Raleigh's plan for that horse Maurice paid a fortune for, San Lucar. You might be on a collision course there, should it all pan out."

"That's looking miles ahead," Jimmy said. "Anything could happen before then."

"Yes, we all know that. But the plans are laid."

"Who will Tom ride?" Tessa murmured.

"Interesting point. He's talking about leaving Raleigh, going freelance."

"If Buffoon carries on the way he's going, Tom will choose him," Sarah said.

Tessa knew that plans in racing nearly always went awry, but the possibility outlined by Sarah made her blood race. To beat Maurice in the Grand National! That would be the biggest prize of all. Even if they didn't win (that was an impossible dream) – but just to beat San Lucar, to *show* Maurice. Dreams indeed!

Jimmy and Sarah were already talking about something else, showing how remote the chances were of the outlined meeting taking place. Tessa half-listened, hugging her arms round her knees, the ideas jostling in her head . . . what might or might not happen. The rain beat on the windows, the cigarette smoke made a thick haze, mingling with the steam from Sarah's washing which hung over the glowing stove. It was a slum but, to Tessa, far more inviting than the hot, plush wastes of Goldlands. What was Myra doing without her? she wondered – the needle-sharp thought that spoiled the fleeting satisfaction. Why didn't her stupid mother get a job in a racing stable and get happy? Maurice hypnotized her, Tessa thought. She was scared of him, scared of running away. Scared because he had convinced her she was stupid. Tessa knew how it felt, being scared.

But, if she hadn't known Sarah before, she now appreciated the strength of Sarah's support, the feeling that she was in good hands. Sarah did not suffer fools gladly, and made no attempt to be popular. But she was a staunch friend, and totally committed to her job, with an instinctive understanding of her horses. She was like Jimmy in that respect.

With her looks and style, she could have done anything. Tall, with long legs, she would look superb on a horse if she didn't cramp herself into racing-length stirrups. She rode with strength and grace. Jimmy said she was wasted out of the dressage ring: any horse would "piaffe" himself silly with Sarah's legs telling him what to do. "Dressage! Much too much like hard work!" Sarah laughed. She was totally committed to racing, the daughter of a rich bloodstock breeder who had – it was said – run away from home at the age of sixteen with one of her father's grooms and been disowned. Gilly said she had had a baby, who would now be about twelve, but could not vouch for it. Gilly said one day Sarah would be legging up a jockey in the paddock and the jockey would look down at her and say "Mummy!" and fall into her arms. This tack-room gossip was intriguing, but Tessa knew it didn't do to believe everything Gilly said. She believed the bit about Sarah running off and being disowned – that was fairly well known – but the baby. . . ? And who was the groom? Nobody knew, not even Gilly. Sarah, at sixteen, must have been gorgeous, with her mass of chestnut curly hair and her violet-purple eyes, before her features hardened and her skin roughened. Now she was more handsome than beautiful, with an unquestionable authority about her – a good person to have on your side, Tessa thought. She wasn't going to ask her about the groom, not ever – it would be too dangerous. She loved Sarah. If she had been a boy she would have been in love with her. Sometimes she thought Jimmy loved Sarah, but with Jimmy it was hard to tell, he never revealed anything about himself. They were well matched in that respect. When they were together, talking, in the caravan, they never made Tessa feel unwelcome. She did not feel an intruder.

But Jimmy said, "If you're going to stay, we'll have to get you a caravan of your own. Show those council people you've got a home."

He brought one home the next day, behind the Land Rover, and parked it next to Sarah's. Everyone helped furnish it, and Tessa fetched her precious things from her den in Maurice's Home Farm, including her photo of Shiner, and for the first time in her life felt she belonged somewhere. Her small space was her own, all she needed, secure and private. Even Maurice could not touch her here.

But his long arm reached out, sending down the social services people. They didn't like it, but were overwhelmed by Tessa's support group and the Battleaxe's good report. Sarah stood over them, exuding moral virtue, and there was little they could find to argue with. She was not employed by Peter Fellowes; she did not receive a salary; her mother paid for her keep; she was not in danger of sexual abuse; she was a hard-working pupil . . . "What better can you ask?" as Sarah bluntly demanded.

When they had gone, Sarah said, "They have your record – violence, that knife, being excluded from all those schools. You mustn't blot your copy-book any more, it all goes down in writing."

"It was Maurice that sent them."

"Yes. That man's bad news. Pity he's into horses. That San Lucar is a good one, they say."

"Yes. Greevy says. And Tom."

The danger over, horses were the subject. Tessa, liking her new living arrangements, came out of her depression.

Peter confirmed that Buffoon was pencilled in for the Grand National the following year.

"He can run over the National course in November – there's a race then, just one circuit. And if he shows us he's good enough, he can go in for the big one. I think it's optimistic myself, but he's the right type for it. He'll stay four and a half miles, and he can jump. Mr Cressington's not a complete fool."

"If I were ninety-six, I'd want to get on with it," Sarah said.

It was the same programme as San Lucar's. San Lucar – or Lukey, as he was known – was the one horse of Maurice's that was proving worth his huge price. Greevy said he was a very kind and genuine horse, and the yard was full of optimism for him. Tessa could pick him out on the gallops, a big bright bay horse exuding power, built on classic chasing lines. Another head-turner, like Crowsnest. (But Crowsnest was resting, with tendon trouble.) These immaculately built and bred horses were the ones that fetched the big money in the sales, their looks and winning relations making them valuable. But they didn't always win.

"You get a freak like Buffoon – he might beat San Lucar. That's racing – we've all seen it."

Peter was being optimistic, not one of his notable characteristics. He laughed.

"You'll lead him in, Tessa – you'll be the right age by then. Think of it!"

"She'll be on a stretcher in First Aid, passed out," said Jimmy.

"Yeah, me too," said Peter.

The gloom cast by God Almighty's death was quite quickly eclipsed by thinking ahead, as always in racing. On with the next . . . what might happen . . . it kept the spirits high and the pulses racing. On a bright cold spring morning, high on the downs, facing up to the gallops, it was impossible to feel downhearted. The horses were at the peak of their fitness, the shine over their muscled bodies proclaiming their well-being, along with the bucking and pulling and eagerness to go. In spite of the setback with God Almighty, the stable was winning races with Catbells and a new horse called Gamekeeper, White Smoke and even the Littlun – properly called Cantata – who had won a claimer at Huntingdon. Peter Fellowes' reputation was growing, and Buffoon's appearances always caused comment, because of his ugliness and undoubted character. He walked round the paddock with a benign look in his eye, completely untroubled, showing no excitement at all, lolloping down to the start in his lazy canter, lining up as if called in for a riding-school beginners' class.

"Takes him a couple of miles to get going." The crowd was beginning to appreciate this, not only his jockey.

When the season finished in May, Buffoon had won four races and been placed in three. He was turned out to rest in the big field that sloped down to the river, with Lucky, two other horses and a herd of cows for company. Tessa spent hours with him in the paddock, lying in the grass with his big grey lips tearing at the grass-roots round her head, talking to him, dreaming of the days ahead. Sarah told her it was dangerous to love a horse too much.

"I know," Tessa said, and went on loving him.

She took her exams, going into school to sit near Jackie Barstow, and finishing with good passes in everything. The Battleaxe was proud of her.

"You have a very good brain. Don't waste it," she said, looking round rather doubtfully at the rustic surroundings.

"No."

Tessa asked Peter if he would apply for a jockey's licence for her. Her sixteenth birthday had arrived: the time was ready. Peter duly got it for her.

"But it doesn't mean," he said sternly, "that you will get any rides. The owners won't like it. They'll want an experienced jockey. I will try for you though. Perhaps on the Littlun, because you know him so well. I'll tell his owners he loves you and will do as he's told."

"Win."

"Yes. And if he wins, it'll make it easier to get you another ride. I'll try and find the right race for you."

"A load of crocks," Wisbey said.

"You put it so kindly," Sarah said.

But Tessa knew all this without having it spelt out. She knew how incredibly difficult it was for a female to make it as a jockey. And to make it good enough to ride Buffoon – her life's ambition – was hardly on the cards at all, not now Buffoon was a winner and the public put their money on him. The public expected him to have a top jockey.

"I will help you all I can, but expect nothing."

"No," said Tessa.

But in her heart she expected to become a good jockey and for Buffoon to win the Grand National. That was all.

14
Taking Failure

*H*er first race . . . she was trembling so hard she had to clench her teeth to stop them clattering. But it was cold – call it shivering. All the jockeys had white, pinched faces. She was the only girl. The men looked sideways at her, but when she weighed out Tom Bryant came over and put an arm round her shoulders and gave her a squeeze.

"Good luck! Keep out of trouble."

He wasn't riding in her race, which was for apprentice jockeys, but his kind words were noticed by the others, and Tessa recognized the respect in their eyes. The top jockey was her friend. Her teeth stopped chattering.

"Once you're aboard out on the course, you forget about being nervous," he said. "It's the same for us all."

Well . . . maybe. Tessa smiled. She was riding Cantata – the Littlun – and she knew him as well as she knew Buffoon, so it wasn't like being thrown up on a strange horse. Jimmy had elected to be his lad, and was leading him round the paddock, a taut little liver-chestnut gelding with the wind in his tail. His price was twenty-to-one.

"There are some reasonable horses in this race, and much more experienced riders than Tessa. Don't expect too much."

Peter was in the paddock with the horse's owners, a kindly pair of old hunting ladies who believed in "giving the gel a chance".

"We'll all have a nice drink together afterwards, whatever," they said. "What a jolly day!"

Imagine Maurice saying that! Tessa thought, speechless, when they shook her hand. She tried not to show how terrified she was.

Jimmy legged her up.

He said, "Winning's not everything. Keep safe, that's the main thing, for the horse too."

"Have a lovely time, dear," said the owners.

She rode the Littlun – Cantata for now – every day, after all. He had no bad ways and as soon as she was on his back she felt her confidence soar, just as Tom had predicted. Jimmy led her out, wished her luck and let the horse go. Cantata was a pony compared to Buffoon: he felt so different, slippy and spry. Riding Buffoon out on to a gallop was like taking a bus out on to a motorway, knowing there was miles of room to get going in the fast lane, in many ways easier than handling the nippy little hurdler who was now showing a great keenness to get on with the job. Tessa sat tight and held him in against the rails, terrified of being carted before the race had even begun. But she wasn't the only nervous rider. Cries of alarm and swearing echoed all round her. It was a big field and many of the riders were far less well trained than she was.

Everything she thought she knew went out of her head once

the race started. The astonishing power of the galloping horses all around her was overwhelming, the pounding of hooves and the crack of brushwood when they jumped . . . placing the horse, seeing a stride in that mêlée – even seeing the jump – was beyond her. Stay on, stay there . . . that was all she could think of. The wet mud flew in her face, spattering her goggles, but the little horse knew what to do. The field thinned out ahead as Cantata galloped on and by the time Tessa heard the noise of the crowd above her own panting breath there were only two horses ahead of her.

Another one was close, coming up fast. She glanced round and saw a furious red face beside her, then there was a crack on her knee, and she was flying through the air with the horse apparently vanished from beneath her.

She never knew what happened. Even on the video, afterwards, it looked like a collision over the last jump, but the other jockey escaped unscathed and came third. Tessa knew she should have been third, might even have been second or first, but for the ignorant rider who barged her. But the pain in her wrist was too agonizing to bother about objecting. She walked back, trying not to cry (Tom Bryant never cried), choked with fury and disappointment. Jimmy had caught Cantata and said cheerfully, "No harm done. Great race – you'd have been in the frame."

The old ladies were full of praise, even Peter was smiling. Tessa couldn't understand them at all. She could not speak, she was so angry. Yet they were praising her. She wanted to kill that jockey. . . She would make sure to find out his name. . . The pain flooded up her arm so that she almost cried out loud.

She could not hide it. She had to go to hospital and be X-rayed and be told her wrist was broken. She wouldn't ride for six weeks. When she was alone on a trolley in an empty corridor she let go the tears that choked her and sobbed into the hospital linen. Six weeks! To make such a hash of her first race!

"Only a Tom Bryant could have sat that mistake," Jimmy said when he collected her later. "The horse went right down on his knees. What are you so cross about? The arm, yes, that's a shame, but it wasn't anything you did wrong. You've got to learn to take it."

He was stern with her, but Tessa could not take such failure. She would not speak, and slammed into her caravan without even going to see Buffoon.

"Oh my!" said Gilly. "Our prima donna's back. I suppose I've got to do her horses?"

"I'll see to the Littlun," Jimmy offered.

They left her alone, hoping the sleeping pills she had been given were doing their work. There was no light on in her caravan. They tapped softly on the door but there was no answer and they went away.

But Tessa sat on in the dark, the pills untouched. Her arm hurt, but not so much as her spirit. Maurice would know what had happened; Greevy would tell him; how they would laugh! The thought made her shiver with pure rage. She thought she didn't mind being beaten, but the humiliation of the day overwhelmed her.

The stables were done and it was silent outside, Wisbey's noisy motorbike having departed. Only later, just before bed, Peter would come out and with his torch look at every horse in the stable, to see that it was calm, eaten up, and well. Sometimes Jimmy. Tessa liked to see the torchlight flickering from box to box, hear the soft voice talking to the horse. She often went out to Buffoon in the evening, and sat in the straw talking to him, fending off Lucky who always thought she might have a titbit. She liked to see the two of them lying down together, nose to nose. They did not get up when she entered, but Buffoon's nose would quiver with a soundless whicker of affection. He loved her above all others, she knew that.

But the way things had gone today, she knew she would never ride him in a race, her great ambition in life. She would never be good enough. She hadn't been able to handle anything at all, just let it happen all round her. She cried.

From the lane came the sound of a car approaching. It came into the yard and stopped. Some one for Peter, Tessa thought. But suddenly there was a loud knock on her door and a shout.

"Hey, anyone in? You dead?"

The door was yanked open and a figure entered, tripped over the doormat, swore and groped for the light switch.

Tessa blinked and leapt to her feet. It was Tom Bryant. She gaped.

"Came to see how you were," he said, smiling. "All nice jockeys enquire after the wounded, did you know? And you aren't on the phone, so I called round. What are you doing sitting in the dark?"

Tessa shrugged, shook her head. He no doubt saw the tearstains on her face and was taking in her bedraggled despair.

"Oh, come on, it's all good practice," he said. "It happens to us all. If you can't bounce back, you might as well give up now. Imagine it happening – the last fence in the Gold Cup, when you're five lengths ahead—"

That had happened to him, Tessa knew, a couple of years ago. She had to admit it did put it in proportion. She gave a shaky smile. She was astonished at his visit, knowing he had had five rides that afternoon and was probably pretty tired. Yet he was bothering. . .

"You shouldn't have come. I'm all right."

"They said your wrist is broken."

"Yes."

"Bad luck. You'll have to learn to fall off properly. It's all part of the trade."

He sat down on the end of her bed and grinned cheerfully. Tessa wasn't used to seeing him in social mode, not since the dinner party at home, and had never guessed that he might include her in his circle of friends close enough to take this sort of trouble for. It was balm to her despair, to be cared about by Tom. Tom was the best, and handsome with it, but quite free of conceit.

"The way you are," he said, "so single-minded – potty – you stand a chance. Of making it. You're really mad now, aren't you? Furious with yourself. Want to get on again – show them – it's the right feeling. To be angry. If you're not angry with yourself you're no good."

That was news to Tessa.

"The others think I'm stupid."

"No. The others might say that, but they respect you for it. They none of them want to suffer, do they? Jimmy doesn't, yet he'd be at the top in no time if he chose – he's such a horseman. A natural."

"He likes eating, he says."

"Yes." Tom's face dropped. "I can't eat. At least you'll never have that problem. That's the worst one."

Tessa looked sideways at Tom. His face was drawn, she noticed, and had lines in it that made him look thirty, not twenty-two. He was fair and blue-eyed, the classic English public schoolboy, the sort you read about in old books. The only one she knew.

"Why did you become a jockey?"

"Oh, horses are in my family. Hunting, point-to-pointing. I rode point-to-point and my dad had some good horses so I won and got noticed. I never wanted to do anything else, not ever."

"What if you'd been no good?"

"I'd have kept trying, I dare say. Lots of them are hooked on it, and not good enough, or lucky enough, to get the rides, but they keep on trying. They ride duff horses and get hurt. I admire them. I've had it easy."

"I want to ride Buffoon."

Tom laughed. "We all know that! Highly unlikely, I'd say. I want that ride!"

When Tom had gone, Tessa sat on, dreaming. She wondered if Tom liked her, in a soppy way. Why had he called? She found it hard to understand kindness. She did not think of boys, in the way other lads talked about sex – she never listened, or cared. There wasn't room in her head, and her feelings were used up on anxieties, ambition, Buffoon. . . "You never relax, do you?" Wisbey said. "You never laugh."

"What is there to laugh about?" she retorted. She remembered Wisbey rolling his eyes. Was there something wrong with her?

Yes, her wrist was broken and her career in ruins before it had started. She got into bed and lay awake, staring at the stained ceiling of her caravan.

15

Disaster

$\mathcal{B}$uffoon hitched his massive quarters on to the edge of his manger, sighed gustily, rested one hind leg and stood staring into the square of twilight through the open top door. What do horses think about, creatures of little brain as they are said to be? The large unfathomable eye, bright, blank, gazes giving back no clue. In the depths of Buffoon's eyes an almost indiscernible shadow lurks. He is aware of it, does not know that other horses do not have it, does not wonder when he stumbles over small jumps which he scarcely sees. He hears the word "clumsy" in reproach and doesn't know its meaning. It does not worry him. Horses at rest do not worry. They do not think of things they should have done, ways of improving themselves, what is going to happen to them when they are old. The unfathomable eye registers nil. The horse is well fed, worked only to a pleasant sufficiency, feels well, has his friends within sight. His mind is blank.

Buffoon is sometimes asked to work very hard. He is surprised but, when coerced, finds he enjoys it. Not something he would do without – coercion – but, willing and friendly beast that he is, he will do it to oblige. They seem to want it. When he comes back they pat him and kiss him – that girl kisses him – and he knows he has pleased them. He likes them. They feed him and are kind to him. He is contented. He doesn't know what it's all for, save it comes up regularly. His mane is plaited (boring!) and he is led into the horsebox and after that he knows exactly what is going to happen: a drive, long or short, a new stable yard, strange companions, a lot of bustle and tension, to which he responds, becoming a bit fidgety, anxious to be out there, to be where it's all happening, out on that wide river of green grass where he can take hold of his bit and go. This seems to be what they want of him. He likes it, it comes naturally, it's bred in him. If he didn't like it, they couldn't make him do it. He knows that, so do they.

Does he think of it when he dozes in the evening? No, he only thinks: Lucky is there, everything's all right. Take Lucky away and his life would fall apart. Great horse friendships are tedious for owners. Mostly owners try to wean friendships away, to avoid difficulties, but racehorses are allowed their foibles. Racehorses are special. They get the best of everything in life in exchange for the test of courage, the asking of all they can give, as often as the trainer sees fit. They live as herd animals and run as herd animals, their natural way of life, and very few would rather be riding-school hacks or ladies' pets.

Not that Buffoon knows anything about a different way of life. Not yet. He accepts. He yawns. He is at peace.

He doesn't know he is going to run in the Grand National.

Tessa told him, every day, while she was grooming him, but it meant nothing to him. Her voice was soft and loving, and he listened with one long ear held back, liking the sound. Her ant-like energy had worked up a golden burnish on his pale coat . He stood patiently, unlike some, not even minding the ticklish places behind his elbows and up round his stifle. She washed his mane and tail more times than any other horse had its mane and tail washed in the stable, and he stood happily, not minding. She hosed his legs off after exercise and rubbed them dry with a supply of elegant towels filched from Goldlands and, if it was cold, wrapped them in warm bandages. No horse could be given more.

Peter the trainer was nervous as a coot about the Grand National. Old Mr Cressington was adamant that the horse should run but Peter thought next year would be better.

Jimmy said, "But you'll say that next year as well. Don't be so funky. The old man might be dead next year. It's not like running a horse which isn't capable just to please the owner. Buffoon is capable all right."

"He's not ready."

He had missed a preliminary race over the National fences because of a bruised foot at the time, which troubled Peter. But it didn't trouble Jimmy.

"He's ready. He's made for that race. Stays for ever, great jumper, great heart. Stop worrying."

But all trainers worried. How could they not?

Tessa worried. She did not see how she would get through the great race, watching. Her heart would give out, beating so hard. Wisbey said she would pass out in his arms. She could not put God Almighty out of her mind, and the fear that Buffoon might –

"Horses get killed in potty little hurdle races if they're unlucky," Sarah said harshly. "It's stupid to think a horse like Buffoon is any more at risk – he's learned to get his legs together, he never panics, he's as safe as they come. You've got to get your brain round this, Tessa. You're in the wrong business if you can't take it."

Tessa knew all this. They told her all the time. It made no difference.

Buffoon, the ill-made, bad-coloured, ugly son of Shiner, was now a racecourse favourite, a freak horse on his long, ungainly legs who never ran a bad race. He didn't always win, but he never let anyone down. The longer and tougher the race, the more likely he was to come home in front. For all these reasons he was high in the betting for the Grand National. Not the favourite. The favourite was Maurice's horse, San Lucar.

"Of all the likely scenarios, this is the craziest coincidence," Gilly said in the tack-room, after exercise. "That Tessa's horse – in the biggest race of all – is going to come up against Mucky Morrison's."

"They're first and second favourite in the paper this morning," Wisbey said.

"Buffoon's first and Lukey's second," Sarah said.

Tessa found this hard to believe. "Buffoon first!"

"It's a housewife's thing – the people who don't know

anything are putting their money on him because he looks like a giraffe. For a lark," said Wisbey.

There was an element of truth in this, but Tessa hit Wisbey with a metal curry-comb and cut his cheek.

"Tessa!" Sarah was furious. "It's time you grew up! For God's sake, can't you take a joke?"

"You know she can't. Not about Buffoon," Gilly said.

"It's lucky you live on your own in that caravan. If you'd still been at home with Mucky and Greevy . . . I wonder. . ." Sarah's eyes sparkled. "I bet they don't like playing second fiddle to our old Buffoon."

Tessa herself had wondered about this. Was Maurice as furious as she hoped he was, that his great horse was ranked with hers? She thought she might go up and see her mother in the afternoon, keep her fingers crossed that Maurice wouldn't be there. There were rumours about a falling-out between Raleigh and Tom Bryant. Myra might know the inside story. Tom hadn't said anything.

She was lucky. Myra was alone, eating chocolates and reading a love story in front of the fake coal fire. The room was very warm and Tessa remembered how she was always falling asleep in this house.

"Oh, darling, what a sight you look! If only you would come home again, you would get looked after properly!"

"No fear!"

Tessa thought her mother looked a sight too, in her shiny dress and high heels. (What a waste of a life! How could you

153

do anything dressed like that?) Tessa wore jodhpurs (rather dirty) and an old Barbour jacket Sarah had thrown out (not without reason), and a red polo neck jersey from Oxfam.

"How can I come home, with him here? I came to see if he's getting excited about the Grand National."

"Well, of course he is. It's all he thinks about. He put an enormous bet on when the horse was only twenty-to-one and stands to win a fortune if Lukey wins. Not to mention the prize money. He's very agitated about your horse – everyone seems to fancy it all of a sudden."

"Did you know Buffoon is out of Shiner? Declan bred him."

She didn't know why she threw this at Myra suddenly. She had never mentioned it before or told anyone at the yard of her link with the horse. Myra stared at her, amazed, and then burst into tears.

"Oh, my dear, you and Shiner, that's what went wrong, wasn't it – leaving Shiner? I've always known it, Shiner and your daddy, how you loved them – especially Shiner—"

She wept. Tessa didn't know what to say, embarrassed, wishing she had held her tongue about Buffoon's breeding. Her own emotion at seeing Shiner's name on Buffoon's passport was long forgotten. Tessa no longer dwelled on the past, only the future.

"I do miss you, Tessa. If only you'd come back here!"

"Oh, Mum, you know I can't. Talk sense. I'm only down the road if you want me, no distance. You could come and stay in my caravan and ride out with us – you'd love it. You rode well once. Why ever don't you?"

"Oh, don't be so silly! Maurice wouldn't stand for it. How can I?"

Tessa shrugged. It was useless talking to Myra. Why ever had she come? Only to find out about San Lucar.

"Who's going to ride him? There's a rumour Tom Bryant's fallen out with Mr Raleigh. Is it true? Peter wants Tom for Buffoon, so we thought there might be a chance if he's not going to ride San Lucar."

"You know how it is, it's all Maurice's fault. He's hard on Bryant and Tom hates riding for him, because there's always so much money on. I'm afraid Maurice only cares about winning. It doesn't matter if the horse is half-killed of exhaustion as long as it wins. And Tom won't ride like that. He's refused to ride Lukey in the National, Raleigh's furious and Greevy says he's going to get the sack."

"He'll ride Buffoon!" Tessa's heart leapt.

"Raleigh says he can afford to turn down the ride on Lukey because he knows he can ride Buffoon. But I think he's going to lose his job over it."

"He can get any job he pleases, surely? Or freelance."

"Raleigh's the top trainer though. Largely through Maurice's horses. Tom says Raleigh would like to give up training for Maurice, but if he did he'd lose at least four really good horses. Maurice has been very lucky with his horses this last year or two, but he needs it – he's a heavy gambler and a lot of his investments have gone wrong lately. He's really depending on winning with Lukey."

"More fool him. Horses aren't like that. And the National, of all races – you need the luck."

"Well, you can't tell him that, can you? It's very fraught round here at the moment. I'll be glad when it's over."

"Only a fortnight." Tessa knew she would too. The anxieties were getting to her.

Shortly afterwards the season would finish. Tom could afford arguments now, at the end of the season. Next season, a fresh start, and the quarrels would be forgotten. Tom would no doubt be back with Raleigh.

Tessa was pleased with the information she had picked up. The rumours were true. They usually were in racing. It sounded as if Tom was going to ride Buffoon, whatever it cost him. Did he really prefer him to San Lucar? He must do, else he would have timed his quarrel differently. Tessa was filled with a burst of proud, quivering emotion and flung her arms suddenly round the surprised Myra. The top jockey had chosen her Buffoon for the greatest race of them all! Out of all the horses in the world!

"Oh Ma, that's great news – if Tom rides Buffoon!"

Greevy stood in the doorway suddenly, and heard Tessa's exclamations of delight. Tessa might have guessed – he too took a couple of hours off after lunch.

He said, "Don't count your chickens before they're hatched. It's not settled yet." And to Myra, who now looked embarrassed and frightened, "I suppose you've been shooting your mouth off to the opposition?"

"Don't talk to my mother like that!" Tessa hissed at him. "She can say what she likes. She didn't tell me anything I didn't know already. It's all in the papers, Tom being fed up with your place."

Greevy seemed to soften. He sighed and shrugged. It occurred to Tessa then that he was in a dreadful situation, the buffer between Raleigh at work and his father at home. No wonder he looked so wan! She laughed.

"You ought to come and work at our place. It's all sweetness and light in our yard."

Greevy scowled at her.

"I sometimes wonder. . . " He shrugged again.

He certainly had grown up since she had last had to do with him, Tessa thought – no longer gangly and pimply, but broadened out and tough-looking. He must work hard in a big yard like Raleigh's, and Raleigh was known as a hard taskmaster. She was surprised he had stayed with it. No doubt commanded to by his father. But he was his own man now . . . surely he wouldn't dance to Maurice's tune for ever?

"Your horse well?" he asked, friendly now.

"Couldn't be better. And yours?"

"He's fine. Yes." And he actually smiled.

"I'll see you at Aintree then."

"Yeah. I dare say neither of them will win. A forty-to-one will beat them both." And he actually laughed.

Tessa was amazed.

When she got home she reported what she had found out to

Peter, and Peter said, "Yes, I know all that. But apparently Maurice is now bribing Tom to ride Lukey. So the story goes. Something huge. Tom hasn't decided yet."

"He wouldn't! Not a bribe! Not Tom!"

"Oh, come on, Tessa, he's a young man with a girlfriend, a house to buy, a dangerous job. . . You might think money doesn't matter but most people set a lot of store by it, believe me."

"I'll ride Buffoon then!"

Peter laughed. "If only you could! He's easy enough. San Lucar is a very difficult ride, and Tom knows him so well, that's why they're so keen to have him. If we don't get Tom, it doesn't really matter, because Andy will step in, and Buffy will go the same for anyone."

"We must have Tom!"

"Well, he's the best, yes. I want him, sure."

Everyone knew that whichever horse Tom decided to ride would be the favourite. He was riding at the top of his form. Journalists and photographers came to Sparrows Wyck to take notes about Buffoon, and Tessa was photographed cantering up the gallops, looking like a flea on the great horse's back. Now in his prime, he was seventeen hands high, all legs. The pundits shook their heads.

"Don't know how he does it, made like that."

"He'll walk over those jumps, all the same."

"Got to wrap his legs up first!"

"What a freak!"

They daren't criticize him to Tessa. They took note of his spitfire lad, and released the story that she was the stepdaughter of Maurice Morrison-Pleydell, owner of San Lucar. Then the gossip writers wanted her story, but she locked herself in her caravan and refused to speak to them. At Goldlands they were turned away by George before they could get to the front door, on Maurice's orders. Some of them camped out on the front lawn and Maurice got security men with Dobermans to deter them – successfully.

"Sooner it's over the better, all this fuss," Peter said. They all agreed, the extra work of making the place look respectable for the publicity beginning to pall. Tessa took to sleeping in Buffoon's box. She did not trust Maurice one inch to play fair when so much was at stake. Walter the lurcher's kennel was parked outside the door and Walter reluctantly kept guard, a shaggy ear cocked to the nonsense Tessa talked to Buffoon as she lay curled up in her sleeping bag. Tessa kept her bread-knife hidden under the straw in the corner by her head, but nobody knew this.

Buffoon was at the peak of his form. When she rode him out every morning Tessa could feel the power of him, even at the walk. Peter secretly worried that Tessa was not man enough now to ride the valuable and highly-tuned horse, but Jimmy resisted his doubts.

"There's a link there that's worth far more than ordinary horsemanship. He trusts Tessa. He would never go against her."

"She looks so fragile up there!"

Jimmy laughed. "Tessa – fragile? You're losing your mind!"

Tessa showed no signs of blooming into curvaceous femininity. She was honed and angular, all steel. Peter thought she was too small to impress owners as a rider, in spite of her undoubted talent, but he had managed to get her a few rides with kindly and unambitious owners, and she had clocked up three winners. Although she loudly despaired, they all told her three winners was a good haul for a teenaged shrimp like herself. With that she had to be content. She might get a few rides at the fag-end of the season, after Aintree, if she was lucky. But she couldn't think beyond Aintree and the Grand National. None of them could.

Five days before the race Tom Bryant rang Peter to ask if he could have the ride. He had refused all blandishments from Maurice, and Raleigh had given him the sack. The stable was jubilant. Tessa wept with joy. Now she was so excited she could scarcely sleep. The papers were full of Bryant's "disobedience" and Buffoon became the clear favourite.

Buffoon was to be driven to Aintree early on the Friday before the big race. On Thursday Tom said he would come over and ride him out at exercise and talk tactics; so on Wednesday Tessa had her last ride on him before the big day.

The weather was damp and warm, the going perfect, the sun shining. Tessa rode with the others, Peter included – a long, quiet ride, with just trotting up the long hillside, a short pipe opener over the rise, and a leisurely walk home. Tessa tried to relax, but she was so happy and excited that she felt she might explode. Buffoon, she could tell, was puzzled by the tension, but it did not get to him, lazy beast that he was. As they came down the last muddy track into the yard she was thinking: the next time I do this he will have won – or not won – the Grand National. It was almost too much to take in.

Nothing was any different as they slipped out of their saddles and ran up the stirrups. Tessa led Buffoon into his box, shut the door behind him and went across to the gate to fetch Lucky. Lucky was nearly always waiting to come back in, but today he was not standing in his usual place. The spring grass was coming through and Tessa knew how greedy Lucky was; she thought he had gone away down the field to find the best grazing.

But when she looked for him, there was no sign of the little pony.

She went back to the yard and shouted to Jimmy, "What have you done with Lucky?"

Sometimes Jimmy used him for his own purposes, to calm a youngster. But Jimmy said, "I haven't had him. What's wrong?"

"He's not in his field."

"Who put him out there?"

"I did, like I usually do, before we went out."

Tessa's heart was now beginning to agitate with fear. "Where is he?"

"Steady on. He can't be far away. Don't be daft."

Jimmy came back with her to the gate and they looked across

161

the large field. It was undoubtedly empty. But at the far side a gate that gave out on to the lane swung open.

"Blast! He must have got out," Jimmy said.

"Someone's let him out!"

"Someone's taken him. Even if it was open, he wouldn't go, not of his own accord. Not away from the others."

Now even Jimmy looked worried. Behind them in the stable yard they could hear Buffoon kicking on his door and whinnying for his friend. This was always the way if Lucky was slow coming back in.

"You go back to him and keep him calm, and I'll get the car out. Tell the others." Jimmy moved sharply.

Tessa ran.

Seeing her, Buffoon let out a shrill whinny. Already there was alarm in his voice, and he stood weaving his head backwards and forwards over the door. Then he struck out with a foreleg, crashing into the woodwork.

"Stop that!" Peter bawled. "Tessa, go to him!"

But Tessa was there already, at his head, talking to him. Everyone saw what had happened and the alarm spread. The other horses were hastily rugged up and left, and everyone scattered to find Lucky. Wisbey fetched straw bales to line the front of Buffoon's box with, and then brought a small feed in a bucket. But Buffoon would have nothing to do with it, pushing the bucket over, sending the contents flying. Left to himself, he walked round and round the box, whinnying.

"Oh my God!" Peter moaned. "Just what we don't want!"

Tessa stayed with Buffoon but was nearly trampled to death. She could do nothing to calm him. Already a dark sweat was breaking out on his flanks.

Gilly came back and said the others were still looking.

"But there are tyre marks by the gate. Looks like a trailer or horsebox has been parked there just recently. Peter thinks he's been pinched. He thinks it's inside knowledge – you know, to upset him so he won't be able to run –"

"It's Maurice!"

Tessa leapt to the corner of the loosebox and snatched her bread-knife out of its hiding-place.

"I'll kill him!" she shouted. "I'll kill him!"

Gilly screamed, "Don't be so crazy!"

She held on to Tessa as best she could but Tessa wriggled free, shot out of the box and went tearing away out of the yard towards Goldlands.

Gilly chased her, but it was no good. Tessa was fast, and her anger gave wings to her heels.

16

The Big Race

"Tessa, for heaven's sake! Have you gone mad? Maurice is at Aintree, he went up last night. He's not here."

Myra was shocked by the distraught appearance of Tessa wielding her bread-knife, shouting for Maurice.

Tessa sobbed, "He did it! He arranged it, I know he did! It's just the trick he would pull – he is so vile! He arranged to get Lucky taken away——"

Tessa was breathless and hysterical, and Myra calmed her down as best she could, removing the bread-knife at the first opportunity. She gathered what had happened from Tessa's wild raving, and understood the seriousness of it.

"It must be someone who knows Buffoon's dependence on Lucky. But most people in racing know it, Tessa, it's not a secret. The papers have reported it – they like those sort of sentimental stories – and all the lads in the the racecourse stables have seen Lucky, haven't they? It's not Maurice – how could he do such a thing when he's already at Aintree?"

"No, not himself. But he's paid someone to do it. Or did Greevy do it? Did Maurice make Greevy do it?"

"Greevy went to work as usual. How could he have done it?"

"He could have! He could have sneaked away!"

"You said the pony was taken in a horsebox. How could Greevy possibly have driven away from work in a horsebox? He's on the gallops every morning at that time. Calm down, Tessa! You're talking rubbish!"

"I bet it's Maurice. Somehow it's Maurice. Because San Lucar's got to win for him – you said so yourself. All that money!"

"Well, I can't say he wouldn't do such a thing, I'm afraid." Myra shook her head. "It's a clever trick."

"Yes, it is. It's diabolical. Buffoon won't eat without Lucky. He'll fret himself stupid and be useless by Saturday."

"Perhaps you can get him another companion –"

"It won't work! You know it won't."

Tessa didn't intend to stay. Now her visit was in vain, she wanted to be back with Buffoon. He needed her.

"It might be OK when you get back. They might have the pony," Myra said soothingly. This wild Tessa terrified her. "Do be sensible, Tessa. You can't go round flourishing a knife like that. You'll end up in prison."

"If it *is* him – I'll kill him. You'll see!"

"Tessa, stop it! You're being really stupid."

But Myra's words fell into thin air – Tessa was already away, scampering across the garden, leaping across the ha-ha and away down the green valley. Greevy might have done it, she thought, at Maurice's instigation, but it wouldn't help to go crashing into Raleigh's yard. Her hysteria was wearing off and she was trying to think more rationally. And yet, the last time she had seen Greevy . . . she did not think now that he would stoop so low. Not even for his father. Unless Maurice had bribed him? Like he had tried to bribe Tom. Maurice thought money could buy him everything.

Back at the yard, having found no trace of Lucky, they all agreed with Tessa that Maurice could well have had a hand in it.

"He's definitely been taken, and the reason is obvious," Peter said. "It's a devilishly clever way of getting at Buffoon without doping him or drugging him. But the effect by Saturday will be the same. He'll be drained of all his enthusiasm if he carries on like this for two days."

Peter was white with misery. All his worst fears had come true. Buffoon was kicking the walls of his box (now padded all round with straw bales) and whinnying at intervals with a high-pitched, distressed call. Midday feed and haynet were untouched.

"He can't go on like this for two days," Jimmy said, for encouragement, but they all knew he could.

"Let's try him with something else."

They borrowed a small pony from a friend of Gilly's but had to rescue it from getting kicked after a few minutes, also a calf and the lurcher Walter. Buffoon would have none of them. Peter sent a message to the police, offering a large reward for the immediate return of Lucky. He had it put out on the local radio, but nobody replied, except all the national press wanting the story. San Lucar was back to being the favourite the next day. Tessa stayed with Buffoon all night but he never lay down. He stopped screaming and kicking, but restlessly walked round his box, and dozed only for a few minutes at a time. He did not touch his evening feed, nor eat up at breakfast. Stripped of his rugs, his huge frame was already looking gaunt and tucked up. When Tom Bryant came down in the morning his face fell when he saw him.

"I won't hold you to the ride, lad, if you want to be out of it. You could still get back on San Lucar, I dare say," Peter said. Peter looked worse than the horse.

"No way, not for that swine," Tom replied. "I'll ride your fellow."

"I've a mind to pull him out. He won't do himself justice."

"You can't! It's not a good enough reason – not for the general public. They won't understand. They'll think you're mad."

Mr Cressington was adamant his horse would run. He didn't understand either. Peter was locked in an impossible situation and they all knew it.

Tom rode out on Buffoon, and he went well enough, but still did not eat up at midday. They all knew that his chances of winning the big race were draining away by the hour.

"He's as fit as he can get – this apart – and he's got a great heart. Let's not be too pessimistic," Tom said bravely. "Take him up to Aintree and distract him. There's nothing else to be done."

So Tessa loaded up all Buffoon's gear and her own gear (minimal) and packed it into the horsebox, and they got ready to go. Peter was driving and Jimmy was coming as well as Tessa. The others had to stay behind and watch the television. The fraught little group saw them off, not the cheerful waving bunch that they should have been, but sad and anxious-eyed.

"At least it's better to get moving," Peter said, as they ground out down the lane.

But Buffoon was an uneasy passenger, not his usual dozy self. Tessa kept going in to talk to him, scrambling over the back seat but, although he had stopped whinnying and kicking, he was a troubled horse. The two brothers spoke little and the atmosphere in the cab was grim. Tessa tried to keep herself quiet and dignified because she knew they hated her histrionics, but it was an effort.

The weather was grey and dirty, but good for racing. Not heart-lifting. The motorway threw up a filthy spray and the approach to the famous racecourse was uninspiring, through a busy, built-up area.

"It was in the country when they built it," Jimmy remarked. "In eighteen thirty something. Times change."

They drove into the horsebox car park and Peter turned off the engine. The race meeting was in progress, for racing took place for two days before the Grand National Saturday, and the atmosphere was familiar. Horses were coming and going and being washed down, walked out to cool off. Lads and girls, hurried and overworked, were leading out immaculate beasts, carting basketfuls of gear and buckets of water and getting shouted at by little bandy men in flat caps. The remembered atmosphere was comforting. They went to look for Buffoon's allocated box, and checked in. The stables were built of old red brick, rows and rows of them built round adjoining yards. Some of the boxes had the names of past winners and the date painted on the door, but Buffoon's had no such distinction. They unboxed him and Tessa led him in and he started walking round immediately, tossing his head and pawing at the bedding. Usually he went straight to the manger, or fell asleep. Under his rugs the sweat was darkening his spring coat, a bad sign. After he had had time to settle Tessa put his feed in the manger, but he would not touch it. He now had not eaten for two whole days. With no one to see her, Tessa wept.

In the morning, early, she rode Buffoon out to exercise in the middle of the course along with several others, and the press and television cameras followed them. Everyone knew the story of Buffoon losing his friend Lucky; it was the news of the day, with many conjectures about the reason and the likely outcome. The horse's price in the betting was falling steadily. Peter told Tessa not to say a word to the press, and he came out and gave a brief outline of events, and offered no opinion. He knew Tessa would tell the world that it was Maurice's doing if she opened her mouth.

But the big gaunt horse was looking bad, tucked-up and ribby, and although he exercised in his usual fashion Tessa could feel his unhappiness. Everyone knew that even the slightest setback in training could affect a horse's chance in such a tough race; the only person who didn't appreciate the seriousness of what had happened was loony old Mr Cressington and his hard-faced daughter. They trundled over to say that they had put half their life-savings on him "at a very good price" and Peter hadn't the heart to tell them that they were on a hiding to nothing.

"Well, who knows? Anything can happen in racing," Jimmy said when they had departed. He smiled his quiet smile and said to Tessa, "It's not the end of the world, you know."

But to Tessa it was. She tried to remember that these things had to be taken on the chin in racing, and realized that Tom Bryant's situation was far worse than her own, that he had turned down the ride on the now clear favourite for poor old Buffoon! She knew that Raleigh had offered the ride back to him, and Peter would have let him go, but he didn't ask to change.

The day was grey and blustery, the going good. People were pouring in to the course and the atmosphere was heady; it was impossible to suppose that this was just another day's racing. Tessa kept telling herself it didn't matter.

"Leave the horse alone," Jimmy said. "Come and walk the course, take your mind off it."

"You're joking!" She had to laugh. Seeing those jumps in close-up was not going to reassure her.

"Remember," Jimmy said, "Tom will be up there, seventeen hands high. They don't look nearly so bad from a big horse."

It was good to be in Jimmy's company, always soothing. No wonder hyped-up horses came to Jimmy for re-schooling, learning to relax in his calm company. Tessa felt the magic working on herself, getting away into the country and away from the sight of Buffoon walking round and round his box.

"These things blow over," Jimmy said. "He can run in the National for years yet, he's only young. And he'll learn something today, and so will we. It's not the end of the world."

Tessa saw the sense of his words, and was pacified. She did not realize that she was looking as gaunt as her horse, her face thin and pinched with anxiety, frown lines across her forehead. She looked at the fearsome jumps and told herself that she wanted to be a jockey, that women rode in the Grand National and one day, if she was worth her salt, she might line up in this famous race. She would have to stop worrying, learn to control her runaway emotions. Walking out into the country with Jimmy was really good for her, putting things in perspective. She was such an idiot compared with Jimmy. He never got upset. He was always steady and optimistic. She saw that Peter, a worrier like herself, depended a lot on his brother's support. She even laughed.

Jimmy grinned too. "That's better. Expect nothing. It's more fun. You can't change the world."

The morning seemed to go on forever, then the first races. Tessa could not eat, like Buffoon. The noise of the crowd surged in and out of the stable yard on the gusts of wind and the horses looked out over their doors with their ears pricked, sensitive to this unusual excitement. Tessa plaited up her horse, then offered him titbits in her hand, but he blew them away into the straw. He was quiet now, but unhappy, she could tell. She put her arms round his neck and talked to him, and he stared out of the half-door, listening with his long waggy ears, the purple depths of his eyes full of anxiety.

At last the time came to put on his bridle and take him out towards the paddock. Tessa followed San Lucar, who looked magnificent and was tearing to go, needing two lads to hold him. But Buffoon went calmly and stopped patiently for Lukey's antics in front of him. The crowds round the paddock were dense and the paddock was too small to take all the runners comfortably, but Tessa winkled Buffoon on to the asphalt path and got behind a quieter horse than San Lucar. Peter had gone to fetch Tom's saddle from the weighing-room and she had to keep a look-out for him, to go into a saddling box. Now there was so much to think about that she forgot her troubles. Buffoon's apparently steady walk was strong enough to make her breathless as she scampered at his side, hearing the comments of the crowd as she passed, mostly, "That's the one that's lost his pony friend."

At last she could see Peter beckoning, and led Buffoon out of the paddock towards the row of saddling boxes. Jimmy was there to help and they tacked the horse up between them while he stood quietly. He never made a fuss, unlike most. Sounds of kicking and swearing came from the next box.

"That's Lukey using up his energy," Jimmy said happily. The big bay horse had white lines of sweat on his neck already, a bad sign. Maurice wouldn't like that.

"That's in our favour, at least," Peter said. He threw the rug back on and fastened the roller. Buffoon was number five.

They took him back into the paddock and after a few minutes in the crush the jockeys started to come out. Tom winkled his way towards them and ran his eyes critically over the horse he was to ride.

"He doesn't look too bad now. Settled enough anyway."

"Well, let's keep our fingers crossed," Peter said. "He's not eaten up, that's the worry."

He legged Tom into the saddle.

"Let's get going. It's all OK once you're out there," Tom said. "I'm still glad it's this one I'm riding."

Tessa could feel the tension rising by the minute. They had to lead out on to the course in number order, no mean feat getting organized as the stewards barked orders. Jimmy came with her, although Buffoon was still calm, and Tessa was glad to have the company, feeling extremely inexperienced amongst this impressive company. Now, when they came out on to the course, Buffoon took hold and dragged her forward, but Tom had a hold of him, and stroked his neck soothingly.

"Not yet, old fellow. We've got a parade first. Then you can go."

Most horses got impatient as soon as they were on the

course, and the parade was a nightmare of plunging, trained-to-the-minute horseflesh, being forced into a straight line, led by a couple of retired winners who were the worst behaved of the lot. The crowd loved it, as the commentator rolled out the names one by one. Tessa looked up and saw Tom's face taut with anticipation, pale and spark-eyed. As the first horse turned and was let go to canter down, Buffoon started to pull and prance. Tessa hung on grimly.

"He feels good," Tom said.

"He's forgotten that wretched pony," Jimmy said, and laughed. "Let him go, Tessa."

Tessa unclipped the lead and Buffoon gave a great leap forward. Tom went with him, balanced and secure, and Tessa and Jimmy watched the familiar red hindquarters pound away down the course. Now the anxieties were forgotten and Tessa felt all her old optimism come flooding back. Anything could happen! In the Grand National, that was the norm. It wasn't like other races.

They retreated off the course and fought their way up to the corner of the stand where Peter stood in the crush. It was hard to move and they could see little, but at least there was a huge television screen which was showing the action. Horses were all over the course, some still going down and some coming back, having had their pipe-opener down as far as the first jump. Now the tapes were being stretched across for the start and the horses were beginning to circle round in readiness.

Tessa stood with the two brothers, feeling herself start to tremble as the horses lined up. The crowd hushed. Tessa could see Buffoon, not pressed into the front, but lined up around the middle.

"They're under starter's orders!"

Straggling across the whole width of the course the untidy line began to move forward. The sun came out from behind a cloud and gleamed on the bright colours. The tapes sprang up. The crowd's roar went up – "They're off!" – and seemed to power the field with its breath, blasting them into the bend at what seemed a terrifying pace.

So fast! Tessa knew it was always a scramble to see light for the first obstacle in such a large field: to fall at the first was a disappointment too far! But it was hard to catch sight of the Cressington colours in the mêlée. Peter had his binoculars up but his fingers were trembling as much as Tessa's. All they could do was listen for possible fallers over the commentary – two at the first but not Buffoon – then none at the second and on to the big ditch which was a tough one. But now Tessa could see Buffoon, well-placed by Tom to avoid trouble, and she saw his huge jump, so big she was afraid for a moment that Tom was unseated. But no, it had gained him several lengths and he was coasting now, still in the middle.

It seemed easier now the fraught start was over and the first few jumps cleared. . . Survival was all now, and winning a remote dream as, perhaps, it always had been. Anything could happen in this race. The fear and doom was replaced by pure excitement and the joy of seeing their horse taking these big jumps apparently in his stride.

Peter said, "If he doesn't make it this year, there's always next! He's loving it. He's an Aintree horse!"

Buffoon soared over Becher's, landing so far out that he went right up the field. But at the Canal turn he lost it again by his ungainliness. Smaller, nippier horses slipped up his inside while Tom had to steer his big mount steadily round to keep him balanced, losing ground. San Lucar was running a blinder out in front, galloping relentlessly and jumping fast. Tessa ground her teeth, thinking of Maurice's adrenalin running up in his champagne box. . . To have all that money at stake must make it terrible, she thought. As if it wasn't enough just to love your horse, your heart in your mouth for his bravery, testing it, your own heart thumping in tune. "Why do we do this?" Peter said out loud, but he was laughing. All the distress of the past few days was quite forgotten.

When the field came down towards the stands on the first circuit they were beginning to string out. A group of six or so were bunched in front, led by San Lucar, and then a straggle to another bunch amongst which was Buffoon. Tom had got him on the inside now, saving ground, and he seemed to be going very easily, his long stride making him look relaxed compared with some of the others. As they came to the biggest jump on the course, the Chair, in front of the stands, Tessa found herself shaking again. She saw Tom sit down and drive, asking him, and Buffoon flew, once more landing well out. He danced over a fallen jockey, gathered his long legs together and powered on.

"He's a natural," Jimmy said. "Whoever'd have thought it?"

176

They went past towards the water-jump, right in front of where they were standing . . . close enough now to see that Buffoon was pulling quite hard, to see the grimace on Tom's face as the horse took off a full stride too soon and sailed over the water with another vast jump. Now he was closing on the leading bunch, belting round the bend near the start and out into the country again on the second circuit. Behind them on the wind came the receding frenzy of pounding hooves and the cries of stable lads trying to catch loose horses pulling up near the stables. Tessa tried to calm herself, but it was hard to stand still, breathe, not have hysterics. Just to stay sane . . . Even Jimmy was showing signs of excitement.

"He's doing you proud, Tessa. Whatever happens, he's shown class."

Bechers loomed again. Tessa watched the television screen and saw San Lucar go down on his knees on landing. His jockey clutched frantically at the horse's ears but Lukey ducked his head again, the jockey flew off over his shoulder and the big horse continued alone.

Tessa screamed with joy. Buffoon flew over, making the jump look like a pole on the ground.

"Well, that's the opposition gone. It's anybody's now," Peter said.

The field was now well and truly strung out. Out in the far country the spruce flew from the big hedges as tired horses ploughed through them. Buffoon was now in the leading group, with only three horses ahead of him. Tessa was unashamedly clutching Jimmy's arm, but he said quietly to her, "Don't bank on it, Tessa. This is where three days without food will find him out."

All the horses were tired now, jumping raggedly, their jockeys holding them together. Tom was sitting quietly, niggling with his heels, but Tessa could see that the big horse was failing, the heart going out of him. His stamina, his great strength, had been sapped by the misery of the past three days. He came round the home turn and into the long straight to the finish, but three other horses were in front of him and going farther away, and as he struggled in their wake two more overtook him. Tessa's heart died with him and the tears ran down her cheeks, but she was smiling at the same time for his bravery. He had given his all. Tom did not ask him for any more, but just held him together to help him over the last two jumps, going for the big holes cut out by his predecessors. The horse came home with his ears pricked, loping slowly up the run-in to finish seventh.

They all ran out on the course to meet him. Not winning did not matter at all any more. The horse had done brilliantly.

"My God, I reckon he could have won! If that damned pony had stayed around!"

Peter was his old self, all the worries of the past few days rubbed out. Tessa was dancing, hugging the sweaty neck, hugging Tom as he slipped wearily from the saddle.

"What a ride! He was great, really great!"

Tom tugged off his saddle and the cloths, his face wreathed in smiles. Peter, remembering his duties, was looking round for the Cressingtons, but there was no sign of them in the crush, so he turned back to the horse, patting his neck, looking him over for injury.

"He could have won, I reckon," Tom said, "without that Lucky business. Next year, eh?"

"Next year. I'm booking you now," Peter said.

"I made the right choice. What a bollocking Ferdy's going to get from our friend Morrison! I wouldn't be in his shoes now!" He turned back to Buffoon and kissed him on the nose. "He's a wonder, Tess! And you too – such faith!" And he gave her a kiss too, gathered up his gear and went off to weigh in.

"He gave him a great ride," Jimmy said.

A lot of people were standing round, gawping and eavesdropping, and now one of them came forward and stood by Buffoon's head. But it was Tessa he was looking at. Tessa looked up, stared, trembled. The shock hit her like a bolt of lightning.

"Tessa?" he said, not sure either.

"Yes?" A whisper.

"This is Shiner's boy, isn't it?"

"Yes."

"I bred him. And you too!"

The sudden breaking of the lop-sided smile showing the tooth broken in a fight, the amazing sparkling eyes laughing at her . . . Tessa could not believe it. After all this time, her father! After years of dreams, odd quirks of memory, the terrible regret, the anger at his defection . . . it all rolled away now in what felt like a blast of golden sunshine. She was too stunned to speak.

Declan put his arms round her and covered her face with whisky-smelling kisses. She could tell he was fairly drunk as usual, but it didn't matter. She buried her face in his dirty jacket, not wanting to come up, not wanting anyone to see her out-of-control face. But they were surrounded by a crowd, and Buffoon's reins were in her hands.

Declan was happily proclaiming to all and sundry, "My little girl! This is my girl Tess, and this is the horse we bred from her little old mare, eh Tess? The little old mare with no eyes. My, how she loved that mare. Didn't you love old Shiner, Tess, when you was just a little girl?"

Tessa wanted to die.

She loved him just as much, but not here, for God's sake! Blathering away, on a whisky and Guinness high, he was revealing all the good reasons for the family break-up. Peter and Jimmy were looking on, astonished.

"Declan Blackthorn?" Jimmy enquired.

"The very same, sorr!"

He was sounding now just like a television Irishman, away on one of his spiels. "And this is my own little Tess, my little lost girl, my baby – and my horse too, the ugly great brute I cried over the night he was born—"

"Oh Dad! Shut up!" Tessa muttered, surfacing. "Not in front of all these people."

She could see Peter and Jimmy smiling. The Cressingtons were trundling towards them, no doubt to talk about the loss of their life's savings. Peter turned away with a groan.

"We've got to take him back to the stables, Dad," Tessa said desperately. "Can we talk later?"

"I'll be in the bar, my darling. Come back to the bar and have a word before you go. My little long-lost girl—"

A group of equally happy and inebriated Irish friends were waiting to take him away, and Tessa watched him depart with a feeling of relief mixed with terrible pain. What a man! It was like the past coming up and slamming her between the eyes, nothing like the romantic dream she had nurtured of her father all these years. It was how he was, had always been, why her mother had left. Why ever had she dreamed otherwise? It was all plain now.

Jimmy said, "All you need, your long-lost daddy after a day like this! Take it easy, Tessa."

He could see her state.

"He's drunk!"

"It's a great drinking day for the Irish, Aintree. Give him a chance. You can look for him before we go, when we've done the horse."

Tessa stumbled back to the stables, leading Buffoon. People jostled them on all sides. Somewhere in the crush she saw another face from the past – Mrs Alston. Was she dreaming? But no, at her side was the Battleaxe, and as they went by the two ladies waved their race-cards at her and shouted, "Well done, your horse, Tessa!"

Were they drunk too?

Tessa felt more drunk than any of them.

Buffoon! What a horse! Could winning feel any better, when he had run his great heart out like that? But for losing Lucky, who knew. . .?

The quiet Jimmy was wreathed in smiles.

"We all laughed at him, didn't we, when he came? Your beauty! Did you know your dad bred him? Is that why you wanted him?"

"Only when I saw his passport. Not the night he arrived. The dam, Shiner, was my dearest —" She choked.

Covering up, Jimmy chatted quietly. "Declan's name isn't in the passport as breeder. Only a stud name."

"He called it a stud. Just a row of tin sheds. The rain came through. . . " She went there when her parents quarrelled, she remembered, and sat under the tin sheets in one of the few dry spots, talking to Shiner.

"Shiner had no eyes," she said.

"No eyes! That why your father had her? She was a reject? Should have been put down."

"Yes. He insisted. He raised her."

"Because of her bloodline? He's not stupid, your father. She's got a great bloodline. That's where he gets it from. Not his sire, who was useless."

"Declan could never afford a decent sire."

Talking about it calmed her. By the time they had worked

on Buffoon and got him dry and comfortable, watered and fed, Tessa was getting back on an even keel. She could see they needed to start for home, and that Buffoon was now, the excitement over, starting to fret for Lucky again, but both Peter and Jimmy knew she had to see her father again, if only to say goodbye.

"I won't be long," she promised.

But it took her ages to find him, and when she did he was surrounded by his pals and at the singing stage. She stood amongst the noisy, jostling throng in the swaying tent of one of the hard-drinking bars and watched him raising his lovely tenor voice in an obscure Irish folk-song, of which he had a huge repertory. How she remembered that song!

And she knew she couldn't speak to him. It would be too awful, in that company. He would be maudlin and dreadful. She watched him, and the tears of her long devotion to his memory filled her eyes. What a day! She didn't need a Guinness to feel drunk herself, reeling in her roundabout of emotions – up, down, round and round like a circus carousel. The noise and the atmosphere were unbearable. She turned away. If he wanted her, he knew where to find her now.

But she guessed he would never come.

They were on a high now it was all over, the horse safe, the worries at rest. They could talk for ever about whether he would have won or not if he had had no setbacks, but for now there was the tidying up to do, the horse to be washed down, the owners to be found.

Jimmy came back to the stables with Tessa. Tessa kept thinking with a delirious joy of Maurice seeing his jockey come off at Bechers. The thought of him losing his fortune was euphoric. Every time she remembered the poor jockey shooting off over the horse's ears she laughed out loud. It was the loveliest thing she had seen for a long time. She would go up to Goldlands and visit, and gloat. Poor old Greevy. He would be sick.

Peter was shaking his head over the Cressingtons.

"They're more upset about the money they lost than excited about the horse's performance. That dreadful daughter – moan, moan, moan. She doesn't even begin to understand how it works. Did I tell them to put all their savings on? I told them to have a modest bet each way. And then I told them about Lucky and the chances slipping away. What more can a man do? The old man wasn't so cut up. He's got more sense. But that woman!"

And when they were on the motorway, purring for home, Peter said, "I saw Tom later and he said something about getting the vet to have a look at Buffy's eyes. He reckons his eyesight is not all it should be. I must say I was quite surprised. We've always thought him clumsy, but Tom reckons there might be a reason. I hope he's mistaken."

Tessa felt the cold hand close again, as the secret fear that she kept buried in her subconscious was pulled into the light again. She knew all about blind horses. No, Buffoon, not that, she prayed. But she kept her counsel, and changed the subject, saying, "Are there any sandwiches left? I'm starving."

17

The Knife

*B*uffoon stood looking out over his door, whinnying every now and then. Something was missing in his life. He felt ill at ease, anxious. He was not used to feeling anxious. He couldn't eat.

"He looks like a scarecrow," Sarah said.

"He's my beauty."

Tessa had her arms round his neck. But she wasn't enough. A horse knows his humans, but knows his mates better. They are creatures of habit and Buffoon had had Lucky by his side ever since he was a foal. His dam Shiner had not been a good mother to him, and kicked him away from his suckling early on in his life, and Declan had given him Lucky for a pal. When he went to the sales, Lucky went too, and his lackadaisical early owners had had no problems with taking the pony too. Anything for a quiet life. Buffoon had been fortunate. But the habit of Lucky's companionship was now so deeply ingrained that it was more than just the usual bonding.

"He'll get over it," Sarah said. "Eventually. Silly old sod."

Tessa had work to do. She wasn't allowed to spend all day mooning over her horse. Buffoon watched her go, as far as he could see her, which wasn't very far. He was looking through a grey mist, but didn't think it was anything unusual. He fell over things if they were in the way, but mostly there was only a grass way ahead. He never went anywhere else. He had got used to the sudden appearance of large fences, and jumped as big as possible in his surprise. He had a careful nature, and a well-developed sense of self-preservation, learned from his foalhood. It had stood him in good stead so far.

"He ran such a cracking race," Sarah said. "We were going mad, watching the box."

"Tom thought he would have won if—"

"We all thought so too."

He still wouldn't eat, save for desultory picking. He would not eat the bran-mash they made him, nor even a handful of carrots. At least he had stopped box-walking. Or was it because he was tired? Tessa was tired too and her head was reeling. But she could not resist going up to Goldlands to see her mother. And Maurice.

It was late, and when she set off up the valley the stars were out and a bright half-moon lit her path. A slight frost hardened the way, the grass crisp and sharp under her shabby boots. So many thoughts and emotions jumbled in her mind that the walk in the cold air was welcome and she did not hurry. The threat about Buffoon's sight, surfacing again, was something she did not want to think about, and again she tried to sink it under the good memories of the day. If Lucky had not disappeared, would her horse have won? They would never know, but she knew Jimmy thought he would have kept on going. "He stays for ever, that one." The memory of his great golden galloping legs eating up the ground as he came round past the stands on the first circuit would stay in her mind for ever. And his courage, his generosity, his kindness . . . she had stayed with him in his box to settle him, as if she were the piebald pony, and he had rubbed his big bonehead against her shoulder affectionately, to tell her he had done his best. What did he know about the Grand National and what it meant to win the biggest race in the world? He only did as he was asked. She could not imagine her life without Buffoon.

As she approached Goldlands she felt a thrill of delight go through her. She could almost find it in her heart to be sorry for Maurice, remembering his poor jockey's frantic effort to stay in the saddle. Tom might have sat it. Maurice would know that. Tessa hoped he wasn't going to take it out on her poor mother.

They were sitting in the lounge, waiting for dinner, drinking. Tessa could feel the wrath even as she opened the door, a heavy air of tension. They were both well into the whisky. Tessa saw that her mother had been preparing herself for Maurice's homecoming and was now in a loony maudlin state, her eyes full of tears. Maurice looked wiped out, his face sunk in, like an old man, Tessa saw. Her reaction was of savage pleasure.

"Greevy not home yet?" She felt she must tread carefully.

"No. What do you want? Come to show your sympathy?" A heavily sarcastic query.

"No. I came to see Mum. And get some dinner, with luck."

"I shall have words with your boss tomorrow, about getting his hands on my jockey. Very underhand, and Tom broke his contract. I've a mind to complain to the authorities —"

"It was nothing to do with Peter. Tom chose."

"Tom would have sat that peck. The horse didn't fall, for God's sake! I was robbed of that race. The bloody jockey. . ."

It was all that Tessa had expected. No word of praise for their horse, no suggestion that he might have handled the situation better, no joy at Lukey's great performance, no sympathy for his jockey . . . only self-pity and blame. The atmosphere was so bad that she wondered if it was worth staying after all. She had seen what she wanted. But when Maurice went off to the bathroom her mother said desperately, "Do stay for a while. I can't bear it when he's like this! He's lost a fortune and this mood will last for weeks. He can't afford to lose so much money. I told him he was mad, but he was so adamant that he had the winner."

"Well, he had too, I imagine, if Ferdy had stayed aboard. The horse ran a blinder."

"And your horse ran so well! You must have been pleased."

"Yes, he was great. But there's always next year. Neither of the horses got hurt and Lukey's fantastic. What more does he want?"

"It's the money, mainly."

"Yes, well, he's made his racing like that. He's just stupid if he bets more than he's got. How can he ever enjoy it?"

"Well, that's Maurice, I'm afraid."

Tessa stayed for the dinner, which was wonderful, roast pork with lots of crackling and gravy and roast potatoes. In the bleak caravan world at Sparrows Wyck such luxuries were impossible. She and Sarah shared a tin of corned beef or made cheese on toast most nights, but tonight she felt her emotionally-battered self needed the goodies Goldlands could supply. Several glasses of Maurice's rare wine also lifted her spirits. If only the company were Peter and Jimmy and Sarah and Wisbey – what an evening they would have! The others had been euphoric at Buffoon's performance, although they all knew he might have won if . . . they would never stop wondering this. The eternal question.

"I don't know why you're so miserable – you've got a great horse," she said to Maurice at the end of the meal. "There's always another day. He's only nine."

"Don't you patronize me, my girl! What do you know about ownership? All you staff, you just take your wages and gossip your time away, it's just a game to you. Don't tell me how I should feel."

"If your horse got killed, all you'd think about is the insurance," Tessa said witheringly. "If you were nicer to your staff, they might be happier to work for you. Tom, for instance."

She thought he was going to hit her, but he was too far gone to get up from his chair.

"Get out of here! You make me sick. You only come up here

to see how much you can wheedle out of your mother – I know your tricks."

"Oh Maurice, don't! I love to see her, she's all I've got!" Tears trickled down Myra's cheeks. Tessa wanted to scream. Her *stupid* mother, to put up with such treatment! She was just like a rag doll, no stuffing at all.

"Yes, you don't think I come to see *you*, do you, you selfish, stupid old git!"

It was now essential to depart. Tessa ran, bursting with the joy of delivering these words. He couldn't touch her now – she was her own person, with her own home, her own wages, and her good friends. She had everything and he had nothing. But her mother! As she leapt over the ha-ha, the problem of her mother brought her up short. Oh God, her mother . . . would she never see sense? Myra's hopeless tears distressed her. She walked more slowly, turning over the day's doings, but the events were a tired and slightly inebriated jumble now. The moon was floating behind a gauzy cloud, and an aeroplane's lights blinked like moving stars across the downs. Tessa stood still, sniffing the cold air.

And as she stood there, contemplating her life, a small noise penetrated her consciousness. So familiar, it caused a start like an electric shock to fix her rigid. She could feel all the hairs standing up on the back of her neck. A distant whinny . . . no, not Buffoon's anxious noise, but the answer he had been fretting for: it was Lucky's voice. It came from the old buildings of the Home Farm where she had once made her den. It was unmistakeable. It came again, very faint, but Tessa knew she was not mistaken.

"Lucky!"

She ran. Galvanized, she leapt over the frosty grass towards the dark huddle of buildings on the skyline. All the time – why hadn't she thought of it? She had known all along that it was Maurice's plan, she *knew* it was . . . the diabolical timing! Her breath was bursting her lungs as the slope steepened to the brow but she ran even faster, choking for air. The swine! The evil bastard!

"Lucky!" she screamed. "Where are you?"

But she knew her way around the yard and where the likely loosebox was, and ran down the row of darkened doorways, peering over the swinging half-doors. A familiar little head suddenly stuck out in front of her, and a now piercing whinny of recognition blasted her ears.

"Oh, my little darling!" She flung her arms round the pony's neck, and dragged open the door.

The loosebox was full of dirty bedding, but there was hay and water; the pony had not been ill-treated. Tessa got hold of his forelock and led him out. She was shaking now with anger.

"You know your way home! Come along! Quickly!"

She dragged him by his mane out through the gate and on to the down and faced him down the long hill home.

"You know the way – off you go! Go and whinny at the gate and they'll come running!"

She gave him a thump on the quarters and he trotted off, letting out a few bucks as he went. Then he broke into a canter, straight down the path for Sparrows Wyck. Tessa watched him, shaking. She knew she should have gone with him, but the compulsion within her was too strong, the hate rising like bile. She was shaking with violence. She turned and ran back across the field to Goldlands. The lights still shone in the room she had just left. The curtains undrawn, she could see Maurice deep into the whisky, moaning away at Myra. She hated him then so much that she stopped, frightened for herself. For a second she knew she must follow Lucky, cool it, go home. But then she knew she couldn't. This had happened before and she knew it led to disaster, but it was beyond her powers to pull back. It was as if she was standing back watching herself, and knowing what was going to happen.

She was ice-cold now, and calm. But trembling like a trapped hare.

She went in through the kitchen door and into the dining-room. The pork joint was cleared away on to the sideboard and the carving knife lay beside it. Tessa picked it and walked over to Maurice. She heard Myra scream and saw, for one glorious moment, the look of abject terror on Maurice's face, and then she stepped forward and thrust the knife with all her power into his chest.

"That's for you, from Lucky. From Buffoon. From all of us. From *me*!"

And then there was blood all over her and Myra screaming, and screaming and screaming.

And Greevy came in.

And she knew she should have gone home with Lucky.

Part Two

1

"This place is killing you"

The raindrops ran slowly down the window-pane, something to watch, something to do. Sit on the end of the bed looking out. There were bars over the window but she didn't really see them any longer. She wasn't going anywhere.

"In here for violence! You must be joking. She hasn't the strength to lift a teaspoon, let alone a carving-knife."

The parting words of her last visitor (a do-gooder) lingered on the air, deepening the worried look on Ma's face. Ma ran the place. She was a sort of aged Sarah, frightening on top but, deep underneath, kind. The place was for wild girls and Tessa regretted that she hadn't come here at a time when she might have enjoyed it, before all the Buffoon business, when she was looking for trouble. But now the company meant nothing to her. She shut herself away and stared out of the window, refused to go out, refused to talk, wished she was dead. Doctors came to see her and gave her pills for depression, but they didn't make any difference. Something had died in her. No one would believe it was a horse.

Buffoon had been sold shortly after his Grand National. Mr Cressington had had a heart attack and died and his creditors took Buffoon to the sale yard. A vet had diagnosed incipient blindness through cataracts on both eyes, and one of his legs had swelled up with tendon trouble after the race, so nobody was much interested in buying him. He went to a dealer with a doubtful reputation and now no one knew where he was.

Tessa's friends at the yard found it very difficult to tell her what had happened. Jimmy came with Sarah. Sarah told Ma it would break her heart. Ma said she'd never heard of such a thing but now, two years later, she was beginning to think Sarah had been right. She was arguing for Tessa to be released.

But the crime had been sensational at the time, especially in the racing press. Tessa had been given a heavy sentence.

What happened that night was something Tessa had blanked out of her mind. Save for the one thing. The look on Maurice's face when he lay on the floor with the knife sticking out of his chest. Greevy had pulled her away and held her struggles in arms suddenly as strong as iron shackles; Myra was screaming the house down, and Maurice had looked at Tessa with what she remembered only as *satisfaction*. It ate into her, Maurice's satisfaction. The knife hadn't gone in far enough. Greevy had stopped her, and Maurice knew, even at that moment, that it was enough to put her away, and to do him no lasting harm. After that look, self-pity took over and he moaned and wailed until the paramedics and the police arrived in a cacophony of sirens and blue flashing lights. Tessa sat watching, numb. Myra needed sedating, Greevy rose to the occasion. The few years coping with race-horses at Raleigh's had taught him how to deal with emergencies. Unfortunately Maurice was not allowed to bleed to death.

The racing world and the national press exploded with the story. The print dared not say it, but it was freely remarked in Newmarket, Lambourn, Middleham, Malton and Epsom that the man deserved what he got, and pity the knife hadn't gone farther. Big spenders in racing weren't always likeable, but got what they wanted. Greevy knew what Raleigh and the yard thought about his father but had learned to live with it. He had grown away from his father, influenced by the people he now worked with. It wasn't easy for him, pulled in two directions. He had come to admire Tessa since they had lived apart, and his horror at what she had done was more for her than for his father. He knew, with her record, that she would suffer far more and for far longer than his father. And he was right.

"She didn't kill the man, after all – a stroke of luck for the child. Not for want of trying though. We've tried every approach, but she's the most stubborn character we've ever come across. She responds to nothing."

"Didn't they say she had a jockey's licence?"

"Well, she had. Whether she's still got it after stabbing a leading owner is another matter."

"It would give her direction, a job like that to go back to."

"They want her back. She's certainly got good friends."

The powers-that-be were finding Tessa tiresome and expensive: shortly she would be in a psychiatric hospital, and

Ma said there were better ways to spend public money. Nobody saw her as dangerous. It was domestic, essentially, they said. Domestic was – well, domestic. A private war.

While they argued Tessa went about the routine like a zombie, speaking to no one. All the other girls left her alone. She did what she had to and spent her time lying on her bed reading rubbishy novels. She did nothing wrong.

The Battleaxe came to see her, and once came with Mrs Alston. Tessa was shocked into attention.

"You got what you wanted from me that time," Mrs Alston said, smiling. "I thought you were pretty bright. What went wrong?"

Tessa fell back on the old defence of saying nothing.

"Was it the horse?" Mrs Alston said softly.

Tessa's eyes filled with tears but she still said nothing.

The two teachers ended up talking to each other. They made their farewells and walked slowly outside to their car.

"That girl," said the Battleaxe, "is all heart, all brain. What is she doing in a place like this?"

"But violent too. She hasn't learned to contain it. The stepfather deserved it, of course; I've not met anyone who didn't smile with satisfaction at the story. Tessa just did what many, many people would have liked to do."

They shook their heads. They did not mention the obvious, that the girl needed someone – or the horse – to love, it was too apparent. To love her.

"The mother once told me that Tessa thought – thinks – the

world of her father, although he's never come by nor near since the family split up. I wonder if there's any chance of getting him to visit?"

"After such a long time?"

"The shock of it, you never know. Besides. . . " Mrs Alston shrugged. "It's his business, after all. His girl. It just might get a reaction."

"Maybe we could trace him. It shouldn't be all that difficult."

They put the idea to Ma. Ma got in touch with Myra. Myra rang old, half-forgotten friends, and second cousins once removed, and the Irish racecourses, and sent the message out on the horsey grapevine of Ireland: Declan Blackthorn, ring home. The number she gave was the yard at Sparrows Wyck. Myra had no wish for Declan to turn up at Goldlands. Myra was not convinced it was a good idea but no one had come up with anything better.

Declan came over, as usual, for the Grand National meeting. He won a lot of money and got very drunk. In his pocket he had the address of the institution where Tessa was confined. Two days after the Grand National he got in a taxi and gave the taxi-driver the slip of paper. The taxi driver said the address was two hundred miles away but Declan merely said, "Drive on!" and fell asleep on the back seat.

It was just about opening time when they arrived at their destination and Declan needed a whisky or two to give himself courage. He asked to be put down at the nearest pub. He needed time to try and work out how old Tessa would be now. He remembered seeing her at the Grand National. She had looked about ten. Could she be only ten? This seemed a bit odd for a would-be murderer and he wondered if he had heard Myra correctly. But no, he had heard the story in Ireland. It had been all over the racing press: his Tessa stabbing Mr Maurice Morrison-Pleydell. He had been much congratulated. He had taken credit. He sat on in the pub, smiling to himself. What a girl! A chip off the old block. He and Myra had bred good stock. Myra . . . oh God! Myra. . .

He ordered another drink.

Some racing men came in and he got talking. The evening wore on and then it was too late to visit. He went to a cheap hotel to spend the night, and in the morning couldn't remember where he was or why. He had lost the bit of paper with Tessa's address. He went to the railway station to find out where he was, not liking to ask, and a train came in so he got on it, hoping it might be going in the direction of Ireland.

When he got home three days later he remembered why he had gone to that place. But it was too late by then.

Neither Ma nor Mrs Alston were surprised at the failure of their quest for Declan Blackthorn. When Mrs Alston visited again three months later she had thought of something else.

"That jockey, what was his name? The one that rode her horse in the Grand National? I think he was called Tom Bryant."

"Tom Bryant? I've heard of him."

"Perhaps. . .?"

"It might be worth a try. I'll get in touch."

Tom had a bad conscience about Tessa. He hadn't visited because – hell – going into a girls' madhouse wasn't his cup of tea! He got mobbed enough as it was by far saner girls than Tessa's companions. And what to say about Buffoon? He must have been put down by now, and how could anyone tell Tessa that? Peter and co had a conscience about not buying him back at the sales, but he had gone for more than they expected. Once bought, he would have been nothing but expense and trouble, neither of which Peter could afford. It would be hard to face Tessa's questions.

Tessa was under everyone's skin; they could not forget her. Tom thought of her radiant face, taking Buffoon's reins, and the eyes that seemed to consume him. She wasn't like any other girl he'd ever met. He would have liked to have had a bit of fun with her, like he did with most attractive girls he came across: he would have liked to kiss her, properly. She intrigued him. But there was an invisible fence round Tessa that said "Keep Out". As Wisbey once said, it was "like she's inside barbed wire". Tom thought she hadn't grown up yet, she was a late starter. She had never learned about relationships like ordinary, loved people. But she was almost eighteen now and physically maturing and perhaps, when she had come through this thing, she might . . . well, love him like she had loved that horse? He had to laugh at himself, thinking that. No man could be so lucky.

So when he had a phone call from someone called Mrs Alston, he promised her he would go. He told her he felt bad about having to be told.

But the woman said, kindly, "I know it's hard. I understand. But please go."

Ma knocked on Tessa's door and, after a moment, opened it.

"A visitor for you. Called Tom," said Ma. "Very handsome."

"Tom!"

This time there was a positive reaction. Tessa panicked.

"I can't see him!"

"Why not?"

Because of things she could not bear to think about! But she was obliged to go downstairs with Ma.

Tom was looking out of the window (also barred), fidgeting nervously with the window blind. He turned round and stared at her, smiled uncertainly.

"Hi. Tessa? God, you look awful."

Ma said, "That's a fine welcome, I must say. I thought you were here to cheer her up."

She went out and shut the door.

"This place is killing you! Sarah told me. I should have come ages ago, but it's worse than hospital – you know – visiting . . . I'm pretty useless. But *being* visited – it matters. So I'm a bit of a shit really."

He had been injured several times like nearly all jockeys and knew about hospital visiting.

"Sarah says you're in a decline."

Tessa shrugged.

"You can't do this to yourself, Tessa. You've got to be ready when your time's up to get your licence back."

"I don't stand much chance of that."

"Don't you believe it. What he did was criminal. Just as good as doping. The Jockey Club takes all that into account, after all. They couldn't prove it was him, but everyone knows he paid someone to do it. And it wasn't Greevy, surprisingly."

"I wish I'd killed him."

"Damned good try, all the same." Tom laughed. "I don't think he got many sympathizers visiting *him* in hospital. Raleigh never went."

He sat on the edge of the table where the magazines were laid out and looked at her seriously.

"Come out of it, Tessa. Get some beef on yourself. You'll never be able to ride again unless you buck up your ideas."

"No one will give me a ride, even if I get my licence back."

"They will, you know. Everybody cheered at what you did – everybody thought it was just what he deserved. Nobody will say it in so many words, I suppose, but you'll find you have a lot of friends."

This was a surprise to Tessa.

"You don't get anywhere by being sorry for yourself," Tom said sternly. "Especially if you're a jockey. Think positive."

"I suppose Sarah told you to come?"

"No, she didn't actually. She told me you were a mess, that's all. She's disappointed in you. She told me that ages ago and I've only just got round to calling. I had to come this way to ride out for Parmenter. I'm on my way back to Wincanton now, got four rides there this afternoon. Pity I can't load you up and take you with me."

For a brief moment Tessa was roused out of her lethargy to wish – fiercely – that she could go with him. The sound of the crowd, the smell of sweaty horse and damp leather. . . Tom's gaunt face was suddenly so dear, remembering him sliding off Buffoon on the hoof-scarred Aintree turf. Tears pricked her eyes and she turned away and looked out of the window.

Tom said softly, "Don't do this to yourself, Tessa. We want you back."

"Oh Tom!" she wailed. The tears streamed down her cheeks. She turned towards him and he came over to her and put his arms round her and she buried her face in his chest. It smelled of horse sweat. It was wonderful to be held in such a strong grasp, so foreign to her nature, but so comforting. It felt like opening up a great crack in her shell, a mortal surrender.

At this point Ma opened the door to issue in another visitor for somebody else, but when she saw what was happening she withdrew quickly and closed the door silently behind her, taking the visitor to another room. Tessa behaving like a human being was what she was always praying for. Might this be the breakthrough they were all hoping for?

When he departed, she had a close look at the young man who had effected this surprising breakdown.

"You look familiar. Should I know you?"

"Only if you're a racing fan. I'm a jockey. Tom Bryant."

"Ah yes. That's it. Mrs Alston said she would contact you. I remember now."

"I rode the horse she looked after. The one all the trouble was over."

That made sense to Ma. How lovely if this young man could deliver Tessa from her living death.

"Will you come again? You seem to have got through to her. We're worried about her here, you know."

"I'll try."

"I know you lead a very busy life, but no one else has got her to cry before."

"It seems strange that crying is a good sign."

"Oh yes. She's like stone. But stones don't cry. Please come again."

"Yes. I'll try."

"You will."

Tom was taken aback by the look in Ma's eye. He went away, disturbed by what had happened. Tessa's steely, impenetratable armour – had he dented it? It was only via the horse she had loved, suffered, known joy and sorrow like a normal person. He guessed that what she really needed to come alive again was Buffoon back, but life did not work that way. Everyone knew that racehorses came and went at the whim of their owners, not to satisfy the wishes of their devoted carers. And Buffoon – Tom hadn't heard of him since the Grand National. He enquired after him, but Peter Fellowes had no idea where he had gone.

"He'll be dead by now, like as not. A bad business all round. I hope Morrison gets his just deserts one day."

"He's lost a lot of money lately."

"Good."

Tom had lost his retainer with Raleigh through refusing to ride Maurice's horses but was not short of offers to ride for just about everyone else. It was hard to slot in visits to Tessa. Luck had been running his way, and he was ten wins ahead of the field towards the end of the season, on the verge of becoming champion jockey.

One morning he rang Tessa's place and asked to speak to her. He told her he would visit after the day's racing. It was to pin himself down, otherwise, without the promise, he knew he would go on putting it off. It was hard enough to fit in everything necessary for his work without sick-visiting, or whatever the equivalent was. Prison-visiting, he supposed, with a dart of surprise. Tessa was as unlike a criminal as anyone he had met. But there had been gruesome stories of the damage she had wreaked on her stepfather that night at Goldlands. The hospital helicopter had winged in while Lucky was still bellowing to be let in down at the farm gate. What goings-on in the sleepy valley!

He went to work and rode five races. Weighing out for the last, he could not help looking forward to the end of the season and a bit of a rest. His body felt parched and strung-up, his nerves twitchy. His last horse did not inspire him with confidence either, a confirmed tearaway which fell frequently but nearly always won if it kept on its feet. With luck this was one of its winning days.

"Let him go, if that's what he wants. It's safer that way," the trainer said. "You can't say he hasn't got the appetite for the job!"

True – just hang on. It wasn't the sort of ride where you had to work for every metre, and come home exhausted. The horse was a character and a favourite with the crowd for its quirky enthusiasm.

The spring shadows lay long across the grass, the low sun making visibility very bad as the course swung round into the West. Maybe that was what caused it. Tom remembered squinting up through his darkened goggles at the black bank of brush looming against a scarlet sky, giving the horse his office to take off, and then the jump coming at him in a most extraordinary fashion, not swinging happily below, but apparently crashing down on his head. He couldn't understand it, nor did he have the chance to wonder what had happened for a very long time.

Tessa had no visitor that night.

Ma was angry, until she read the papers in the morning, and then she understood.

She took the paper with her to Tessa's room and said, "I'm afraid it's not very good news – why your jockey friend didn't turn up last night."

Tessa read the paragraph Ma was pointing at: "Leading jockey seriously injured in last fence fall."

"It doesn't sound too good."

Tessa made a little moaning noise and snatched the paper off Ma. She read: "Tom Bryant is still in a coma this morning after a horrific fall from erratic jumper, Country Cousin. The horse appeared not to take off, ploughing into the bottom of the jump, bringing down the horse behind it which fell on Bryant. Bryant sustained severe injuries to his back and head, and is said to be in a critical condition this morning."

Tessa went white and started to shake.

"Not Tom! Oh, no!" She leapt up and shrieked out, "I must see him! I must go!"

"Tessa, dear, he's in a coma, it says. I shall get you permission to visit him when the time is right. But not yet."

"Oh Tom! Oh Tom!"

Tessa sat on the bed with her head in her hands, rocking backwards and forwards. Ma watched her curiously, pleased to see this response. Tom, having been the first to crack the stone defence, was now, by default, the cause of the crack widening.

"Hush, my dear, I'm sure he'll survive. They are so skilled today with these injuries. I will ring, if you want, and ask about him."

"Oh please! Please!"

Tess could feel the almost forgotten surge of adrenalin coursing through her miserable system. Seeing Tom again had cut into her lethargy, reminding her that the world was still going on out there. And now this shock – she could not pretend any more that she didn't care what happened.

Sarah kept her informed. She called with Gilly in the evening, and they told her Tom was in a bad way, but not going to die.

"I'm going to see him! Ma says I can go. She's going to arrange it."

They were surprised. Going home, Sarah said, "He's done her a good turn, getting half-killed. She's unfrozen."

"Poor old Tom. There must have been easier ways!"

"He visited her when she was down. She remembers that. It's crazy to keep her in that place, it's killing her."

"It would kill me!"

Ma kept her word, and ten days later drove Tessa to visit Tom in her own car. There was a stern lecture about trust, and no monkey business – "Because it will be me that will be in trouble, not you," Ma said. "And I'm sure you wouldn't like that!"

"Wouldn't I?" Tessa said, and smiled.

Ma nearly drove into the ditch.

It wasn't easy for Tessa, visiting Tom.

Tom had always inferred that, when a jockey was down, he needed the support of his jockey friends, still out there. But Tessa knew she wasn't the sort of jockey Tom meant, to go visiting a fellow, she being at the bottom of the pile and he at the top. She was very sensitive to this knowledge. It was more

211

for herself that she was visiting him, because she needed him, more than vice versa. So it was with trepidation that she walked with Ma through the long white corridors of the hospital, up in the lift, more doors, wards, getting ever more frightened. She stopped at one point, and said she wanted to go back.

"Don't be silly," Ma said abruptly.

Tom was in a room alone, lying down. His head was swathed in bandages and he looked as white as his pillow. He looked awful.

"You look awful," Tessa said.

He smiled. "That's what I said to you, isn't it?"

"Start again," said Ma. "Hullo, Tom. How lovely to see you. I've brought you some flowers."

She had too, having bought them from a stall at the hospital entrance. She held the bunch out to Tessa. Tessa took them and smiled.

"Hullo, Tom. How are you? I've brought you some flowers."

"That's better," Ma said. "Give them back to me and I'll go and find a vase for them."

She went out and shut the door behind her.

"There," said Tom. "You could escape now. Tie my sheets together and shin out of the window. I thought she would handcuff you to the bed."

"I don't want to go."

"You ought to want, Tessa. Not out of the window, of course, but work at it. Get out. Do you think I'm going to lie here and give up? It's the same thing."

212

"Be a jockey? Get half-killed, like you?"

"Yeah. I'm no advertisement at the moment, but I'm improving. I'll be back next season."

"Does it hurt?"

"Yeah, it hurts all right. Better for seeing you though."

"I was scared of coming."

"Why scared?"

"Well, I'm not. . ."

No words to say what she was not. She was nothing, wiped out.

"Tessa." Tom put out a hand. She sat on the bed, near the hand, looking at it. Those long, strong fingers, on the reins to Buffoon's stubborn mouth . . . Buffoon never put a foot wrong, not like her. She remembered the euphoria.

"Get moving, Tessa. That's all. Come out of it. It's like you've had a horse fall on you as well. If I can make it, you can too. It's just making the effort. It's really tough, but you've got to."

He was remembering Ma's hard eyes, boring into him, saying, "You will." He was doing as he was told. Perhaps he should have Ma to help him get going too. He needed all the help he could get. More than he could say to Tessa. Even the effort to say this was hurting. God, it hurt – his brain hurt!

When Ma came back Tom was asleep and Tessa lay beside him on the bed, holding his hand.

2

Buffoon

*B*uffoon, against all the odds, was not dead. Not quite.

He had returned home after the Grand National tired, hurting, to his empty stable. They had done everything possible to make him comfortable, but he was unhappy, strung up, disturbed. He blundered round his straw bed, ignored the goodies in his manger, stared with difficulty across the yard to the dark gateway where Lucky should have been waiting for him and wasn't. He had no thoughts. But he wasn't happy.

Later, amazingly, he heard Lucky's voice at the far gate out to the valley.

He put his head over the door and roared back. Lights went on everywhere and they all came running, shouting and laughing. Lucky came bolting down the yard, kicking and bucking, and stopped at Buffoon's door. Buffoon put his head down, whickering deeply in his throat, Lucky was let in, and both of them settled down immediately, Buffoon going to the manger to finish up his feed and Lucky tugging greedily at the big haynet.

"Wherever did he come from?" they exclaimed.

"Tessa will be over the moon when she comes back!"

"Where is she?"

And of the disturbance that occupied the valley for what seemed the rest of the night Buffoon and Lucky took no notice, totally occupied with eating. And then sleeping, lying side by side as usual. Both perfectly contented.

Buffoon did sense that there was a very strange atmosphere in the yard the next day but, with Lucky back, it did not matter to him. He was eating up and had already lost the gaunt look that had so disturbed the betting public. He missed Tessa and whinnied for her once or twice, but Wisbey fed him and all was well.

Wisbey was muttering strange oaths. "A *carving knife*, by gum! It could well have been one of us!" he said to Gilly, and Gilly said, "Might have been you, you asked for it sometimes, you ape."

"I'll be damned careful when she comes back, I can tell you."

"She won't be coming back, will she?"

Buffoon, if he had understood this, would have been sorry. He trusted Tessa and would do whatever she wanted of him, however stupid. But in a few days he almost perceptibly put on weight and bloom. In spite of being lame with a damaged tendon, he began to look like his old self.

But Tessa didn't come back.

The horse did not know what events were taking place around him. There was no way of telling him, when he was sent to the sales, that it was through no fault of his own. He was being dumped, yet he had given his all. He did not understand this, he did not feel bitterness nor indignation at his lot, merely bewilderment. He was sent to the sale ring with Wisbey as groom, and Lucky still as his companion. The stables were strange but he was comfortable, happy even. It was like going racing, and he expected to be asked to race, in spite of having a bad leg. He was used to being asked to do these inexplicable things. But instead of being asked to race he was sent into a round building and led in circles by Wisbey while a man droned on over a loudspeaker and eventually dropped a hammer on his desk which made Buffoon jump. He was then led outside and a long conversation took place between Wisbey and another man.

Buffoon could tell Wisbey was cross with the man. He didn't know it but the man was refusing to take Lucky too and Wisbey was trying to persuade him otherwise.

"I'm a dealer, not a philanthropist," the man said. "The horse'll get over it. They always do."

Wisbey knew this was true, in the end, but his heart was full of pity for the poor old horse going to this crook dealer. Better they had shot him and given the creditors the carcass money, as he told Peter bitterly when he got home. It was a bad evening back at Sparrows Wyck, where Lucky spent the night whinnying, just as Buffoon had a few weeks before.

A bad evening too for Buffoon, transported to a strange stable without Lucky, without anyone he knew. He was totally bewildered. He expected to go home, like after a race, but the horsebox, coming and going during the following days, never waited for him, although he whinnied after it every time it left the yard. He found it hard to see too well where he was, only that it smelled strange and Lucky was nowhere to be seen. He did not recognize the voices of anyone around him, nor the smells of the place, nor the nip in the air. He did not know why he never went out any more. He stopped whinnying after a bit, and they cut his feed down while he was in "box-rest", to mend his leg, so he became dull and bored. Not exactly miserable, but without any of his old zest. His coat was dull and his eyes duller and he stood dully on three legs, his nose in a corner.

In the autumn Buffoon was no longer lame and was advertised for sale. He was cheap. No vet would pass him because of his bad sight and dicey legs.

He needed another year off to cure his leg and an operation for cataracts to cure his eyes, both of which the dealer could not afford.

"I'm in it for a living, for Gawd's sake," he said. He did not dare say he was looking for a mug to buy a useless horse like Buffoon. He had bought him at the sale specifically for a customer who had fancied owning a famous horse, but the sale had foundered, as so many did, and the dealer now only wanted his money back. He knew he wouldn't get it. Memories were short where fame was concerned. He was now just selling an ex-racehorse cheap because he was so ugly. Anyone who asked for a vet's certificate would be fobbed off.

The mug, in the shape of an ignorant but ambitious man

called Campbell, duly came along and took the horse away for his daughter to event.

At last it was Buffoon's turn to be loaded into the horsebox. He went in eagerly, pricking his ears. Memories of journeys to a racecourse lightened his step. He remembered going home, and the security of his old box with Lucky and the half-forgotten voices. That girl who used to hug and kiss him . . . he gave a little whicker as they tied him up, and the lad laughed and said, "Thinks he's going to Aintree again, poor old beggar."

"Knacker's'll be the next journey, when they've found out he can't see."

But when he was led out at the other end, there was no racecourse bustle, no familiar voices, no Lucky. Just a single loosebox at the end of a small field, no other horse in sight. A straw bed and feed were waiting, and a skinny girl fussed about, but didn't seem to know anything. The straw was thin, the feed small, the hay poor. Buffoon's step dragged and he did not even raise an enquiring whinny.

The Campbell family, parents and girl, had coped with Pony Club but knew nothing about seventeen-hand thoroughbreds. They thought they were kind and knowledgeable. They knew you fed hay and cubes and mix, but not how much; they didn't know good hay from bad and bought at a "bargain" price; their farrier was cheap and incompetent, their field ill-drained with more weeds than grass. Buffoon ate it up in a week and when it rained it turned into a patch of mud. He stood in it all day and got mud-fever.

His legs swelled up and grew red scabs. The Campbells were told to keep him in, so he stood in the small stable without exercise for several weeks and grew weary and gaunt. He wasn't used to living alone. He had never in his life been without company. There had always been a yard of horses, even without Lucky. He didn't like this dreary existence but he accepted it, as horses accept nearly everything.

They don't understand they are being ill-treated. They only know they are hungry, or in pain, or miserable, but they accept it. They don't ask why or how long for. They don't wonder what is going to happen to them.

Buffoon just stood looking at the wall, waiting for another small feed, tired of his unpalatable hay. He had memories, but they didn't surface often. Sometimes the sound of a lorry on the road made him prick his ears, and he remembered the racecourses and the excitement and lifted his head for a few minutes. But nothing happened and soon a fly bit him and he scratched, and let out a gusty sigh. If he had heard Tessa's voice again, he would have gone eagerly and looked out and whinnied. He remembered the timbre of her voice. If Lucky had come he would have whinnied. Even Wisbey. But he did not like his new people much. They did not understand what he wanted, although they thought they were kind. They patted him sometimes but did nothing to make him happy.

But when summer came round again and his legs cleared up the girl started to ride him out and take him to a few cross-countries. When Buffoon saw the jumps he raced at them in the way he was used to, but the girl pulled him back, wanting him to go more slowly. He couldn't understand it. The girl had a few lessons, and Buffoon learned that he had to jump, but slowly. Very odd. But he was on his own, not in a herd as he was used to, and it wasn't so much fun. In fact, as he had no neighbours taking off at the same time, he often found it hard to know when to take off, the jump ahead being just a dark blur in his vision. He did his best but often blundered. The girl lost her temper and hit him. He had no idea what for. He had rarely been hit, only sometimes in the heat of racing and then he had never felt it. He found life puzzling, and lost confidence. It was often better to stop than try to find his way ahead. Then the girl got furious and hit him a lot more.

"That poor old nag of the Campbells looks really miserable," they remarked at the Hunter Trials. "They've no idea. . ."

"I think it's half-blind. I told them to get the vet to have a look, but Campbell just laughed at me."

"It's dangerous – he ought to know – putting his girl up on a blind horse."

"Well, there he goes . . . hope they come back in one piece."

The ugly chestnut horse lolloped off into the country. He cleared the first island jump standing in the field and disappeared into a wood. Not long afterwards there was a message on the walkie-talkie for the ambulance.

"Don't start another rider. Spot of trouble up here."

It took quite a time. The ambulance took the rider away and

eventually Campbell came back down to the start leading a lame chestnut horse.

"Bloody thing never even took off! Just went straight through it, turned a complete somersault. She's broken her leg."

"Lucky it wasn't her neck. That horse is dangerous, Campbell. Get the vet to it – it's blind."

"Heck. If it's blind, what good is it?"

"I'd put it down if I were you. Kindest."

"The girl'll go potty if he's put down! She loves it."

("Blow me, I'd never have guessed!" – but the thought was not expressed aloud.)

"Well, don't let her get back on. Too risky by far."

"What shall I do? I've no time to look after it, and now the girl's got a broken leg. . ."

"Put him out to grass for the time being then. Give you time to think. Get a vet –"

"Vets cost a fortune! I haven't got that sort of money."

He went blundering off and the men he had been talking to shook their heads over his ignorance.

Campbell didn't think he was cruel.

But he found a field for Buffoon out in the country with lots of grass and an automatic trough. That was kind, wasn't it? Horses liked lots of grass. Buffoon was turned out alone, and left. The field was large, on the side of a hill, surrounded by prairie fields of corn. Over the summer machinery came and went, and in the autumn the fields were ploughed, drilled and sown, and left. There was a thin hedge round Buffoon's field, not enough to give any shade, nor was it thick enough to give shelter from the cold winds from the North Sea that started to blow in as winter approached. Nobody came near nor by. A minor road led past the gate and sometimes a car went past, very occasionally a lorry. At the sound of a lorry Buffoon would lift his heavy head and prick his ears for a few moments, but the lorries never stopped. That was the only sign of life. Nobody came. It made him anxious. He limped up and down by the hedge where the gate was, wanting to be taken in, but nobody came. He whinnied, but there was no answer. Nobody came.

The horse had grass, water, freedom . . . Campbell was content.

And as winter progressed Buffoon lost hope and stood tucked into the thickest bit of hedge, his scrawny tail clamped down over his quarters. His ribs stood out like the shell of a rotting boat. His winter coat was too thin to give him warmth. Long shivers convulsed his frame when the wind blew.

Campbell would have been amazed if anyone had accused him of cruelty.

3

"Lovely to have you back, dear"

*J*immy brought her home. It was a sunny September day with the sharp tang of autumn in the air. Tessa sat in the car, aware of every passing tree, every golden leaf, every bird tossed into the clear air. She felt delicate, not quite in charge, terrified of not handling it right. Terrified of Buffoon's empty box, her own wayward emotions, never knowing whether they were in hand. She was always being found wanting. When would it change?

"Say something," Jimmy said, and smiled.

"I'm frightened," she said.

He seemed to understand. "Why not? So would I be."

"You've never been frightened!"

"Haven't I?"

He showed so little, yet he was always the one she felt at home with, the one she could depend on.

"Have you seen Tom?"

"Yes. His dad drives him out. He comes up to Raleigh's sometimes, watches the horses working. There's no bad blood there, in spite of the split."

"Is he getting better?"

"Slowly. But nobody thinks he's going to ride again. Not for a very long time, at least."

How did they expect her to be happy? Getting out wasn't everything. But to her surprise, coming up the lane and into the yard and seeing a big banner splayed across the wall, painted apparently with a yard broom, saying, "Welcome back Tessa" made her laugh out loud. And seeing Sarah, Peter, Gilly, Wisbey and old Arthur standing in a row to greet her made her feel like the Queen arriving at Ascot. She could not help but feel her spirits rise to a new level.

They all gave her a kiss, even Arthur, and took her into the tack-room where there was a bottle of champagne and glasses laid out on the big table amongst the riffled pages of *Racing Post* and soapy sponges and old tea mugs. Just like home!

They drank, and told her all the gossip, and then she had to see all the horses, both new and old, and hear who had done what, what was going to happen, what she had missed. Nobody mentioned Buffoon. In Buffoon's old box was a grey mare called Summer Sky.

"She belongs to those two old girls that have the Littlun. They want you to ride her, Tessa – they told me," Peter said. "She's really nice, promising. Yours."

Tessa tried to be grateful, failed. Looking into Buffoon's box and seeing a grey mare there was terrible.

Jimmy said, "Go and get your jods on, girl. We'll go for a ride."

It was the best thing, out on the down with just Jimmy,

not talking, crossing the stream and climbing up the long track to meet the skylarks. Not looking at Goldlands.

"My mother—"

"Your mother is not allowed to contact you. She contacts us instead. We chat to her on the phone. She'll come down and see you when the coast is clear. You are never, *never*, to go near Goldlands, Tessa."

"No."

She was riding one of Jimmy's problem horses, a nice chestnut fellow who did everything she asked.

"He has jumping problems, nothing to bother you," Jimmy said.

He was riding a black thoroughbred mare who kept rearing when its owner rode it, but never reared for Jimmy.

"Rider problem, not horse problem. Tricky to explain to the owner, but I'm taking money for nothing. It's she who needs to go to a problem-mender, not the horse."

Tessa laughed. It was wonderful to be on a horse again, to be on the downs, to smell the grass-scented air. They cantered, fast, over the brow of the downs and came out on top of the world with the whole of the west country, as far as the eye could see, rolling away into a far blue distance. It was heady after the years of incarceration, and Tessa felt herself shivering with joy, just looking and sniffing in the air, and feeling the good horse under her.

Jimmy said, "The cure."

"Yes. The cure."

After that, everything slotted slowly into place. She sorted out her caravan, got on with the work, rode out, got herself fit. The others badgered her to get riding seriously again, to get on with being a jockey, but she was frightened and kept putting it off.

Peter said, "Summer Sky is nearly ready to race. Are you going to miss your chance? You need every chance there is going."

She did not reply. It was too difficult to articulate: the great fear. She hadn't had it before. She had been confident, cocksure. If it had been Buffoon to ride . . . But he had always been Tom's.

Did they say anything to Tom? She never knew, but one evening he drove into the yard to visit her. Her door was open and Walter was standing on his hindlegs trying to lick her face while she was making baked beans on toast. Jimmy never let him jump up, but Tessa liked his kisses and Walter knew it.

"I love you, Walter. Yes I do," she was saying.

"The ice maiden is thawing," Tom said, and laughed.

She spun round.

"Tom!"

"Oh good," he said. "Baked beans."

She had never seen him to talk to since her visit to the hospital. He had a lot of friends and didn't need her now, she was sure.

"I'll do some more toast. I'm sorry – it's only—"

"My favourite," he said.

He looked so different now, his gaunt face filled out, his

226

athletic grace scrambled into a painful crablike movement. Scars still showed on his head where the hair hadn't grown back. But he smiled.

"It's great they let you go."

"Yes, I was lucky. And my job still here."

"Peter's a good guy to work for."

He sat down at the table while Tessa made more toast. Walter came and laid his long nose on Tom's lap.

"How are you now?" Tessa asked. "Better than the last time I saw you, anyway."

"Walking, at least. Not riding yet. I've got to have an operation, then – perhaps. . ."

"I thought—" She stopped herself. The rumour was that Tom would never come back. The operation he mentioned was highly dangerous, kill or cure, or some dramatics to that effect. Everyone was incredibly sorry for him.

Yet he smiled.

"I'm only a young lad yet," he said in a squeaky voice. "I've my whole career ahead of me."

Tessa laughed.

They ate the baked beans and Tessa made tea, and Tom was in no hurry to go.

"And what about you?" he asked. "Has Peter got your licence yet?"

"No."

"You can't afford to hang about. Life is passing you by. Why not?"

"When I wanted to do it everyone said I was mad. Now they all say I'm mad not to go on with it. I don't know what I want any longer. Only one thing, and that's not going to happen. . ."

"What?"

"My horse back."

"Ah."

"I've tried to trace him, but there's no Buffoon in racing any more. He was sold to a dealer . . . I've found out that much. And then, nothing. Nobody knows."

Tom was silent. He could think of no way to encourage her. A horse with cataracts, going blind, a duff tendon, ugly . . . even with his talent, few people would consider him a viable proposition. Tom guessed he had been put down by now.

"You get around – could you see if you can find out anything?"

"Yes, of course. But I wouldn't hold out much hope, Tessa, honestly."

"I do want – so much. . ."

The pony, Lucky, still grazed in the field, companion occasionally to fractious horses, but mostly unattached. The sight of him always brought a lump to her throat.

"It doesn't do to be sentimental in this game. Too much hurt."

"Yes, I've found that." Even Wisbey, she remembered, wept.

"Did you think that, one day, you might ride Buffoon in a race?"

"Yes, I suppose I did. Even with you around." She smiled.

"I think you should get in training, for if he comes back. Because I'm not around any more."

"Can you find him for me?"

"I can try. Perhaps an advert. My father might turn up something. I'll try. But only if you get off your butt, Tessa. You're being really feeble, not wanting to ride again. Suppose I'd been as feeble as you? I'd still be in a hospital bed. I'm going to ride again and look what I've got to surmount – you've got nothing standing in your way at all. Everybody is behind you, wanting you to succeed. And you have the talent to make it, unlike most aspiring jockeys. The only thing you've got against you is being female, but if you're good enough – so what? Show 'em!"

Afterwards, it occurred to him that he was a fine advertisement for the trade, half-killed, exhorting the girl to get up and do likewise. But perhaps he was the one to point out to Tessa her cowardice.

As Sarah said pointedly, "You haven't got anything else going for you, after all. No social life, no boyfriend, no darling parents, no hobbies – nothing. Mucking out all your life. Is that your ambition?"

"Thank *you*," said Tessa.

But it was true.

She asked Peter to try and get her a licence again, and she started to do her getting-fit drill again. Tom promised to try and trace Buffoon, and that gave her a spark of hope. She rang her mother when she knew Maurice was away from home, but only received the usual negative bleats that so incensed her. Once her mother told her that Maurice had hit her.

"All the more reason to leave him," Tessa said coldly.

Greevy had left home and got himself a flat on the other side of the valley, handy for Raleigh's, where he still worked.

"Greevy says leave him, too," Myra said hesitantly.

"Well, then?"

But Tessa dreaded her mother arriving at her caravan door, her most likely bolt-hole. Physical violence might drive her out when nothing else had. Tessa tried not to think about it.

When she spoke of it to Sarah, Sarah said, "Like mother, like daughter. You're just as bad, not trying to better yourself."

That was the remark that really hurt. Like her mother!

She got Peter to accept that Summer Sky was ready to run, that she was ready to make her first ride. She forced herself, scared rigid. She had lost all confidence in herself.

But on the day the support she received astonished her. It seemed no one had forgotten the story of Lucky and Buffoon, and the stabbing of Maurice Morrison-Pleydell by his stepdaughter. The press mobbed her as she made her way to the weighing-room, and all the officials smiled and said, "Welcome back," and the other jockeys, formerly not so friendly, now gave her winks and grins. "Just what the bastard deserved, everyone thought so." The general opinion was aired several times, in confidential whispers. It buoyed her up fantastically, so that when she came out into the paddock where Jimmy was leading up Summer Sky and Peter stood with the "old gels", she felt ready to ride, almost calm. And the mare that she could not grow to love looked beautiful in the cold November paddock, spinning round with excitement, scattering her game old owners.

"Lovely to have you back, dear," they said.

"Have a nice ride, dear."

How lucky she was to be riding for such people, the old hunting ladies who knew what it was, themselves, to ride at a great fence and have the fear of God in your throat. If Maurice had ever given a thought . . . no, don't think of Maurice. Raleigh was in the paddock with a horse. Even he gave her a smile and a good luck nod. Tessa's head whirled. And then she was being led out by dear Jimmy, the mare prancing with the joy of life, and the lovely green river of grass ahead. . .

Summer Sky was young, but had raced on the flat and knew her job. With Jimmy having schooled her over hurdles, Tessa was not afraid that her mount would let her down, only vice versa. But, lobbing down towards the start, she felt a surge of excitement go through her that wasn't just to do with the present race – it was to do with seeing her way to a future, which had never seemed possible before. When Sarah had said, scornfully: "Mucking out all your life?" – it was true that her ambition had been nil. Now, suddenly, she knew there was more in her than that. Tom and Jimmy, great horsemen both, had told her she could do it and she hadn't believed them. Now, suddenly, she did. Even if she was last today, she saw that this was her way ahead.

With all this in her brainbox, she channelled it into proving her cause. She was prepared, this time, for the feeling of inadequacy and panic in the face of what felt like a cavalry charge all round her, keeping her wits together – much more than last time – trying to take notice of what was happening round her as well as just to herself. Where was the favourite? Where the stamina-tester, the one stretching them? How close to keep in touch, when to ask her . . . she was aware now of her job, instead of just holding on in a blur of fierce action. She was being paid to do something, not just sit there.

But Peter had not put her on a hiding to nothing. The mare was good, and fit. She jumped well and gained ground jumping. At the end, having kept a good place by using her brains, Tessa used the last of her strength to ask the mare to go on. They were both as tired as each other but the mare responded gamely and ran on to finish second to the favourite.

Not like last time! Perhaps she was due for a slice of luck by the law of averages, but this euphoria in the winner's enclosure was something she would never forget. Not first, perhaps, but near enough. The old gels were overjoyed, and Jimmy and Peter hugging her, and complete strangers saying "Well done" – it was a magic day. Having seen the light on the canter down, to have fallen or failed would have wiped out her new courage. Now everything was different.

Or was it?

It didn't make Buffoon appear out of the blue. It didn't mean trainers started to clamour for her services. A fortnight later Raleigh offered her a ride on a solid old-timer whose owner didn't expect to win but enjoyed a day out. The day before, according to the press, Maurice had removed all his horses from Raleigh to another smart and up-and-coming trainer called Con Powers. Con Powers had a fast turnover of horses and also of owners, was very successful, but not well liked.

Raleigh was at a bigger course with better horses on the day Tessa rode for him, and it was Greevy who saddled her horse. To her surprise he was perfectly civil, even pleasant.

"You've got a nerve, going into this game. Rather you than me."

"I'm no good at anything else."

"This one'll give you no trouble. He won't win but he'll get you round."

The old owner turned out to be a friend of the old gels. Was this to be her clientele, dear old no-hopers? Maybe she could get their horses up into the frame, at least. It took all her strength and more, but the horse came in fourth, and the old owner was in the winner's enclosure with Greevy, pumping her hand so hard that she thought her whole arm would come away at the shoulder.

"Great ride," Greevy said.

Tessa nearly fainted. Or was it exhaustion? She couldn't speak. Her head was reeling.

But perhaps, after all, she had a future.

4

Rescue Mission

On December, on a cold wet day, Tom drove into the yard at Sparrows Wyck and asked for Peter. Tessa saw him and said Peter was out.

"Jimmy around?"

"Yes, he's in the school. Just finished, I think. Shall I fetch him?"

Tessa was business-like, seeing that Tom did not seem to be calling in friendly mode, but with a purpose. He still could not move very easily, so he nodded at her invitation and stood waiting. He was due to have his operation shortly, and Tessa thought he was scared — who wouldn't be? It required a different sort of courage to face, from galloping towards Bechers Brook, and one she was not sure she would be able to cope with.

Jimmy came and, after a few words, disappeared with Tom into the house.

"I didn't want to say in front of Tessa," Tom said, "but I've found Buffoon."

Jimmy looked up in surprise. "Still alive, eh?"

"Barely. That's the problem. If he comes back here, who will keep him? Tessa's got no money. I wondered if you just wanted to let it go. What will it do to Tessa? He's stone-blind and half-starved."

"Oh Christ!" said Jimmy.

He rolled one of his cigarettes, stared out of the window.

"Kindest to buy him and put him down, no word said," Tom said. "I'd do that, if you want."

Jimmy shook his head.

"It makes sense, I can see that. But. . ."

He pulled on his scraggy cigarette, stared out of the window some more.

"No. He was a great horse. He deserves more. We'll get him back here. Put him down later, when he's had a week or two's cossetting."

"It'll do for Tessa."

"Yeah, well, she'd prefer that way to not knowing. She's tough. She'll survive."

"I'll sort it then, if you like. Give me something to think about, instead of just waiting for—" He shrugged.

"Getting mended? You'll make it," Jimmy said.

"If I'd been a horse I'd have been shot long ago."

"Yeah, well, we're kind to horses. Who are these nerds who've let our old boy go to pot? What's wrong with them?"

"I haven't met them, just spoken on the phone. I saw the horse in the field and recognized him, then asked around. Seems a girl had him for eventing, he got hurt or she did – not sure which – so he got turned out, she got a boyfriend and left

236

home and it sort of went on from there. He's on his own, blind, neglected."

"Christ!" said Jimmy again.

"I'll see to it. Just wanted the OK, that's all."

"They'll let him go, I take it? You can't always take it for granted that people even know how pig-ignorant they are."

"Yes, I asked. If you want him, take him away, they said. Do us a good turn. It's near Newmarket, easy to lay on transport."

"OK. We'll pay expenses. We're not that hard up," Jimmy said. "And go from there."

"And Tessa? Will you tell her?"

"Take her with you," Jimmy said. "You can cope! By the time she gets home she might be back on an even keel. I'm not good with Tessa in extremis. When I think of her going after her old man with a carving knife . . . I often wonder. . ."

"If you're safe?" Tom grinned.

"She's got that streak – yeah. It's not gone away. It's what might make her successful as a jockey – over-the-top commitment. When Tessa wants something – phew! Stand back, put your hard hat on. It's still there, the mad streak."

"In the blood. Her parents are both mad, by all accounts. She's not like an ordinary girl, is she?"

Jimmy laughed. "No."

"I'll make a date with her then. Tomorrow lunchtime OK?"

"Yes. You're not telling her beforehand?"

"No."

"Rather you than me!"

237

When Tom called for Tessa the next day and they departed in his red Mercedes the others watched with open curiosity.

"What is this? The beginning of an affair?"

"What, with Tessa? You must be joking," said Wisbey.

"Where are they going?"

"Tessa doesn't know, she said."

Jimmy came in from the school, on his way to lunch.

He gave the orders: "Move Sky to another box. Clean the box out thoroughly, bed it down, bring Lucky in and groom him and have it all ready for a new occupant."

They looked at him curiously.

"Who is it?"

Jimmy smiled. "Guess."

Tessa had guessed too – the only thing it could be, this magical mystery tour. But she was too afraid to ask. She felt sick with it. Tom was wondering if he was doing the right thing, only re-opening old wounds in Tessa's psyche that were best left alone. The more he drove, the more he thought it was a mistake. But too late now to change anything. He did not say anything, and Tessa was too frightened to, and they drove without speaking, listening to the radio. She knew it wasn't good news, else he would have told her.

It was a cross-country drive, out towards Cambridgeshire and Suffolk. They drove into Newmarket and Tessa felt the tension rising, but Tom took a minor road out and drove out south through the rolling countryside dotted with studs and woods.

They came to a bleak, intensively farmed hilltop, and looked over an empty landscape. Down a long hill, Tom signalled right, and turned up a winding lane. There wasn't a house or human in sight. An arable crop, just coming through, ran uphill ahead of them, unbroken across the horizon, but in the valley a few grass fields surrounded by hedges edged the road.

They came to a gate, stopped. A spatter of rain blew across the windscreen. Tom turned the engine off and the radio went dead.

"Here you are."

Tessa turned blindly and tried to look where Tom was looking. Already tears blurred her sight. On the other side of the field, all alone, a thin horse stood with its back to the hedge, its tail clamped against its quarters. Its head was raised, ears pricked, turned questioningly in their direction. Now that the car engine had stopped and there was only the eternal silence, it whinnied.

"Tom!"

Tessa flung open the door, scrambled out, tripped and fell, scrambled up, over the five-barred gate like a terrier and hurtled across the field shouting, "Buffy! Buffy! Buffy!"

Tom stayed in his seat, groaning. Why the hell –! Yet he knew he could not have lived with any other course of action. Soft idiot that he was!

The rain was cold, Newmarket style. Was it ever warm in Newmarket? Tom eventually groped his way painfully out of his driving seat and staggered to the gate. Tessa was coming back slowly, the horse following with its nose on her shoulder. Even Tom's eyes pricked at the sight, it was so touching – the look on Tessa's face, and the old horse's muzzle trembling with – well, what? What do horses think? Tom wondered. Buffoon was miserable all right, abandoned alone in a completely dark and silent world. But one could hardly imagine he was planning revenge, or remembering happier days, or thinking of his mother. Animals weren't like that. Just hoping someone would come, no doubt. And now someone had. A voice he remembered.

"He's blind, Tom! He's blind!"

The tears streamed down Tessa's cheeks.

"Yes, well, we knew that was going to happen, didn't we? Before he was sold."

"Can he be cured?"

"I don't know, I doubt it."

"Tom!" Fresh floods.

"Shut up, Tessa." Tom glanced at his watch. The afternoons were short and it was already growing dusk, the dismal landscape smudging towards invisibility through the rain.

"It's not all bad. A horsebox is on its way to pick him up, to take him home. He's yours, Tessa. Jimmy said bring him home. We've arranged it."

"Oh Tom! Tom!" She sprung at him, embracing him wildly, nearly knocking him flat on his back. Her tears were wet on his cheeks.

"You are a marvel! I love you! We could never have left him

here, could we? So lonely! And he is blind – how *could* they? To do this to a horse – how could they!"

Lucky, Tom thought, she did not have access to their address, and a carving knife. She was like a flame, the anger torching off her skinny frame, almost hissing in the rain. What an enemy! She flung her arms round Buffoon's neck, crooning rubbish to him, and he nuzzled at her with an enquiring nose, trembling a little in the legs. Poor old nag! Tom remembered the feel of him going over Bechers, the feel of himself too, his old strength and the horse's strength, and the glory of it all . . . and now look at them both, crocked up, on the scrapheap! Self-pity overwhelmed him suddenly, and in the rain it didn't matter if he cried a bit too, terrified of the path that lay before him and tired of pretending he was brave when he wasn't. . . All the fears he only ever admitted to himself in bed in the small hours of the night rose up and threatened to swamp him in that moment, set off by Tessa's emotion. He turned away, rescued by the distant sound of a lorry changing gear as it approached the hill.

"The horsebox. . ."

"Oh Tom, you are wonderful! To have found him! I love you! I love you!"

The kisses for Buffoon now veered in his direction, unabashed, and his mood was blown away, so that he dissolved in laughter.

"You are a nutter!"

The lorry drew up, a Newmarket transporter, and the

driver got down, pulling up his collar against the rain.

"Blimey, what a night! He loads OK, I hope?"

"Yes, but he's blind."

"Poor old sod."

He went to open up the back ramp, and Tom fetched the headcollar he had thrown in the car. Tessa put it on and Tom opened the gate. They led him round the lorry and lifted his hesitant foot on to the ramp. He hadn't forgotten the routine and went up carefully, lifting his legs high, not missing the larger step up into the inside. He blundered in and Tessa tied him up.

"I'll travel with him."

"Don't be an idiot. He knows he's safe in the box. Travel back with me." He wanted her suddenly. He couldn't face that drive all alone, the way he felt now.

Tessa was unwilling, but came. The driver had Peter's address, knew the way.

"See you later, mate."

They went off first, so that they didn't have to overtake the lorry. Tessa watched in the mirror as the lorry's headlights came down steadily behind them. She was overcome with the strength of her feelings, not knowing whether to laugh or cry, only saying, "I never thought this day would happen." She was shaking but not with the cold.

"Don't expect too much." Tom said.

"What do you mean?"

"Think about it. He's not the horse he was, put it like that.

He won't go back to racing."

"He's back though. That's what matters."

"You own him now. He'll be expensive to keep."

"I earn money. I can pay!"

"A blind horse is useless. A liability."

Tessa flared up. "Why did you bring me here then? What do you want me to do?"

"We thought," (Christ, why had he started this?), "Give him a kind ending. Feed him, make him happy. Put him down. What else is there for him?"

"Oh no! I'll make him happy! Why shouldn't he be cured, anyway? You can cure cataracts. They can operate on him."

"It'll cost a fortune! Where'll you get the money from? You know what vets' bills are like. Ask Peter."

"I'll get the money! I'll earn it!"

"Earn it? You've only had three rides so far this season."

"Why are you being so horrible? Why did you bring me, if now you're saying it's all useless?"

She started to cry again. Tom cursed himself.

"I just don't want you to get disappointed, Tessa, to think it's all a happy ending. It isn't really. You've got to be sensible about it."

"I am being sensible! It's you who are being defeatist. You're just the same as Buffoon – all washed up. Suppose we said the same about you – you won't come back, you're finished? What's the difference?"

"I'm not a flaming horse! People might think that about me

243

but they don't say it, because they're not so unkind. Only you!"

"Oh Tom! I'm sorry! I didn't mean it! Not like that! Just that, it's the same really, like you; he must be curable, like you."

"But horses——" Didn't she understand? Horses were expendable and humans weren't. It might not be right, but that's the way it was. But he couldn't tell her Buffoon was expendable. She probably thought she could get him cured, ride him in the Grand National and win it. That's the kind of girl she was.

"Well, it's not my department, the future. I've done my bit. The rest of it is up to you, and Peter, I suppose."

"Yes," Tessa said. "It's up to me. Buffoon is mine."

And an idiotic smile lit up her face, Tom could almost feel it, like an electric fire. What a girl!

In a little while she said hesitantly, "I'm sorry, I didn't mean that. About you being washed up."

"I told you, everyone thinks it. Only you would actually say it, but do you think I don't know it's true?"

"But this operation, it's going to put you right?"

"Fifty-fifty chance. Could make it a lot worse if I'm unlucky. They've spelt it all out and leave it to me to say if I want it."

"But you do?"

"Think about it. How can you turn it down when you've got a job like mine? It's all I've got – want – the job. So I've no choice, have I? But it doesn't make it any more appealing."

Tessa was silent. It was horrible, the prospect.

"I'm sorry, Tom," she whispered.

After quite a long time, she said, "It *will* be all right, Tom. For you. And Buffy. It *will* be. I *know* it will."

Tom grinned. "You make things happen, Tess, I'll say that for you. I'll trust you. I feel better about it already."

And the red Mercedes roared fast through the dusk.

5

"Win for me!"

On the dark and rain they all waited for the arrival of the horsebox. Tom had said he wouldn't wait but go on home, but he waited. The stove flickered in the tack-room, and they sat over the interminable cups of tea amongst the smells of leather and steaming wool and saddle-soap. Tessa could not speak, but wandered out into the yard to stare down the lane. Then she went and leaned over the door of Buffoon's old box, where Lucky was eating the clean straw bedding. Gilly had given him a good groom and he looked like a circus pony, gleaming black and white, in the electric light. Tessa could not stop herself trembling. She was spaced out, hardly in control.

At last they heard the lorry coming up the lane. Everyone piled out of the tack-room and Jimmy and Peter went to let down the ramp. Tessa ran up to untie Buffoon. He was standing head up, ears alert, sniffing the air, all his senses trying to divine where he was, what was happening. At the sound of Tessa's voice he turned his head and nosed towards her. His helplessness gutted her.

She led him out carefully, with Jimmy guiding his front feet over the gap and drop at the top of the ramp. After that he knew the drill and clattered down, letting out a shrill whinny.

Lucky answered him and Buffoon, recognizing the pony's voice, whinnied again, clearly excited. He whirled round on the end of the halter and dragged Tessa across the yard to the door of his old box. Jimmy shot back the bolt and Buffoon ran in, circling the box through the deep straw, reaching out to nuzzle Lucky and making deep whickering noises in the back of his throat. Tessa was not the only one with tears in her eyes. Everyone was touched to see the blind horse, thin as a rake, so pleased to be back at home with his old mate Lucky.

"God, the state of him!" Gilly choked. "Who could let that happen to such a great horse?"

"Any horse, come to that," Sarah said shortly. She, the tough one, blew her nose. "Thank God Tom found him."

"All alone, not a living thing to be seen for miles," Tom said.

Tessa was fetching his feed, tipping it into his manger. Buffoon plunged his nose in hungrily. The watching group took in Tessa's rapt face, silently considering the consequences of the day's events. It wasn't going to be easy, they guessed. Peter wasn't in the game for charity, and keeping Buffoon was going to be a charity. Tessa was unpredictable.

"Is he yours now?" Wisbey asked her bluntly.

"Yes, he's mine. Tom got his papers from the owners."

"Your wages don't cover what it costs to keep a horse in this yard," Wisbey said.

"He's not in training, idiot," Sarah said roughly. "Only keep, for the time being."

"All the same——"

"Oh, shut up, Wisbey!" Gilly said.

"There'll be plenty of time to work it out," Peter said equably. "He's not going anywhere else."

"Only the knacker's," Wisbey muttered, but no one heard him. (Tessa had got her horse back. He never got his back.)

Now Buffoon was settled, everyone gradually drifted away. Tessa stayed leaning over the top-door, watching Buffoon feed. Tom came over and said, "Happy?"

"Oh Tom, yes! Thank you, thank you, thank you! I still can't believe it!"

She turned her face towards him and in the dusk he saw the wild gleam in her eyes, her face suddenly beautiful with her happiness. She wasn't one for being happy very often. What a weird girl she was! Frightening, over the top, with a heart too big for her body. He could do with her on his side, he thought, in the days to come. Anyone could do with her on their side. Lucky old Buffoon.

"It was luck, seeing him. My back route to Newmarket, hardly anyone uses that road. And that I actually saw him . . . the hand of God, you might say. Weird." He shrugged, smiled. "I'll be off now."

"Yes. OK. See you later."

And she turned round suddenly and gave him a hug and a kiss.

"I love you, Tom! Thank you for ever!"

He laughed. He went over to his car and thought, She has no idea what love is, save for a horse. She's had no practice with humans.

The December night drew in, cold and wet, the rain gusting round the corners of the yard. Tessa thought of Buffoon out in that lonely field all by himself in the winter cold, and wept for his past miseries, his present salvation. She sat in the straw and talked to him as she had in days gone by when he was tough and strong and bulging with muscle. Now a warm rug covered his bony frame and his eyes were blind, hiding his spirit, but they were together again, the three of them. The two animals stood with their noses together, each resting one hind leg. Tessa slumped in the thick straw in one corner, content just to watch, and to talk to Buffoon. She felt ecstatically happy. It was Sarah who came to winkle her out, her torch stabbing across the yard.

"Come on, Tess, he's not going to run away! Have you eaten?"

"No."

"I've made a corned beef hash. Come and share it."

Tessa got up and went back to Sarah's caravan.

"Happy day!" Sarah said. "Look, a celebration!" She opened a bottle of Guinness and poured it into two glasses.

"Here's to the old horse. To Buffoon, your beauty!"

"And Tom for finding him."

"And Tom for finding him."

Tessa hadn't realized how hungry she was. Sarah made a good hash and it was good now, not to be alone. Her hopes and fears tumbled out of her, for Buffoon's future, but Sarah would not comment on it, and in her excitement Tessa did not notice her reticence. She was laughing and talking too hard, unbuttoned by the Guinness.

"Now, perhaps," Sarah said, "you will put your mind to being a jockey again. Now you've got a horse to keep. Peter will want paying."

"Yes, I will!"

"If you hadn't got the talent you wouldn't get much encouragement here. But they all say, Jimmy especially, that you could make a go of it. If Jimmy says so. . ." Sarah shrugged and laughed. "And I think so too. You don't see it often."

"Tom said it too."

"Well, there you are. Tom should know. Poor devil, he's going for his operation next week."

"He's scared."

"So would I be. The job means everything to him. From what I gather, he's been advised to stay content with how things are. He's improving, but very slowly, and not much chance of getting back into the game. The op is very risky, could make things a lot worse. But if it succeeds, he'll be riding again within the year. That's the story. He'll be a brave man to go through with it."

Tessa remembered that it was Tom, visiting her, that brought her back to life again during her imprisonment. He had done so much for her! She owed it to him to help him if she could. But he had so many friends in high places . . . he was scarcely going to need a neurotic visit from her.

She went back to bed, exhausted with the emotions that had

shaken her day. The images went round and round her head. Would she ever forget that first glimpse of Buffoon across the field, trying to work out what was happening from the sounds caught by his long rabbity ears? The eyes unseeing, that were once so bold and bright . . . Tessa had come through bad times herself and vowed now that she would get Buffoon through this. Cataracts could be removed.

"It'll cost a fortune! Who's going to pay?"

Everyone said it, from Peter down.

"And not always successful, and you still have to pay the money."

"And afterwards, anyway, what good will he be?" Wisbey said what the others were too kind to say.

Tessa knew she could never save up enough money from her wages, not now that quite a chunk was docked for Buffoon's keep. Only getting rides might help, but how long would that take? Who would lend her money on the slender proposition that it would be paid back from her riding fees? The only person she could think of was her mother.

"I'm going to ask my mother," she said to Sarah.

"Don't go up there!"

"No. I'll ring her. Or go when he's away."

"If *he* finds out. . ." Sarah was worried.

"He'd kill her probably. But why should he find out? She has an allowance – she must have, to buy all those vile clothes."

"Do be careful, Tessa. You might get her into bad trouble."

But Tessa had only one thought in her head. Every day she

groomed and fed Buffoon, and turned him out in the field with Lucky where he grazed happily, following the pony devotedly. When she went to fetch him in he came at her call, his big ears pricked with pleasure. If his eyes could have shown anything, they would have shown his new interest in life. His coat started to shine again, and the ribs began to cover with flesh. Every day he looked more his old self, although, without the riding, he had no muscle. And – "Let's face it, Tessa, you might call him your beauty, but nobody else could call him even half handsome," as they all said. All legs and withers.

"But you showed them, didn't you?" she said to him. "You're the best."

Her dream was to have him back in racing, but she had no money for training fees and everyone told her he would never come back, even if the operation worked. "He'll be too old by then." But her dream did not go away. Tessa knew how to live on dreams.

Peter said she could ride Summer Sky at Uttoxeter, and Raleigh asked her to ride again at Market Rasen. They were being kindly, she knew. From the way she rode for them depended whether she might get a ride from someone else. She had made a name for herself in racing all right, but for stabbing an unpopular owner, not for her riding. Not *yet*, she told herself. She thought of Tom's determination. She owed everything to Tom.

She got his parents' telephone number from Raleigh and

rang to enquire after him. It was in the racing press that he had had his operation two days ago, but no comment as to the outcome. Someone she supposed was his mother answered the phone. Tessa felt very nervous. His mother might think she was one of Tom's silly fans – he had quite a number.

"How is Tom?" she asked abruptly.

"Who are you, dear?"

"Tessa Blackthorn, a friend." She hadn't the nerve to say a fellow jockey.

There was a pause, and a rustling of papers. Then the cool, gentle voice said, "He's come out of the operation well. But no one quite knows what the outcome will be yet."

"I would like to visit him."

"Well, he's not having any visitors just yet. What did you say your name was?"

"Tessa Blackthorn."

"He left me a list of people he would like to have visit him, when he's ready. He said only people on the list. I see you are on it, almost at the top. So I'll let you know, dear, when you can go."

Tessa was amazed. Near the top of the list of Tom's friends! He must have been delirious when he wrote it!

She remembered to give Peter's phone number and gabbled, "Give him my love." She had never thought to send anybody her love before. She rang off, feeling deeply moved. Near the top of Tom's list! She couldn't get over it. She didn't tell anyone, not even Sarah. But she told Peter to expect a call from Tom's mother sometime.

Meanwhile, in spite of strong advice to the contrary, she went up to Goldlands to visit her mother. Gossip had it that Maurice was in America.

"What if he walks in?" Sarah asked. "You take the stupidest risks."

"He won't."

She walked up there one evening, and went in quietly the back way. Maurice's car wasn't there, so she felt safe. Her mother was watching the television as usual, and was overjoyed to see her.

"Oh, I miss you so, Tessa! And all the time I know you're only down the road, so close!"

"You don't think Maurice would have me back, surely?"

"No. He'd kill you as soon as look at you. He never forgives, you know that. How are you? Is everything all right?"

She guessed Tessa hadn't come to make small talk.

Tessa told her about Buffoon, and his need for the operation.

"But it costs money I haven't got. I need to borrow it off you, Mum. I know he gives you a whacking allowance. And I'll pay it back faithfully, every time I get a ride."

"Oh Tessa!" wailed her mother, in her usual hopeless way.

"You can, surely?"

"Without him knowing? You know what he's like about money. Nothing escapes him."

"But you can buy what you like, can't you? Say you're having

254

golf lessons or something. Or – or driving lessons. Whatever. Buying a wedding outfit —"

"He'll want to see it."

"Show him one you've already got. He won't recognize it. You've got thousands of outfits!"

Myra's lip trembled. "I'd do anything for you, Tessa. You know I would. But —"

"You're frightened of him, aren't you? I always knew you were. How *can* you stay here —"

"Oh, don't start that again —"

Tessa bit her lip. No, it got them nowhere. Start again. Her best wheedling voice.

"He doesn't watch every penny, surely? Not when he's got so much?"

"No. Sometimes he doesn't bother at all. And then sometimes, over something quite petty, he goes berserk. I suppose there is a way of covering up that I'm giving some to you. But giving it to you – of all things – that would send him really up the wall."

They strove to think up a plan. Her mother was willing as long as she wasn't found out.

"Perhaps I could do it with clothes. A really nice dress from a top house in London would come to almost the same. And I've got one from Dior that he might not recognize, if he asks. I've only worn it once."

That much for a dress! Tessa thought of Sarah hearing the news and had to stop herself laughing.

"Could you? Really?"

"Well, I'll do it for you. I wouldn't do it for anyone else. For Declan's horse!"

"Oh Mum, if he comes right again – he's mine now! They say he won't ever race again, but why not?"

"Because you won't have the money to keep him in training!"

"I will, if I get the rides."

"You've got to be good! And it's so dangerous, Tessa; it's not a job for a girl. Oh, why do you get such crazy ideas? You're just like your father."

"Good. I'd rather be like him than Maurice."

Her mother laughed. Her eyes sparkled. Tessa got the impression that she was quite excited to have something to do, even something so risky, to interrupt her excruciating boredom.

"Look, you can take a couple of hundred now, out of the housekeeping. It's cheap here when he's away. All that drink! And he won't be back for a week."

"Why don't you come down and see us? Ride out one day?"

"Oh, you know I can't."

Tessa shrugged. But when her mother gave her the two hundred pounds in cash her spirits leapt with joy. She stuffed the notes into her jods pocket.

"I've got two rides coming up – that'll make it five hundred pounds. And if I win!" Another ten per cent on top. "Ma, I'll pay you back in no time, honestly."

"I'd do anything for you, you know that, Tessa."

Anything but move out of her stupid zombie life . . . Tessa was glad to get out of the stultifying house, and galloped back home over the rough wet grass.

She went into Buffoon's box and showed him the money. The stable was warm out of the winter night and Buffoon was snug under an old quilted rug. He was lying down, but didn't bother to get up, used to Tessa's frequent visits.

"There, we're on our way, Buffy."

Footsteps outside surprised her. Sarah stuck her head over the door and said there was a phone call for her from Tom's mother. "She said would you ring back."

Tessa, used to shocks, thought Tom might have died. Her hands shook as she dialled the number on Sarah's mobile.

"Hullo, dear," came the gentle voice. "If you would still like to visit, Tom would love to see you."

"Oh yes! Yes, I will! When?"

"Tomorrow afternoon? He said only if you're not racing."

"No. I'm not. I'll come. Of course I'll come."

"Say three o'clock? It will only be for a short time."

"Yes, I'll be there."

When she had rung off, she wondered how — the hospital was miles away and she had no transport. But Sarah said she would take her, and wait while she visited. Peter would give her the time off.

"How is he? Has the operation worked?"

"I don't know. She didn't say." She hadn't asked. How stupid can you get?

"Well, at least he's still alive," Sarah said. "Go and *will* him to get better, Tessa. You've got such a power in you."

"He did it for me," Tessa said. But Sarah didn't hear, or, if she did, she did not understand.

The next day they drove in Sarah's old banger some fifty miles to the enormous hospital which had decided the jockey's fate. Sarah said she would wait in the car park. She had brought the form book with her and was happy to be stranded with a spare hour or two to study it, while Tessa tried to find her way through miles of white corridors to Tom's bedside. He was in a room alone, and his mother was there with him. She got up to greet Tessa, a well-dressed, roundish woman with a country look, and the same clear blue eyes as Tom.

"I'm so glad you were able to get here. It's such a journey. I come from the other direction else I could have picked you up. But Peter said he would bring you if Sarah couldn't. Everyone is so kind."

"They all like him so," Tessa said bluntly. "It matters."

Mrs Bryant smiled. "Yes, it matters. Your visit matters too. I'll leave you alone. I want a cup of tea."

She went out without saying anything to Tom, who lay on his back with his eyes shut. Tessa went up to the bed, wondering if he knew she was there. He looked terrible, as grey as the hospital linen, with frown lines of pain making him look older than his years.

"Hi, Tom."

"Hi, yourself." His voice was almost a whisper. It was hard

to credit that this washed-up wreck had ever ridden in the Grand National.

"How is it?" Tessa asked. "Are you cured?"

"They don't know yet."

"Oh Tom, you've *got* to! There's nothing else – you've just *got* to. To ride Buffoon again."

Tom almost laughed. Tessa saw the surprise, the pain the amusement caused him, the impatience with the pain, the agonized frustration in his eyes. She was so moved by his plight that she took the hand lying on the sheet and kissed his fingers. The long strong fingers were now as white and soft as a lady's. She cared that he got better as much as – more than – she had wanted it for Buffoon to come out of the shadow of death. Her whole being willed it for him, to be back to his proper self, riding and laughing up on the downs with the wind in his face and a great horse beneath him. He *had* to come back! She could not bear to see him so wiped out.

"Tom, you must!"

"Are you riding? Racing, I mean?"

"On Saturday. For Peter."

"Win, Tessa, For me. If you win . . . it'll work out."

"It's on the television. You can watch it."

"Every move. I'll watch."

"I'll ride for you, Tom. I'll try as hard as you. I'll win for you."

"Winning is tough."

She thought he was talking about what he had to win – his

life again. She could see, now, what it took. It was what separated the winners from the losers – luck apart. Never give in. It made her see what she had to do, to get what she wanted, fight them all. She *would* be a jockey. No more doubts. Tom was her inspiration.

"You'll win, Tom! We both will."

She told him about Buffoon, but he drifted away into sleep, as if the effort of exhorting her had been too much. She knew that, in those words, he had put his whole strength. She felt tired too, washed out by emotion. It all mattered so much!

"Oh Tom, I love you! Live, for God's sake!"

She bent down and kissed his face, laying her cheek on his for a moment.

When his mother came back she was standing by the window looking out, pretending to be cool.

"Oh dear, I hope your visit hasn't been a waste of time! He does fall asleep in the middle of a sentence sometimes."

"No, we had a good conversation."

"He's very ill, of course, but the doctors are optimistic. As far as they can tell, the operation is successful. We're all very hopeful."

"He will get better. I know he will."

Mrs Bryant was surprised by the conviction in Tessa's voice. "We didn't want him to have this operation, my husband and I. We tried to talk him out of it. I suppose we were wrong. But caution comes with age."

Tessa found her way out and went back to Sarah in the car

park. She tried to pretend it had just been an ordinary visit, but inside she felt that Tom's few words had sorted out all the muddle in her head, about the future. Failure wasn't on the cards.

6

"He won't die?"

When Tessa was legged up on to Summer Sky in the Sandown paddock the following Saturday, her mind was only on Tom. She wasn't nervous this time. She wasn't wondering what other people thought, she didn't see the curious eyes noting that she was that hapless thing, a girl wanting to be a jockey.

"OK?" Peter asked, nervous of her steeliness.

She did not answer him. He thought she was on another planet.

"Has she taken anything?" he asked Sarah nervously as she departed down the course.

Sarah laughed. "Frightened she'll be dope-tested?"

"Sometimes I can't fathom that girl."

"Join the club."

Sandown was a class course and Summer Sky was only moderately fancied. Her price was ten-to-one. It was a sharp, cold day and the going was good, which suited the filly. She was very fit. She knew Tessa, and she was eager to run, and she felt an electricity from her rider which excited her. To many of the jockeys the race was a minor hurdle on a tough course, not anything to get too steamed up about, nice to win but of no great account. To Tessa it was the test of everything that mattered. It was for Tom. Herself. Buffoon. Sky did not know this, but she sensed it.

It was a fast-run race, and Tessa did not know if Sky's stamina would hold out. The run-in from the last at Sandown is famously gruelling, long and uphill all the way to the line. She kept Sky in mid-division, steadying her tearaway spirit, but not enough to discourage her. Her mind was cool compared with her first race – what a lot she had learned in so short a time! – and her concentration was deadly. She kept an eye on every competitor in sight, and found a good stride at every jump. Sky felt full of running, enjoying herself, in the mood to try her heart out. Tessa knew she was no faintheart. And it mattered – how it mattered!

Coming up towards the stands, hearing the crowd's roar, Tessa had four horses in front of her, and the rest of the field beaten. Perhaps the crowd thought she was beaten. But Tessa could feel Sky's courage responding to her urging, getting to the point of pain but battling still, because of the others in front of her. The others were tired, as tired as Sky, but the two in front thought they had done enough and the two behind them knew it, fading fast.

"Come *on*, Sky!" Tessa muttered, and rode with all her heart, sinew and muscle agonizing, breath searing in her throat. Sky flew, past the two in front and up to the quarters of the other pair. There was barely fifty metres to go. The nearest horse cracked, rolled sideways and lost a length and Sky's nose went up to the favourite's girth. No, she couldn't lose by a head! Tessa drove the filly with all her failing strength and was past hearing the roaring crowd, drowned out by her own pounding bloodstream. Her knee touched the favourite's jockey and they passed the post locked together.

"Photograph. Photograph," came over the loudspeaker.

The other jockey put out a hand in congratulation. "Great riding," he said, but not patronizingly. "I think you got it."

Tessa was past talking. When Sky at last pulled up, she had to rest, lying over the horse's withers, trying not to fall off. She was shattered, the blood pounding in her ears. She could not speak. Is this what it took to win a race? She felt it had been the Grand National at least, yet it was only a potty two-mile hurdle. She had so far to go! She took in great lungfuls of air as they walked slowly back, not wanting to face the winning enclosure in a state of collapse. Congratulations buzzed in her ears from her fellow jockeys: they were taking it in remarkably good part, being beaten by a girl.

Peter and Sarah came running up, alight with excitement. Peter looked like a boy, flushed red, reaching up to take her hand.

"You were brilliant, Tessa – to get up like that! You rode like a champion!"

"Like Tom," Tessa said. "For Tom."

If only he hadn't fallen asleep when the television was playing!

"You'll get asked to ride, after that, I'll put my shirt on it. I knew you could do it. But none of us expected to win!"

The owners kissed her and kissed Sky and the press gathered round, camera lights flashing. The television commentator bustled in. What rubbish she told him Tessa never remembered. It was all she could do to speak at all. She wanted to say something to Tom, but her Tom thing was private, not to be aired to the public. Tom would know. He would know why she had ridden so well.

She went home in the horsebox in an exhausted dream. She thought she was in cloud cuckoo land – what she had done. She knew it was her riding that had got the filly up, game as the filly was. Good jockeys won races that poorer jockeys lost. That was why they were asked to ride more often than the others. But girls . . . she knew, because of the state of her, that she would have to work on getting stronger.

But Peter said, "Riding in races will make you stronger. You will get the races after this."

But Sarah said, "Only from trainers who've got brains. Lots will still say a girl can't do it."

"She'll get enough." Peter was convinced.

In the evening Tessa went out to Buffoon. At the sound of her voice he turned his poor grey eyes towards her and pricked his ears. A soft knuckering in his throat, almost inaudible, told her he was pleased. She put her arms round his neck and laid her face in his scraggy yellow mane. She was so tired!

"You will be cured, Buffy my beauty, and come back, and I will ride you."

That was her dream, more impossible than any of her

others. But today she had made one step towards it, proving she *was* a jockey. Tomorrow she would ring up the vet in Newmarket and take the second step: ask him to see Buffoon, get his opinion.

But when she did so, the first question was, "Is the horse insured?"

"No, he isn't."

"Ah."

"I know it's very expensive, but I have the money," she lied. "I want him cured, even if you don't think it's worth it."

"Ah."

But then he said, "I'll have to see him first to make an assessment. The operation isn't always advisable. But make a date with my secretary and we'll go from there."

Tessa made a date for a fortnight away.

When she rang off she was shaking all over. She daren't tell the others. She knew what they would say. She scouted round Goldlands in her spare time to see when Maurice's car had departed, and then she went in and told her mother what she had done.

"You've got to lend me the money! Don't you see – I will pay you back easily! You saw me at Sandown? Well, people want me now. There's no risk at all. But I need it soon!"

Her mother complained bitterly at Tessa's insistence, but promised to do her best. Tessa thought Myra was fast becoming a nervous wreck and feared for her future, but this worry was of no account compared with her others. She had to tell the others of her plans because she needed the horsebox to transport Buffoon to Newmarket. Peter was aghast at the news.

"Who's going to pay? It'll cost an arm and a leg!"

"My mother's going to pay for it."

"Does Morrison know?" Sarah asked curiously. "I bet he doesn't!"

"My mother has her own money," Tessa said stiffly.

"It's what Morrison gives her though, isn't it? He'll go mad if he finds out!"

"He won't find out."

"Tessa, you're taking a risk, aren't you?"

Tessa didn't reply.

Jimmy said, gently, "You know the operation is a risk too? It's not always successful. And a big horse like Buffoon – he might die under the anaesthetic."

Tessa could not accept this. Nobody died in her book. Tom didn't die. Tom was getting better. Buffoon would get better.

"He won't! He won't die!"

They all looked at each other over her head, the same dubious expression in their faces. Even Jimmy.

When Tessa was alone with Jimmy she said, desperately, "It's not a bad idea, surely? To make him see again?"

"No. He deserves it. But what for, Tessa? He'll never race again. He'll be too old by the time he comes back. All that bad treatment, starvation – you don't expect him to be the same horse as he was? I think you think he'll race again."

Tessa was silent. Jimmy was right.

"To be a hack, perhaps. Because you dote on him so. Fair enough if you've got the money. He'll be at the vet's for at least a fortnight, could be a month. It's really going to cost you – so many drugs, alone. And then the anaesthetic, not only to lay the horse out, but to immobilize the eye – imagine!"

He pulled a sheet of paper out of his pocket.

"I looked it up, photocopied it for you. Read it."

Tessa took the sheet reluctantly. The words ran together as she read: "A two-millimetre stab incision is made into the cornea, near the limbus . . . the cystotome inserted through the incision is used to tear and remove the majority of the anterior lens capsule . . . ultrasonic waves break up the lens into particles which are aspirated from the eye. . . The major problem associated with intra-ocular surgery in the horse is post-operative inflammation . . . the act of incising the eye causes a cascade of events that, if not modified, can end in. . ."

Tessa moaned.

"You just want to put me off!"

"You're not easily put off when you want something, are you?" Jimmy shrugged. "You would get over it, if he was put down. He's had a fair life, after all. The operation is so risky, and you have to pay, even if it fails."

All good arguments. Tessa dismissed them instantly.

"It's what I want. Above everything."

Save Tom. And Tom was getting better. His mother had rung and told her he watched her win on Summer Sky. And then he "turned the corner" his mother said. "It was odd," she said. "As if your winning did it for him. When you came to see him I didn't tell you, but we were all very anxious. He was so ill. He had no other visitors, only you. And then——" On the phone her laugh sounded carefree, like that of a girl. "Yes, the operation is successful. After all our doubts and worries!"

Peter grudgingly gave Tessa permission to hijack the horsebox to take Buffoon to Newmarket. Jimmy offered to drive. Tessa had made sure the date wasn't one of their racing days. Or *her* racing days. She had three rides booked for trainers whom she had impressed at Sandown. And in spite of all the doubts she was as happy and excited as the horsebox purred along the motorway as if she were going on a good day out. Not a hospital appointment. She had got things moving: she *was* a jockey, Tom was getting better, Buffoon was going to be cured. And her mother had promised to pay.

"It *will* work, I know it will," she said to Jimmy.

"It's only the start of your master plan," Jimmy pointed out. "You've set yourself some mountains to climb, gel."

Tessa gazed out of the window at the rolling Essex countryside, green now with winter corn, and wondered what it would be like to have no mountains to climb: she could just be a stable-lad, after all, with blind Buffoon at grass, a comfortable berth in her caravan, nothing to worry about. A happy life, with people she liked. She had come a long way since coming to Goldlands, but she was never satisfied. Was something wrong with her?

She asked Jimmy.

He grinned. "I'll make a list. Remind me tonight."

He told her to leave the chat to him at Newmarket. "They'll put you down as unhinged, the way you carry on."

"You are so kind," Tessa said, and laughed.

But when it came to the point she was glad. She stayed in the lorry while Buffoon was unboxed with his friend Lucky and put into a stable. She was shaking, and nobody had said anything yet. This was the state-of-the-art horse hospital where millions of pounds were spent on horse health, because the horse in Newmarket was big business. If Buffoon was found to be a lost cause here, there was no hope for him. If he was considered fit to operate on, he would be booked in to return later. Today they took him home. Suppose, the next time, he didn't come home? Tessa was seized with a fit of the shivers. She remembered Tom . . . Tom came home. Tom was out of hospital now and on the road to full recovery. He was even setting himself a date to ride. If Tom could make it, so could Buffoon. Why did they laugh at her dreams?

It seemed an age before Jimmy returned.

He gave her a nod and said a groom was bringing Buffoon back. He was going to make a date for the operation with the secretary. He disappeared. In a few minutes a girl came round the corner leading Buffoon and Lucky, one on each side. Tessa leapt out of the cab to help her.

Buffoon had a way of walking now, when he was in a strange place, holding his head high and to one side, ears tightly pricked so that they almost touched each other. When Tessa saw him, hesitant with a strange person, she felt sick with love and anxiety for him. He was so utterly dependent now, trusting, lost. She ran to take him. The girl smiled.

"Funny, with this littl'un . . . I remember. . ."

Tessa knew she was thinking: this is the girl that stabbed Mr Morrison-Pleydell. It always brought her goodwill.

They boxed the two animals and closed the ramp and the girl went away. Tessa went and talked to Buffoon, who was now pulling at his haynet, content.

He had always like travelling. The noisy interior of the lorry held no horrors for him. He turned his head towards the sound of her voice and his nostrils rippled with the familiar greeting.

"Next time you come out of here, you'll see where you're going," Tessa said.

But her eyes pricked with fear. If he comes out of here, seeing, she thought . . . whatever happens afterwards is of no consequence. I shall have what I want most in the world. Now, after Tom.

Jimmy came back and climbed in the cab.

"Well, you've done it now, for better or for worse. He'll do the operation next month. I just hope you'll get the money OK."

"Oh, yes, it's only an advance, after all. I'll pay Mum back."

Jimmy grimaced at her confidence, but said no more. They drove home, not saying much, the windscreen wipers moving hypnotically across the view in front of them.

7

The Operation

*T*essa did not win her three booked rides, nor was she placed. She was paid her fee for riding, but there was no ten per cent for winning, and the fees looked small beside the cost of Buffoon's operation.

Jimmy said, each time, "You rode well. Money's not everything."

"It is!"

"Those horses weren't expected to win. You won't be offered winners very often, Tessa, let's face it. There's too many guys out there after the winners."

Owners and trainers had been pleased enough, treated her kindly, and she knew in each case she had ridden well. So much depended on it! And with each race her strength had increased. But her impatience, her ambition outstripped any feeling of satisfaction. Thank God her mother had promised the money!

Myra rang Sarah one night. Sarah called Tessa to take the call.

"I've got it out of the bank," Myra said. "It's in an envelope behind the hot water tank in the bathroom."

"Oh Mum, you are marvellous!"

"When the coast's clear, you must come and collect it."

"I will. As soon as possible."

What a relief! Another hurdle cleared. Tessa could not believe her luck. Sarah was more cautious.

"What if Mucky finds out? He'll come down and shoot you."

"How can he find out?"

"It's what it's for – Buffoon. When you think what he did to stop Buffy winning the Grand National . . . unbelievable! He's a mad man. Dangerous. He's got San Lucar back in action, I see."

"Shall I ask for the ride?" Tessa laughed.

Sarah grinned. "Tom won't be long, from what I hear. Have you seen him again?"

"No."

"I thought he was a special friend of yours? He asked for you in hospital?"

Tessa did not reply for a while, then she said slowly, "It was different then."

Sarah did not enquire farther. Her interest had touched Tessa on a sensitive point, for she did not know what her relationship with Tom was, and had put it out of her mind as something too difficult to cope with. They had had a need for each other once, but now things were straight again they had got on with their lives. Tom spent his days in physio, getting his strength back, determined to be fit by the start of the next season. Tessa knew this via the grapevine. She could not help thinking about him at times, but thinking about him seemed to make her miserable. She didn't know why. It was an area of confusion, and best forgotten. As if she didn't have enough!

The day for taking Buffoon back to Newmarket drew inexorably nearer. With a fair amount of collusion in the stable, Tessa found that she was booked to ride a new horse, Gamekeeper, at Worcester on the same date.

"I won't be able to go with Buffy!"

"Bad luck," they all said.

Jimmy was taking Buffoon. Peter hitched a lift for Gamekeeper in Raleigh's horsebox and Tessa travelled to Worcester with Peter in his car. The morning was busy and Tessa had no time to take an emotional farewell of dear Buffy. As she led him into the horsebox Peter was already shouting at her to hurry. Her mind was in a turmoil.

"Just think of your ride," Peter said crisply as she got into the car. "It's what you're paid for."

Tessa knew that she depended a great deal on the Fellowes brothers' goodwill, and tried to do as she was told. Not think of Buffy. She sat thinking what a lot she took for granted these days, that she actually belonged somewhere, for a start. Once she had thought that would never happen. She rarely thought of her father any longer. In a way Peter was a father figure, she realized with surprise. She could sit by him in the car for miles without a word being exchanged, in a completely family sort of way, taking him for granted. She relied on him completely; his word was law. Technically he was her boss, but she knew he was more than that. It had never struck her before, what a big part of her life he was.

She glanced sideways at him, and saw a rough-hewn, preoccupied face, untidy hair, tired grey eyes. She saw that he wasn't one of the smart trainers like Raleigh who attracted the smart, rich owners, but a farmer sort of man, not all that articulate but completely honest and as much a master of his job as any of the smart ones. He wasn't married and lived a home life with little comfort, like they all did at Sparrows Wyck. Funny, Tessa thought, how well she seemed to know him, and yet didn't know him at all. They only ever talked work. A bit like Tom. Tessa felt disturbed, feeling suddenly that people had done quite a lot for her but she had never thought about anything except her own way ahead. Even with Buffoon. Although they all thought she was mad and had said so, they had still laid on the horsebox to take him to Newmarket, and Jimmy's whole working day was wasted doing it.

"You are good to me," she said suddenly.

Peter, startled, threw her an amazed glance and the car swerved. Then he laughed.

"What have I done, to earn that?"

But Tessa could not explain. It was like the Tom thing, impossible to articulate. She felt herself going red, embarrassed.

Peter said, "Perhaps I think you're worth the trouble. We get our money's worth out of you, after all."

It was a strange day. The season was nearly over, with spring cheering the sodden courses, all the trees in flower and the racegoers out of their winter woollies, smiling in the sunshine. Tessa tried not to think of Buffoon, but she felt she was carrying out her jockey role in a dream. Her mind could not take it seriously. She was in limbo. Yet the racing was what mattered.

Gamekeeper was a young horse she rode at home, and he was in the race to gain experience. Nobody expected him to win. But he went well and finished sixth out of twelve. The owners weren't there and Peter was pleased with both the horse and Tessa.

"You rode him well. He enjoyed it. Well done."

At least it had kept her mind off Buffoon.

When they got home a strong evening sun was casting shadows across the yard. The horsebox was back, parked in its usual place, Walter lying snoozing with his nose on his paws. He jumped up and came to meet Tessa, who could not resist going to Buffoon's empty box and staring in. It was all set fair for his return, clean and neat.

"You must come back, Buffy," Tessa said to it. Tears came into her eyes. If he came home all right, she would never wish for anything more in her life.

She said to Peter, "Can I go and talk to Jimmy?"

She never went to the house ordinarily.

Peter nodded and Tessa walked up through the yards and knocked on the open door. Walter came with her. Someone shouted, "Come in."

Jimmy was sitting at the table in the old-fashioned, very used-looking kitchen, reading a newspaper. He put it down, smiled.

"Well done on Gamekeeper. I bet Peter was pleased."

"Yes. What about Buffy?"

"Nothing to report. They have things to do before the operation, to get him ready. Two or three days."

What on earth had she expected?

"You can't wait? Tough," said Jimmy. "Just keep your fingers crossed. It's unlikely anything will go wrong, after all. We had to say all that to warn you – it *can*. But he's in the best hands possible. We'll ring later in the week. Patience, Tessa."

She smiled. She had to.

"Thank you for taking him."

A strange day. She ate something, talked to Sarah, went out to Buffoon's box again. It was still light, the sun sinking over the dark silhouette of the down. She called Walter from the kitchen doorstep and walked up the track towards Goldlands, not to call, but just to be somewhere quiet. The spring dusk was full of promise. If Buffy were to die . . . she had no other love in her life. What would she do? She had eschewed love for humans long ago, and given it first to Shiner and then to Shiner's son. But now, disturbingly, humans were impinging on her armoured isolation, and she was discovering that she could not free herself of feelings she was unused to. The image of Tom Bryant would not go away. And today she had felt that strange compunction to tell Peter that she appreciated his kindness.

And towards Jimmy there was always a . . . what? A soft feeling? What would one call this betrayal of indifference? It was impossible to put a name to. All manifestations of what might be considered, by some people, as love. And Sarah too . . . but Tessa thought she didn't love people. It was confusing.

She talked to Walter when he was at her side, which wasn't very often, and told him her thoughts about Buffy. Now she was on the paths that she had ridden with the horse, his dear ways choked her to think of. She knew she was a stupid sentimental fool but she also knew that really tough hard-boiled men cried over their horses and she was in good company. What did it matter when there was no one to see? She went down to the river and, passing the log that the silly old fool had stumbled over because he never saw it, remembered Tom saying something about his sight then, so long ago. Remembered the feel of him slowly getting under way into his great galloping stride and lifting her over the ridge of the down like thistledown flying in the wind, the first time he carted her. But so kindly. She had never been afraid of Buffy. He was the kindest horse in the world.

The river flowed strongly in the bottom of the valley, trailing its green weeds, smelling of nature untouched, rank and ambrosial, secret, elemental. Tessa stayed there for some time, listening to it, unceasing, stroking her difficult thoughts. Whoever, whatever, died, nothing stopped the stream's coming, the spring rising. It just went on. One was of no consequence in the universe. Did anything matter at all?

A blind horse . . . rubbish. One for the knacker's.

"Oh Buffy!" she cried out loud.

Walter came back, soaking wet and muddy, and laid his long nose on her knee. Tessa laughed at him then, and got up and started back for home, feeling comforted. What by, she didn't know.

Buffoon had Lucky by him, which was the only good thing. He was frightened now of going to a strange place, frightened of being abandoned. This wasn't a racecourse stable, but it was a yard with other horses which he could smell and hear, which comforted him. But there was also an atmosphere of tension and unease, of pain and distress, and strange smells which made him nervous. He kept his nose close to Lucky, and was pleased that the grooms were kind.

"This is the horse that ran in the National. That lost the pony – do you remember?"

They were mucking out, pushing him out of the way with gentle hands.

"Yes. The ugly one. Poor old beggar."

"The man that brought him in said his dam was blind. Had no eyes at all. Born like it. Weird, isn't it?"

"It doesn't follow, does it? Must be a freak coincidence, that he's blind too but with something quite different."

"I saw a foal here once, born blind. But it was put down."

Buffoon sensed sympathy, felt less nervous. But what was he here for? Was he going back to his proper place, like after racing? He remembered his abandonment all too clearly. He wanted Tessa. Her voice meant everything to him. But he got strange-smelling men, and needles, and sedatives, and his brain started to fail just like his eyes, so that nothing had meaning any more. Only his nose rested on Lucky's withers, and Lucky stood unmoving, looking after him, his friend.

They wouldn't let her ring up the morning after the operation.

"If he'd died they would have rung us. You know what we think of interfering owners. It's just the same. Leave it," they said.

They gave her lots of work to do. Ride out first lot, ride out second lot, spring-clean the tack-room, disinfect two empty boxes, take a convalescent horse out for a quiet walk, let it graze, cut the grass round the caravans. After this, she thought, I can take anything. None of the jobs took much brain work. Her brain was free to picture Buffoon lying inert on a great operating table with green-garbed figures bending over him, the dreaded anaesthetic – so much for so big a horse – hissing into his lungs. Sometimes it killed them, she knew that. But he was only a horse, she kept telling herself. Unlike Tom. A useless horse, what's more. They all said that. It wasn't as if he was a National winner. Not even a San Lucar.

"San Lucar won yesterday," they told her.

He had been at a classier course than Worcester, won a classy race. Maurice was back in the money. Lucky Maurice.

He might win the Grand National yet. Not like useless Buffoon.

The clock crawled through the afternoon.

"Can we ring now?"

Tessa pictured them, the job done, having cups of tea, filling in forms.

"Got to ring about that horse." But sitting there, all the same. It was four o'clock. Half-past.

The secretary rang.

"So sorry, we didn't get round to doing the operation today. An emergency came in. Tomorrow probably. We'll be in touch."

Jimmy laughed. Tessa hated him, and wept some more, and Sarah took her in hand, took her into her caravan and made strong tea and gave her a good talking to.

"Grow up, Tessa. I thought you were well on the way, until now."

"You don't know what it feels like!"

"I do, Tessa. Believe me, I do. And for a man, not a horse."

Tessa was silent. Where did that leave her now? Sarah's secret, private life that none of them knew about. Sarah, who was so beautiful and marvellous, never seemed to have a man. It must be by choice. Gilly, who was far from beautiful and not marvellous at all, seemed to have them by the dozen.

"I'm sorry," she said miserably.

"I do know what it feels like and it's truly awful but you just have to be patient."

Well, that wasn't one of her virtues, for sure.

But, late, late in the afternoon when she was in the depths of despair, the man himself rang up, very jovial, and said the deed was done, everything looked promising, no hitches, the horse was fine.

"Give us a few days. We'll keep in touch."

"Champagne!" shouted Jimmy, and brought out two bottles of beer. Everyone cheered. Tessa couldn't believe it was over.

"Give or take complications, of course," Jimmy added.

"Complications?"

"Oh, come on, Jimmy, think positive," Sarah said. "Give the girl a break. Here's to Buffoon winning the Grand National!"

They all roared with laughter, save Tessa. A little knot of her inside gave a lurch. They wouldn't laugh, if she had anything to do with it! She was mad, of course, they were always telling her.

Were there complications? If there were, they didn't let Tessa know. But Buffoon didn't come home for a long time. The bill got bigger every day. They kept telling her he was fine, but what they said to Jimmy she never knew. On a Saturday, almost at the end of the season, she got a ride at Sandown in a modest two-mile chase, from a trainer whose horse only liked women.

"We'll give it a try," he said. "You're good for a girl."

Not really patronizing, just honest, Tessa thought. The horse behaved perfectly, and down at the start a fellow jockey, surprised, said what a pig it was as a rule.

"What's your secret?"

"Trainer says it only likes women."

"Just like me," the jockey grinned.

But the piggy horse came second, and the trainer was pleased, and Tessa knew he would ask her again. But second! Only wins counted and she was tired of seconds.

When she got home, tired, her eyes turned as usual to the empty box in the yard – to see the big chestnut bonehead looking out. Buffoon saw her and whickered in recognition. He *saw* her! His eyes were dark and shining again, as if he were a two-year-old.

"Buffy!" she shrieked, and ran towards him.

Lucky's nose inched over the door, whinnying to be noticed, and Tessa threw her arms round their necks, ecstatic.

It was the best day of her life, even better than her first win.

8

Myra Leaves Home

*B*uffoon was put out to grass to recover, along with Lucky and the horses that stayed at the yard for their summer holidays. The season was over. Tessa paid Peter for Buffoon's grass keep, a modest amount, and sent off the enormous cheque for Buffoon's operation. The money behind the hot water boiler just covered it.

"Next season, Mum, I'll give you all my riding fees. All my winnings! I'll pay you back in no time."

Myra was still worried Maurice might find out. Tessa could see that she was afraid of him now. Did he knock her about? His temper was growing worse all the time, and Tessa thought he did, although Myra denied it. But she would.

After a few weeks on the lush valley grass Buffoon looked like a different horse. His fine summer coat shone like polished copper, the flesh filled out over all his prominent bones and high-sprung ribs. Tessa feasted her eyes on him, leaning over the gate. He would come to her out of pure affection when he saw her, not just for a bucket of food, quite a rare thing in a horse. He had the sweetest, friendliest nature of any horse she had come across. The others even agreed with her in this.

"Soft as butter," Sarah said.

"I'm going to start riding him again," Tessa said. "Get him fit."

There was time now, in the summer, with no racehorses to exercise. Sarah, Wisbey and Gilly were going to other jobs for the summer, and there was just her and Arthur to look after the at-grass horses and keep the place tidy. Buffoon was no longer convalescent, and Tessa longed to be on his back again.

The first time, Jimmy rode out with her, to be on the safe side.

They saddled up and went off up the track towards the gallops, Walter loping ahead. It was only walking, for Buffoon was totally unfit. Tessa knew it would take hours of walking and then slow trotting to get him back in shape. In shape for what?

Tessa could not shake off her ambition to have him back in racing.

Jimmy guessed it, although Tessa said nothing.

They rode up the grass track on to the down in silence, feeling the spring breeze on their faces with its smell of distant hawthorn blossom and sweet-flowering grass. The clouds sailed serenely over the hill. Two hares ran away ahead of them, big as dogs, luring Walter. He chased them but they jinked and he lost them, too big to turn as fast as they could. By the time he had stopped and turned they were almost out of sight.

"He'd never have won the Waterloo Cup," Jimmy said.

"Good. I love hares."

It was wonderful riding her dear horse in this lovely place. If one turned one's eyes from the ugly blot of Goldlands on the ridge, this valley was pure paradise. Tessa thought, I really do belong here. It's all because of Shiner. Finding out that Buffoon was her son made me stay. She had hated it, she remembered, until then.

Buffoon remembered the gallops and pulled to go up the hill, thinking he was there for a workout, but Tessa told him otherwise, and they gained the top at a walk. They pulled up there, and sat for a moment taking in the blue distance.

"You needn't have come. He's as good as gold," Tessa said.

"I like it. What we all need more of. Pure pleasure."

"I'm going to ride him every day."

Jimmy didn't say anything, but on the way back he said, "What are you planning for Buffoon?"

"Just to get him fit, happy."

"What for?"

"To ride."

"Ride where?"

Tessa didn't answer.

"He's too old now, Tessa, to race."

"Horses win when they're old! McVidi, Eastern Emperor – sixteen!"

"Freaks. And not turned away during their prime years, and starved."

"A little race or two, why not?"

"Tessa, think it through. Peter can't train him for nothing. It's not fair to ask him. Registering him in your name, getting your colours, all the extras – it costs a mint before you've even started. Why is it only rich people have racehorses? Or have them in syndicates, a share of six or twelve? You will never, never be able to afford it."

"Peter can have all my wages, every penny! And my riding fees, everything!"

She had given away her private plans now. Jimmy had guessed them anyway. This thing at the back of her mind, to ride Buffy on the racecourse, to ride him over the big jumps with the roar of the crowd in her ears . . . She had seen enough, done enough, to make the ambition a realistic proposition, drawing a veil over all the problems Jimmy was describing. And the money was owed to her mother . . . the money she was so glibly promising to Peter.

"I only mention it," Jimmy said, "because I know the way your mind works. And how fierce you are when you want something. It's called nipping it in the bud."

Tessa was silent. Whatever he said, she knew the dream would not go away.

"Enjoy what you've got. You've got him safe and happy, more than any of us thought possible."

"You said put him down!"

"I know."

"Now you say . . . it's the same, not thinking it can be done – it can be!"

"At Peter's expense. It's hardly fair."

"Not if I earn the money."

"No, but such a lot of money. You've no idea."

"But if I train him myself, ride him in the afternoon, in my spare time . . . Peter needn't spend any time on him."

She had thought about it such a lot, all her waking time, how she could do it.

"If he runs under Peter's name, Peter's got to take a hand in it. Don't be stupid, Tessa. I just want you to see sense."

"You always said to me, about being a jockey, if you want something enough you can do it. I want this."

"Fine, being a jockey. But putting Buffoon in training will *cost* Peter. You will never have enough to pay for it. And he's a soft guy. He'll fall for it if you keep on at him, the way you are."

"I'll get him fit, whatever you say."

Jimmy laughed, looking at her set, angry face.

"Poor Peter," he said.

But he was wise enough to know that his argument would go home, for Tessa's independence was total. She had never expected favours.

After that Tessa rode Buffoon alone, every day, in her hours off. She never took him out in her working time, even when there was little to do. Quite often she took him out late, in the long summer evenings, returning in the dusk or near-dark. She loved the evenings, with the fall of the dew bringing the scents out of the ground and the first stars shining over the roofs of the farm below. Buffoon went kindly, as if he too was enjoying his come-back to health and work, and riding alone was a peculiar pleasure, quite different from the exercising in a string of horses that they had known before.

After a month or so she was trotting, and then cantering, as the muscle came up under the shining golden coat. She was never happier, feeling the horse's returning strength as he stretched out up the long hill. How she loved him! And how nearly she had lost him! And now he was truly *hers*, not just her horse to do, to look after for someone else. Sometimes the happiness rose up in her so that she thought the top of her head would blow off.

One evening as she rode home down the long valley she sensed that something was wrong in the yard below. The lights in her caravan were shining, but no one would go in there, surely? Even a burglar wouldn't turn the lights on.

She trotted on, curious, and noticed that there was a long trail ahead of her in the dew, as if someone had run down the valley. No one came that way but herself.

She went through into the yard and rode Buffoon over to the field gate where she quickly slipped off his saddle and bridle and let him loose. Leaving the tack hanging on the gate she turned and ran to her caravan. The door was open.

"Who is it?"

Rather tentatively she entered.

Myra was lying on the bed, face down.

"Mum!"

Tessa ran to her and knelt down, putting her hand on her mother's shoulder.

"What is it? It's Maurice, isn't it? Oh Mum, what has he done to you?"

Myra was too far gone to weep, to have hysterics in her usual way. Her lips were cut and bleeding, her eyes swollen and half-closed, and she was moaning softly. When Tessa went to turn her on her side towards her, Myra screamed in pain. Tessa guessed that her ribs were broken.

"Did he do it?"

"Yes. He found out——"

"About the money?"

"What it was for."

Myra could scarcely make herself understood through her bleeding lips.

"Mum, stay here. I'll go and get some help."

She ran to the house and hammered on the door. A surprised Peter came out.

"What's wrong?" Alarm came into his face as he saw Tessa's distress.

"What is it?"

"Please come! It's my mother! Maurice has half-killed her!"

Peter shouted for Jimmy and they both came running. When they saw the state Myra was in Peter said, "She needs an ambulance."

But Myra screamed out, "No! No!"

"They'll get the police in, a case like this," Jimmy said.

"I won't go!" Myra sobbed. "I won't! I'm all right here."

Tessa could see her point. She wouldn't want public interference either. The hospital would get the police, surely? Peter and Jimmy understood too.

"She can't stay here though. We'll take her into the house, in the spare bed. Get the doctor to her."

"Not the doctor!"

"Let's get you comfortable at least."

She couldn't argue about that. Peter and Jimmy were used to treating accidents, and helped her skilfully to make the journey across to the house. Their mother was alerted, and in the kitchen Myra's face was bathed, the blood cleaned off, strong hot tea administered. Tessa hung over her mother, who suffered the pain stoically. It was only the idea of going public with her injuries that made her shout and scream. She made no murmur at the sting of the antiseptic and the agony of the broken ribs.

Peter said, "We'll get the doctor in the morning to strap up your ribs. We'll tell him you fell off a horse."

This caused some amusement. Even Myra almost laughed. But Jimmy said quickly, "No laughing! That's what hurts the most."

"You're not going back, Mum. Not ever," Tessa said.

"She can stay here till she's better," Mrs Fellowes said. "No hurry to move out."

Remembering Jimmy's words about exploiting Peter's

292

kindness, Tessa said quickly, "She can stay in my caravan. I'll look after her."

"She's better here for now."

Tessa did not argue. The solid walls of the old farmhouse compared with her tacky caravan were more inviting by far. The guest room was large and homely (when had it ever had guests before? Tessa wondered) and Peter and Jimmy got Myra up the stairs and into the bed without hurting her too badly.

"I'll stay with her," Tessa insisted. "I can sleep in the same bed. It's big enough."

They agreed with that, and Tessa went out and put Buffoon's tack away and got her things. She was seething with rage against Maurice, working out ways to get even with him – how to hurt him in the way he hurt others. She was too much improved to think about another knife attack, but the desire to get revenge flamed inside her. This, above all his displays of cruelty and arrogance, was the worst yet. And she had seen it coming, and – worst of all – it was her fault. It was a part of what Jimmy had warned her against: that her own crazy ambitions were starting to impinge on other people, the people she was closest to. She felt very disturbed, hating her part in it. And yet. . .

"He did you a good turn," she said to Myra. "You'd never have left the place otherwise. You're not going back."

"He wouldn't have me back! He said so! What shall I do? Oh Tessa, what shall I do?"

"Live your own life!" Tessa said fiercely.

And even as she said it she knew her mother had no one to

turn to but herself. It was now her turn to take on other people's troubles, instead of giving other people the burden of her own. Her world was turning upside down all of a sudden and she didn't like it.

Jeez, what am I getting into? she thought as she lay on the edge of the big bed. And yet she had wanted her mother to leave Maurice for years.

The next day the doctor was called to Myra (who had fallen off a horse) and he strapped up her ribs. He knew who she was and they all knew that he knew how she had come by her injuries but nothing was said, only the grim remark on leaving, "This ought to be reported, you know."

"Yes," they said.

Myra with her tough upbringing recovered quite quickly and it was decided she could live in Sarah's caravan for the time being. She was welcome to go on staying in the farmhouse, but she didn't want to put upon the Fellowes. Now she had left Maurice she had turned back to her old independent self. She cried a lot and kept saying, "Whatever shall I do?" but between these bouts of self-pity she made herself quite busy round the place, tidying the grass round the caravans, sweeping the yard, cleaning out the tack-room. She stopped wearing her layers of make-up and changed into the old jeans she found in Sarah's caravan.

One day a new horse came into the yard to go into training for the next season. His name was Galaxy and he was fat and lazy and kind. When Tessa went to fetch Buffoon for her afternoon ride, she suddenly had an idea. Galaxy needed exercising too, and why shouldn't Myra ride him out with her?

She asked Peter.

He said, "OK, but Myra rides Buffoon. You ride Galaxy."

"My mother's a good rider. Was a good rider."

"Good. She might be very useful in that case."

After Myra's initial protests, which Tessa bore patiently ("I can't! I haven't ridden for years! Don't be silly, Tessa! What an idea!") she was eventually persuaded to change into a pair of Sarah's old jods and gaiters and venture out to mount Buffoon.

Tessa was determined that her mother wasn't going to ride Buffoon more than the first few times, because riding Buffoon was what Tessa's life was all about. But to get Myra riding it was worth it. Peter and Jimmy were in the yard when they mounted and set off, probably to see what Myra was like, but pretending to be doing something else. Although she was so rusty, they could see by the way she mounted and rode through the gate that she had the seat of an old pro. In her teens she had made her living riding out racehorses in Ireland. It was a skill that did not go away, like swimming and riding a bike, although, being Myra, she was making exclamations of dismay about how weird she felt after all these years.

Peter said, having watched them ride away along the track, "She could be useful."

Jimmy laughed.

He added, "She's a very attractive woman, now she's happy."

Jimmy raised his eyebrows, but didn't say anything.

Tessa enjoyed watching Buffoon walking beside her, seeing him as other people saw him (although with her rose-tinted spectacles). He was said to be an ugly brute. Certainly he was no picture of a perfect thoroughbred, no delicately-veined Derby winner, but in his very presence, his great bones showing through, sliding impressively under the satin coat, Tessa saw, not ungainliness, but power. His stride was long and easy, the withers enormous with miles of horse in front of the saddle which gave the rider a fine sense of security. Two long ears twitched with interest at passing birds and flying hares, and back to the voice, kindly, and the large, resurrected eyes shone with well-being.

"So he's Shiner's colt, this one?"

Myra, now she was riding him, found him more interesting than before.

"Yes. Declan must have bred him."

"Ah, what's become of the man, I wonder? Down the drain, I dare say, with all the drink. And Shiner – she'd be an old girl now. How you did love that filly when you were little!"

Tessa did not want this conversation. She had long ago drawn a veil across the pain of leaving Shiner, which had traumatized her life. (How could a horse traumatize a life? she wondered, now.) She hated her past and did not want to think of it now, yet Buffoon tied her to it.

"Let's trot," she said, as the track rose to the hill, and she watched Myra posting easily to Buffoon's long stride as if she had been riding for the last twenty years.

Perhaps Myra could have a job in the yard when the horses came back into training? She could earn her keep! Already she looked like a new woman, out of her stupid tight clothes and with her hair all wild again, just as Tessa remembered her as a child when she laughed and shouted. Maurice had as good as stifled her in that dreary house before he finally duffed her up. Now she was free again. She seemed to realize it herself, sending Buffoon on into a canter as the hill steepened and laughing out loud with enjoyment. Tessa kept Galaxy back as he wasn't fit but he didn't fight her and Myra waited at the top.

"I'd forgotten how good it was, to be on a big horse again!"

"You could ride out, Ma, when the horses come in, and earn some money."

"I could think of worse!"

Tessa hadn't seen her mother so happy for years. It made her laugh too. Perhaps she would learn to stand on her own two feet again? She hadn't whinged for quite a while, apart from the "I don't know what will become of me" chant. But when Sarah came back and claimed her caravan Myra would have nowhere to live. Tessa knew that there was no way she could share her caravan with her mother.

But no doubt that was a problem that could be resolved. For now the future looked promising.

A Stable Hack

*T*he problem was resolved in a way that brought astonishment to the yard at Sparrows Wyck, and not least to Tessa. When Sarah came back, Myra moved out, into the farmhouse. Mrs Fellowes packed her bags and departed for a "nice little bungalow in the village, what I've wanted for the last twenty years" and Myra took over. And then it was quite plain for all to see that Peter and Myra were falling in love with each other. It was mutual, sudden, a flowering of two bereft and needy characters thrown into each other's path. Peter had never thought of taking a wife, Myra had been stultified by Maurice. Her arrival awoke in Peter a passion he had never guessed himself capable of. There it was! The stable was gobsmacked.

Sarah and Tessa decided there ought to be a party!

"Tell 'em all! Don't keep it under wraps!" Sarah exclaimed. "It'll only be gossip if you don't make it clear."

"Peter Fellowes and Morrison's wife!"

It was the talk of the county, with goodwill behind the astonishment. Nobody knew Myra, Maurice having kept her under wraps all their married life, but when she appeared beside the quietly proud and happy Peter, she looked radiant. The colour was back in her cheeks, her black hair loose and shining, her eyes matching an emerald green dress she had chosen with Sarah which set her Irish colouring off to perfection. She looked to Tessa like the mother of her childhood, more than ten years younger than during her internment at Goldlands. In fact, beside her, Tessa suddenly felt drab and forgotten. It was young people that fell in love in that shouting way, not one's mother and employer! How could she ever have credited that Peter might become her stepfather?

Tessa was as surprised as everybody else.

Wisbey and Gilly said they had seen it as soon as they arrived back in the yard and Tessa must have been blind.

"But she only looks at that Buffoon of hers. She wouldn't have noticed," Wisbey scoffed. "She's in love with that horse."

The party was a great success, staged in a local country hotel. Technically it was a stable party, a party for the owners, but everyone came. It was autumn, the start of the new season, and everyone was making plans, talking of their new stars, full of optimism. Prospective new owners mingled with yard-lads and journalists, jockeys and rich daughters.

Tessa, who had never been to a party in her life, felt completely out of her depth. She knew she was still the girl that had stabbed Morrison-Pleydell, pointed out like an animal in a zoo. Maurice was still buying horses, and had San Lucar back with Raleigh for the coming year, but no one had seen much of him. No one was complaining.

Tessa stood watching the crowd chattering and drinking.

She had no idea how to dance and realized that she wasn't much good at conversation either. Even her dress was hopeless, one of Myra's that Myra had taken in and shortened with her rather wild sewing. It was black and made her look like a witch. The evil fairy. That was what she felt like.

"Hi, Tess." The voice was hesitant. "You look – fantastic."

She looked up, startled. The voice was familiar, the sentiments not at all.

It was Greevy, himself looking rather amazing in a dark suit, holding a glass of champagne.

Tessa didn't know what to make of Greevy these days. He seemed far more friendly, in spite of his father. Tessa found herself blushing deeply, and didn't know what to say.

"I dare say Myra will be happier with Mr Fellowes than with Dad," Greevy said. "Dad doesn't make people happy, does he?"

What on earth was she supposed to say to that? The understatement of all time.

"I don't live at home any more. I've got myself a flat in the village, walking distance from Raleigh's. It suits me fine. In fact I only see Dad if he comes to the races."

How civilized he had become!

"I like my job, even if Dad did throw me in at the deep end. And you too – you've stayed with it. You've done well. Funny how things work out. That night – God almighty! He deserved it – what he did . . . but I'm glad I stopped you killing him. Where would you be now? Think of that! You owe me, Tessa – saving you. . ."

Greevy must have had a few drinks, to be so forthcoming.

"I wish I had killed him!"

"What, and still be in prison? You're crazy!"

"We all know she's crazy — you just found out?" Another voice broke in, and Tessa swung round to see the tanned, smiling face of Tom Bryant looking down at her.

She had to hide the shock that suddenly electrified her. She hardly recognized him from the invalid she had last seen. He looked so wonderful! Slender and obviously fit, in a fine suit and tie like Greevy, his sky-blue eyes were taking in her miserable figure.

"So, you're swapping stepfathers? A celebration surely? Don't mind Greevy here, he knows what I think of his dad, eh Greevy?"

Greevy laughed. "I've got a good idea. Don't worry, I can take it."

They chatted like old friends while Tessa goggled beside them, heart thumping. What was it about Tom that made her feel so weird?

Then Tom turned to her and said, "Want some fresh air? I don't think you're a party person, not enough practice. Come and take a turn with me outside and tell me what you've been doing. Long time no see."

He took her arm and steered her adroitly through the throng out on to the terrace. They walked down the steps and across the lawn to where a river made the boundary, running slackly in the sharp autumn sunlight. Their shadows lengthened towards it. Tom walked without a limp at all, and moved as easily as a dancer.

"You are better! It all worked?"

"Yes, better than anyone imagined. I've been so lucky! As soon as I was walking again I went to the States, and only came back last week. I've got relations out there, and lots of racing contacts. I started to ride out again, and got myself really fit and learned a hell of a lot into the bargain. It's been terrific. And I've already got some good rides lined up for the season. A year ago I thought my number was up – it's amazing."

"You're so fit. It must help, when you have to fight back."

"Yeah. Jockeys usually bounce back. I'm not the only one. I've just been really lucky. And what about you? And that great ugly beast of yours? Jimmy said he's still around."

"Yes. Like you. Back from the dead. He can see now and I've got him really fit. I ride him out every day. Not with the others. Just in my time off."

Tessa's face lit up as she started to tell Tom the story of Buffoon's rehabilitation. Tom listened gravely. What else had Jimmy told him? Tessa wondered. Nobody at home spoke of her ambition for him. It was just too difficult a hot chestnut to tackle.

"You want to race him again, don't you?" It wasn't hard for Tom to pick up this fact. "You're off your trolley, Tessa. He's too old, beat up. They never come back."

Hearing it from Tom, the words that everyone had stopped

saying at home because it was no use telling her, Tessa felt her world cave in.

"He will come back! You come and ride him! He feels marvellous!"

She looked up at him, white-faced, and Tom saw again the light in those weird eyes and the passion that suffused the small wiry figure. This was what Morrison must have seen, he thought, when she launched herself at him with the knife. In her black dress, throwing out sparks, she looked marvellous.

"But to *race*?" He stuck to his guns. "He's too old now, to start again."

"It's what I want."

Tessa always got what she wanted. In the end.

"No. You're deluding yourself."

"Look at you – nobody thought you'd come back."

Tom laughed. "No? Well, I'm young, haven't you noticed? And lucky. Besides, I'm not a horse."

"Come and ride him, and see what I'm saying. He feels just like he used to."

"Well, I might. To humour you."

To humour himself, perhaps. Was it possible that Tessa might learn to love something other than a horse? She gave no signs. One would no more try and steal a kiss from Tessa than enter the stable of a kicking mule.

"I exercise him in my own time. I never take work time on him. I ride him every afternoon, and that's my own time."

"That's a hard day. And what about the race riding?"

"I've got to do as much as I can, because I need the money. I have to pay Peter. If you can get me some rides . . . tell them all how good I am?"

"Yeah, I'll do my best. You work at the riding, that's what's the most important. You could be up there – win a big one. You can do it."

"Mum's on my side."

She was the only one. But she was mad too.

They stayed talking, Tom telling her what he had been up to in America, and it grew dark and they went inside. Other people came to talk to Tom and Tessa left, not wanting any more. It was only three miles to walk home, and now she was wrapped in dreams and glad to be out in the night on her own. She went out through the car park which was completely deserted. An almost full moon glittered on the metal roofs, making it look like a sea. Tessa turned her face gratefully to the cool air.

By the entrance a large white car was parked on its own. There was a man in it, watching her. She sensed rather than saw him. She had to pass close to it to get out of the entrance and as she passed the door opened and a voice called her name.

She stopped, stupidly, instead of making a run for it, and a figure stepped out and caught her by the arm. The grip was painful.

"I want to talk to you!"

It was Maurice, breathing stinking whisky fumes over her.

"My dear little stepdaughter! Come and talk to me, tell me how my darling wife is enjoying herself these days."

He dragged her into the car and Tessa heard the automatic locks click. She sat in the passenger seat, tense, trying not to show her fear. For God's sake, don't start the engine! she prayed. He could kill her.

"I wasn't asked to the party," he said.

"Everyone was asked. It was an open invitation. You could have come if you wanted."

"If *I* wanted? But no one else wanted *me*, did they?"

"No, they didn't."

In the moonlight she could see his drawn, jowly face, and the ice-cold eyes. She was completely in his power. Yet, even in this extreme situation, she could not find the words to sweet-talk herself out of it. The hate rose up like bile.

"My mother is happy now, with Peter! And so is Greevy, now he's left you. And me! We're all happy without you! Can't you see what you are?"

And even while the words left her tongue she was telling herself what an idiot she was.

Maurice laughed.

"You never play your cards right, do you, Tessa? You're still just a spoilt brat as far as I'm concerned. A very nasty spoilt brat with a vicious streak. I am going to see that you get your just desserts."

He put his hand out to switch on the ignition.

Tessa knocked it away. She tried to find her door handle, the panic rising, but knew it was locked anyway. There were headlights coming towards them out of the car park and she turned to scream out for help but Maurice knocked her violently against the window, nearly stunning her. He started the engine. Tessa reached out desperately and put her hand on the horn. She kept it pressed down and screamed again but fear stifled her voice. Only the headlight, flaring now across their struggles, gave her hope.

The car swung wide, crossed in front of Maurice's car and blocked the exit. Maurice, wild and drunk, lashed out at her again as she lunged for the ignition keys. He was so mad he was going to ram the car that blocked him.

The driver leapt out and Tessa screamed at him.

"Tom, mind out!"

She kicked out at Maurice's ankles and swung her fist at his face. Pure rage guided her blows and Maurice couldn't get the car in gear. He roared at her, and she lunged again for the ignition keys, this time managing to pull them out of the lock. The engine died as they dropped on the floor.

"Let me out! Let me out!"

She beat on the windows with her fists, thinking Maurice in his rage was going to kill her. But he sat quietly, breathing hard. Then he bent down to pick up the keys.

He clicked the door locks free.

"Get out," he said.

He leant over and opened the door and Tessa stumbled, half fell, into Tom's arms.

"What on earth's going on? What were you doing to her?"

"She's hysterical. Take her home. Do I have to spell out to

you that she's unhinged? Wasn't she put away for it, for heaven's sake?"

Maurice looked up at them, his face twitching with the effort to keep in control. Sweat beaded on his forehead. Whoever was unhinged at that moment, Tessa knew it wasn't herself. He looked just like the madman he was. She felt Tom's arms tighten round her.

"Are you all right?" he asked her.

"Yes. Make him go. Move your car." Tessa could not bear the expression in Maurice's eyes, boring into her. It brought all the crises in her life spilling back, the black holes she didn't want to look into again.

The urgency in her voice made Tom comply. He drove his car out of the way and Maurice started his car and roared away into the night.

Tom said gently, "What was all that about?"

Tessa didn't want to talk about it. It was too difficult. She shook her head.

Tom said, "I'll drive you home."

She sat silent, unable to make sense of the incident. Perhaps Tom believed Maurice, that she was hysterical.

She just said, "He was drunk."

"I've never understood him. If his horse loses, he takes it as a personal affront. As if all the horses and all the jockeys and all the trainers ganged up together, personally, to beat him. He has the filthiest temper I've ever come cross. You wonder, sometimes, what made him like that. He's a self-made man, so nobody knows what sort of a past drives him. It's just such a pity he has to choose racing as a sport. Rather than yachting or motor-racing, or even golf. It was bad luck, your mother meeting him."

Tessa sat in silence, white as the moonlight. The ice-maiden, Tom thought. He talked to cover up the strange happening which he didn't understand and which Tessa was obviously not going to explain. There was no way having her in his warm car after the party was going to develop into anything but a lift home. Large areas of Tessa were prohibited. Damn and blast Maurice, whatever he had or hadn't done. And Tom was prepared to believe what Maurice had said.

Tessa could not sleep. She blocked out the Maurice thing, wondering if she had, indeed, been hysterical. She had certainly been frightened. Terrified. That was no figment of her imagination. But it disgusted her, that Maurice had the power to frighten her. She would not think of it. She had wanted to think about Tom, but now, after that, she had sensed his doubt. It was spoilt.

The stable yard was quiet, a half moon shining serenely over the big chestnut trees by the field gate. She went to Buffoon's box and let herself in. He was lying down, with Lucky, and neither of them got up, but turned their heads and made welcome snuffling noises. Tessa sat down by Buffoon's head and laid her cheek against his.

"What they say, Buffy. It's rubbish. Even Tom."

As always, what she didn't want to know she blotted out. Being with Buffoon reminded her of what really mattered. Buffoon. She had to believe, whatever they all said. If you didn't have faith . . . what was the point? Nobody believed a horse could win the Grand National three times until Red Rum did it. There were no rules in life that couldn't be broken. She knew Buffoon had a great heart. Hearts didn't change. Did they?

She didn't want to ride him in the Grand National, after all (did she?), only in a small race or two.

And then there was the money. Oh, the money! To be an owner, there were all sorts of unseen expenses before you even started, and when you were an owner there were bills for keep, for shoes, for the vet, for the jockey, for entry fees, for travel in the horsebox. . . Peter, so far, keeping his head down, only docked her pay for the cost of Buffoon's feed, bedding and shoes. Buffoon was still, officially, Tessa's hack, a plaything. Not a racehorse. Just a livery. But if he were to race. . .

"You can have all my money," her mother said.

But what money her mother had was Peter's. She hadn't a penny from Maurice. Never a great one for housekeeping, she worked in the stable rather than in the house and rode work every morning, for which Peter paid her the going rate. Tessa would accept that, fair enough, if her mother didn't want it.

"You're mad, of course," Sarah said to Tessa, knowing only too well her ambitions and agonies. "Tell your mother to divorce Morrison and get a huge settlement. Half of Goldlands, for a start. Then you can keep a racehorse."

"Maurice won't let her divorce him, will he? And lose all that money? His lawyers are all the tops. She can't be bothered with it."

"You've just got to get the rides then, no other way. Three a week at least."

Sarah was the only one now who humoured Tessa's desires. She didn't see – money apart – why Tessa shouldn't ride Buffoon in a little no-hopers race at a far-flung course, just for the joy of it. Or otherwise. She only said it was an awful lot of money for just a fun ride or two. On an old has-been nag.

"But start riding!"

And as the season got under way, Tessa did manage to get some rides. She had shown she had the talent, and she did not make mistakes, her steely determination and intelligence in reading how the race was progressing standing her in good stead. What she might lose in finishing strength she made up for in intelligent strategy. And horses went kindly for her. She got a reputation for handling the funny ones, not what she really wanted. But a ride was another packet towards Buffoon's costs.

She saw Tom at the races. He was too busy now to think about girls. He always had a word for her and she knew that her friendship with the top jockey stood her in good stead. Sometimes she rode in races with him but he was usually well ahead or behind, waiting to pounce. But just sometimes they

310

rode knee to knee, and Tom would give her a wink and they would have a chat. Tessa usually didn't have enough breath to do anything but nod her head in answer, but Tom was always cruising.

Once he said to her, "That horse you're riding, take him on now. Don't hang around. He likes to be in front and he stays for ever."

The trainer had told her to stay up close but not go on until the last bend. She decided to take Tom's advice and go for it. Tom came with her, passed her at one point, riding hard now, head down, no time for chat, but Tessa knew her job with this trainer was on the line now and rode like a demon. As Tom promised, her horse's dour stamina prevailed and Tom's horse, for all Tom's riding, fell tamely away. Tessa won. It was thanks to Tom, but she took the credit from the surprised trainer.

The ten per cent prize money was a bonus. Tessa scraped and saved every penny and by the end of the season had enough to register herself as an owner and put Buffoon officially into training with Peter. Peter said he wouldn't charge her any more than Buffoon's expenses. Perhaps after one or possibly two races she would realize she was on a hiding to nothing. She rode Buffoon at exercise with the string and galloped him with Gamekeeper and Cantata, and he had a job to keep up, finishing last of the three by several lengths. Tessa tried not to show disappointment. Peter said it was good, better than he expected.

Riding back home beside Sarah on Gamekeeper, Tessa tried to be positive.

"It wasn't bad for first time."

"No. But don't kid yourself, Tessa. Put him in a race and you'll see. You can always pull him up, after all. He's yours to do as you like with, that's your bonus."

They all knew Buffoon only got anywhere in races over three miles, for he hadn't the speed to go with the two-mile specialists. He won by wearing down the opposition, by his stamina and heart, not by his speed.

Tessa decided to ask Peter to put him in a suitable race. She had to know. Peter scratched around and found a race at Huntingdon.

"Easy course, no hills, he just has to keep on going."

So this was the day that Tessa had waited for. She was so excited she could not eat nor sleep but, with her caravan to herself, nobody saw. She was sick when she got up. It was April, but cold and sharp with intermittent showers. Jimmy came as "lad", curious to see the outcome, and Tessa shivered beside him in the cab as the lorry sped along the M4. Peter and Jimmy were talking over her head about getting a travelling head lad for the next season. The stable was expanding and Peter had visions of going to the races in a car with Myra beside him like a proper trainer. Not many trainers drove their own lorries.

"We're getting somewhere slowly," he said with satisfaction. He was a markedly happier man since Myra's arrival on the scene.

"Yes. And when Tessa here wins the Grand National on her red elephant we'll really be in the money," Jimmy said.

"Of course," Peter said gravely.

Tessa bit her lip, trying not to cry. She felt terrible! What she had looked forward to all her life (it seemed) was now hurting unbearably. But she knew, when she was up on her darling Buffoon, she would not care what everyone said. It was between the two of them and he would not let her down.

They meant it kindly, Peter and Jimmy, trying to diffuse the tension that had turned Tessa into a zombie, but with no response they went back to talking about future plans.

There was plenty of gossip round the paddock when Buffoon was led in. Tessa knew all the staring was on her and her great ugly horse. There were a few titters but she didn't hear them. She closed herself completely into what she was going to do. Jimmy gave her the leg-up and patted her knee affectionately.

"Great girl, Tess. Enjoy it."

She didn't see him shake his head as she rode away. Peter shrugged and smiled.

"What a kid! Whatever will become of her? She wants so much."

But now she was up on Buffoon with the green course opening up before her for the canter to the start Tessa felt herself come alive again. All her white fear dissolved into a paean of delight for being on her horse, on a racecourse. At last! This had been her dream for ever and now it was

313

happening! She held the connecting reins, feeling the old strength flowing back into her, seeing the great shoulders moving like machinery beneath the arch of her legs. He remembered. She could feel his pleasure too. She wanted to shout and sing. But jockeys didn't do that.

They walked round at the start and the other jockeys made rude but kindly comments to her which was part of the act. Everyone knew she was now the owner of the "red elephant" and no doubt pitied her, but there was no malice, only surprise. (She was a *girl*, after all.) He had been a good horse once, a long time ago. They could hardly remember. Horses came and went in this game.

They went off, not fast, and Tessa lobbed along at the back, bursting with pride and joy. He felt so marvellous! Not narrow and squitty like some, not mean, not stupid, not faint-hearted . . . she had learned to know horses' characters since she had ridden so many. Now she was on a good one, *her* horse.

He jumped cleanly, judging his own take-off, very sensible. Tessa kept him out of trouble. There were twelve in the field and they lobbed along in a bunch, nobody hurrying because there was so far to go. Tessa wondered at one point whether she should go on, but thought it too risky. They had no idea whether his old stamina was still there. Keep with the bunch. Keep in touch.

But as the race opened up and the pace increased she found she couldn't keep in touch. Buffoon felt as if he was galloping his heart out, but he seemed to be going nowhere. One by one the other horses went on until she was last in the field. Buffoon didn't seem distressed, quite happy to keep on going, but the others were into the straight while she was still coming round the last bend. Into the dodgy penultimate fence, and as he landed the winner was going past the post and the stands were full of cheering punters. Hardly any of them saw Buffoon come home.

She had done what she wanted, ridden him in a race, but her spirits were very low on the journey home. Last of all, nothing behind her.

"He went well," Peter said.

"Real old trouper. Jumped a treat," Jimmy said.

She knew they were trying to cheer her up. Knew they were satisfied that their warnings had proved true. Buffoon was a has-been.

"He needed the race," Peter said. "We'll find him another before the ground gets too hard."

They found him another, and he was second last. The bookmakers put him in at a hundred-to-one.

"There," Peter said. "Save your money, Tessa. He can be the stable hack. There'll always be a place for him in the yard."

Tessa didn't say anything, and Peter knew to keep his mouth shut for the rest of the journey home.

315

10

"It's the Grand National you're aiming for?"

$\mathcal{T}$essa did not give up. When all the horses in the yard went off for their summer holidays or out into the field to wind down and get fat on summer grass, Buffoon was kept stabled and ridden out every day. He went out in the field for a few hours in the afternoon or evening but, of them all, he was the only one kept fit and in work. Everyone knew that Tessa intended to race him again in the autumn.

"Maybe it's just because she enjoys riding him in races," they said. "After all, quite a few owners race no-hopers just for the ride. To enjoy."

But Sarah said, "She wants to win."

Tessa didn't say anything.

In spite of her disappointment (and she told herself she was stupid, because the horse's jumping and attitude had been fine; only his lack of speed let him down) Tessa still loved riding Buffoon above all else. Just to be on his back across the downs was to know real happiness. The races had been great too, if only she could have contained her stupid ambition. But her stupid ambition persisted.

"If I expect nothing, I won't be disappointed next time," she told herself.

Expect nothing.

Perversely, expecting nothing, in her first race of the season she came eighth out of twelve runners.

Four behind them!

She rode back beside Tom on San Lucar, who had won by twelve lengths. Neither Tom nor the horse were the slightest out of puff. Buffoon was fine, but Tessa felt badly out of race condition.

"That wasn't a bad run," Tom said, obviously surprised.

"I've been riding him all the summer."

Tessa hadn't seen Tom since last season. He had been back with his friends in America for the summer. He was tanned and super-fit and Tessa was surprised by her own excitement at seeing him again.

San Lucar looked fantastic. He exuded class, and was as beautiful as dear Buffoon was plain. He had large, kind eyes and the air of a star about the way he held his head and pointed his toes. Tessa could not help remarking on it.

Tom gave the horse an affectionate pat.

"Yes, he's a great lad. Pity we can't say the same of his owner."

"Is he here?"

In her fierce concentration on the job in hand, Tessa had not looked around her in the paddock.

"Yes, didn't you see him?"

"No!"

"He saw you." Tom laughed. "I think he was wearing his

317

bullet-proof vest, but he was keeping a good eye on you."

"I thought you didn't ride for him any more?"

"No. In principle I don't. But I love this horse. He's had plenty of leg trouble, more's the pity, but Raleigh's got him just right at the moment."

"You might get a smile from Maurice, winning by that distance! I'll keep out of his way."

All the same she couldn't help a glance over to the winning enclosure as she unsaddled Buffoon. Maurice was, indeed, smiling (no doubt having won a packet with his bets), but he was the same iron-cold customer – not a pat for his magnificent horse nor a word for his lad. Tessa could not help a shiver going through her, seeing him, remembering his grip on her arm, her terror. There was a streak of madness in Maurice. His hair was greying now, and lines of discontent merged into lines of age on his sour face. Raleigh was listening to his instructions with a non-committal expression, saying nothing. He patted San Lucar lovingly, no doubt proud of getting the horse that was prone to injury in such good shape.

San Lucar ran again a week later. Once more he won easily but was reported to have heat in his near tendon after the race. Raleigh instructed him to be rested. The grapevine had it that Morrison insisted he race again in a big race two weeks later. When Raleigh resisted, they had words and Maurice took San Lucar to another trainer. The new trainer entered him for the race and Tom was booked to ride him.

Tom, hating the whole situation, accepted the ride so that

he could pull San Lucar up at the first hint of unsoundness.

Tessa was at the same racecourse with Cantata when San Lucar ran. Peter and Sarah were with her, but Myra had declined to come, knowing Maurice would be there. Tessa rode in the first, coming third on Cantata. She changed and went out to see how things turned out in the big race. Maurice's altercation with Raleigh had been well publicized, and the big crowd was intrigued to see how the day would turn out. They were all on Raleigh's side, knowing that his decision not to run was the right one. Tessa heard the mutterings on all sides.

"Criminal to treat such a good horse like this."

"The man doesn't deserve to own a horse like San Lucar."

Tom listened, poker-faced, to Maurice's instructions. The new trainer was clearly uneasy, saying nothing, probably wishing he hadn't got himself into this predicament. He legged Tom up and watched the horse stride away.

Peter, watching with Tessa, shook his head.

"I'm not a betting man, but I reckon it's odds on that Tom will pull up before he reaches the winning post."

He was right. San Lucar, sailing along in the lead as he took off for the penultimate fence, pecked slightly on landing, recovered, ran on for twenty yards and was sharply pulled up. Tom slipped out of the saddle as the rest of the field pounded past. He came home leading San Lucar, and the horse was clearly lame. The crowd buzzed with excitement and indignation. As Maurice went out with his clearly embarrassed trainer to meet him, he was greeted by several boos.

"At least the horse will get his rest now," Peter said.

He did, but in a form that made Maurice the most hated man in racing. He had San Lucar put down.

Tessa heard the news from Tom. He drove into the yard two days later, on his way home from a meeting, to tell them the news.

"I found out from the lad at his new yard. He was in tears when he told me. Apparently Maurice took the horse away yesterday, said the driver was taking him to some vet in Newmarket, on his instructions. They thought it strange and when the horse didn't come back they rang up the transport firm and were told the horse had gone to the knacker's. It was too late then to do anything about it. The poor old lad had gone."

Tom was nearly in tears himself. Tessa was stunned. But hardly surprised, knowing how Maurice used his racing to make money. A lame horse was an expense with no guarantee of being of any further use.

"But he could have sold him, given him away! Thousands of people would have given him a good home, to recuperate. They loved him!"

"Yeah, I would have put up a thousand or two myself to have saved him from that," Tom said. "The man's a real bastard. I shall never ride for him again."

He went disconsolately across to Buffoon's box and rested his arms on the half-door.

"I sometimes wonder about this game, when things like that happen. To get the insurance money! No doubt some crook vet signed a certificate for him."

"It's not racing. It's people," Tessa said.

"Yes. It wasn't racing that gave your old boy grief, was it? Just some more sick people."

"He loves racing. You can tell, from the feel of him."

"Lukey loved it too. Even when it hurt. I had a job to pull him up. I know now that if I hadn't pulled up he'd have run on and won. And still be alive now."

Buffoon looked round at them from his attention to his haynet. His eyes were large and clear, kind as poor San Lucar's. Tessa remembered how the light went out of God Almighty's eyes, and Wisbey wept. But it happened to people too, all the time. Sarah said you mustn't get it out of proportion. Life was a toss-up for both people and animals. Children died too. Nature was the cruellest of the lot.

"He ran well last time out," Tom said. "You going to prove us all wrong?"

"Yes."

"That's another cert in racing. The unpredictable."

"Buffoon running well isn't unpredictable to me."

"No?" Tom laughed. "Knowing you, it's the Grand National you're aiming for. No less."

"How did you guess?" Tessa tried to sound sarcastic, but was useless at covering up her feelings.

Her private dream. Never to be put into so many words.

But Tom had. She could not answer.

As if in support, Buffoon turned round and came to her, pressing his soft nose against her hand. Tom patted his neck.

"He's a great horse, all the same. If anyone can do it, you two can."

And he smiled at her and, for his faith, Tessa wanted to throw her arms round him and kiss him. But she didn't know how, and kissed Buffoon instead.

That season, Tessa rode Buffoon in eight races. In the sixth race he was second and in the eighth race he was the winner. Tessa was ecstatic and the stable no less so. Buffoon was twelve years old, retirement time. Tessa was now twenty and grown-up, but to the stable she was still their wild child.

"You've done it, Tess, against all the odds," Peter said.

"My girl!" Myra beamed.

"Thank God we can all relax now," Wisbey said.

Sarah said nothing, guessing.

And Buffoon was put out into the field with Lucky and the two of them went bucking and cavorting away like two-year-olds before falling to graze on the fresh tendrils of the spring grass.

11

The Course

Tessa was dreaming. The dream terrified her, and woke her up. Time after time. In her dream she was facing a horse at a big hedge, and the horse jumped, and when they were in mid-air she saw that there was no landing, only space. And they started to plunge down, and there was nothing below, and she screamed and woke herself up.

She didn't tell anyone. There was no one to hear her. The plan was in her head and would not be dislodged, and it was no good to complain that it was giving her nightmares. It was giving everyone nightmares.

Jimmy said, "It's not as if the horse isn't capable of getting round, and keeping her safe. Let her be."

He was the only one so optimistic.

Peter said his reputation was on the line, to enter such an old horse with a girl riding.

"He'll be fourteen. Only one horse has won at thirteen, none at fourteen. It's unprofessional. What amateurs do, to have a day out."

"The Grand National is different from other races, you know that. It's for characters. It's not the Gold Cup."

"He might get killed, then you'll be sorry," Wisbey said.

"Thank you," said Tessa.

She knew that. It's what the nightmare hung on.

"Oh my God!" screamed Myra, "You'll break your neck!"

"It's a pretty dumb idea," said Sarah, "but I can see that you want to do it. It's what you are." Tessa made her feel old.

It certainly gave them something to think about. They all thought: if Tessa wasn't around, life would be much duller.

Peter decided to let fate decide, as it so often did with racehorses. Buffoon missed two months' racing with an infection in the sole of his foot, through picking up a rusty nail, but Tessa kept getting rides by tirelessly badgering people and making sure she rode every horse to the very best of her ability, however untalented it might be. Most people she rode for asked her again, although she rarely got "good" rides. There were too many other jockeys after the good ones. But her expertise and, importantly, her strength improved all the time, and by the time Buffoon got back into racing in January she found herself with far more confidence and skill in the saddle.

January was the first date for entering the Grand National, and Peter agreed to enter Buffoon. It cost a hundred pounds. If they kept his name on the list, it would take three more payments and cost nearly a thousand by the time the race was run. Myra said she would sell her engagement ring, and her wedding ring if need be. She still kept saying Tessa would kill herself but the excitement was too much for her to ignore.

Sometimes Tessa thought, too, that she was mad. When she talked to Buffoon in his box during the cold winter nights she told him she was sorry that he had to belong to a madwoman, who was going to make him work so hard for his living when he could be a happy hack. She put her cold hands under his rugs to warm them on his shining hide, and laid her head against his neck.

"But you like it, I know you do. I can feel it. You feel so marvellous."

Lucky pushed in for attention, and fell to nibbling at her pockets.

"We'll make sure you aren't spirited away this time too. Nothing will go wrong this time."

Maurice was quiet these days. Word had it that he was in financial trouble. Goldlands was up for sale. He had no more horses with Raleigh, and only two with the trainer who took San Lucar. One of these was a dour four-miler who was well-fancied for the Grand National. He asked Tom to ride it, but Tom refused. Then the horse injured a tendon and was out for the season.

Tom was offered the ride on a horse called Marimba who was at the top of the betting for the Grand National. Raleigh had no runners and Tom accepted the ride. Marimba was a stout-hearted dark bay, almost black, with a great jumping record but no certainty to last the long trip. But general opinion was that his class would see him through. He was a great battler.

Sometimes Tessa dreamt that Tom would ride Buffoon if she asked him. Buffoon would get a better ride, stand a better

325

chance, be safer in Tom's hands. But she knew the invitation would be an embarrassment for Tom and he would be bound to refuse, the horse being so old and unconsidered. This knowledge was a relief for she wanted the ride so badly on her own dear horse – the two of them together. . . The thought of it made her blood tingle, even two months away.

The bookies had Buffoon in at a hundred-to-one. He was nearly at the bottom of the handicap. Marimba was on top weight.

As the April day came nearer, Tessa's ambition did not waver. Myra sold her engagement ring and Peter entered Buffoon at the second and third stages, which just left the final commitment. Peter was encouraged by Buffoon's fitness, and his running in two preparatory races in each of which he was third.

"He's a great jumper, you can't ask for more. It's not such a crazy idea, perhaps."

Buffoon had never fallen in his life.

The press noticed this, and loved the story. Tessa was hassled whenever she went out in public, and journalists kept calling at Sparrows Wyck. Tessa got tired of repeating the same thing over and over again in interviews, and posing for photographs.

Buffoon's price rose to fifty-to-one.

Sarah said it was what she called housewives' betting, because of the story, nothing to do with the horse's chance.

"He's still a hundred-to-one, Tessa. Don't get excited. The horses that win are nine and ten years old. No horse has ever won at his age. With a girl on top."

"She's only in it for the ride. Don't tell me she's thinking of winning!" Peter said.

Tessa saw Jimmy and Sarah exchange glances. They didn't say anything. Tessa felt sick, thinking about it. And there were still three weeks to go!

Tessa had offers for Buffoon, from rich idiots wanting to be in on a good story. Grand National horses often changed hands in the weeks before the race, because there was always a pool of rich and optimistic (and crazy) people who wanted the thrill of owning a National horse. The week before the race the press had a new story:

"Morrison-Pleydell buys Marimba!"

In the tack-room they all goggled at the news as Sarah spread out the *Racing Post*.

"He must be desperate!"

"Whatever did he pay? Must have been a fortune."

"I wonder if he's bought Tom Bryant as well?" Jimmy said.

"Tom swore he'd never ride for him again."

"Yeah, but there's no other rides going now, unless he jocks someone off."

"He wouldn't do that, not Tom."

"He'll be asked, I bet."

"Tessa'll ask him, won't you, Tess?" jeered Wisbey. "I bet he'd do it for you."

"I think the deal would have included Tom, somehow," Sarah said. "It's too late to find another jockey now."

It was confirmed later that Tom Bryant was still Marimba's

jockey. On the day they were all starting to prepare for driving up to the Aintree meeting, Tom Bryant called in at the stable to talk to Tessa.

"To see that it's all OK with you," he said. "Wish you luck and all that. It might be busy on Saturday and no time to say all the right things. You feel good about it, I hope? No cold feet?"

"Freezing feet," Tessa said.

"You'll be fine once all the waiting is over. And it's easier for females these days – you're not such a novelty any more. Mind you, you will be if you win."

"You'll be the winner, I dare say. Pity it's for Maurice though."

"Jeez, what a way for it to turn out! The last thing I expected. But I can't change it now. If he starts to give me a bollocking though, for not winning, I reckon I'll pull a knife on him like you did. I'll take one in my boot, in case! Pity – I want to win, but not for that swine."

"The horse will decide it for you."

"Yes. We're useless without the horse. You've got a good one, Tessa. Do it for the thrill – there's nothing quite like it. Keep out of trouble, especially at the first. Follow a good one, or keep clear of the lot. And afterwards, Tess, whatever happens, we'll go to a party together. I'll come looking for you."

Was this her first date? Tessa wondered when he had gone. They would have so much to talk about, one way or the other. A working arrangement, more like. But the warmth of Tom's friendship, his timely visit, steadied her nerves. She felt much more optimistic with Tom's encouragement. He didn't think she was crazy, at least.

She slept in Buffoon's box, as she had done the last ten days. No one was going to pinch Lucky again, or do Buffoon any damage. A good sleeping bag and the thick straw made it perfectly comfortable, with Lucky's heavy breathing in her ear for lullaby and the sight of the moonshine on Buffoon's Roman nose in the bright square of the open top-door to soothe her waking moments. How lucky she was, to have come so far over her rocky path to comparatively smooth going! Sometimes she could not believe her luck, after the despair of her youth. And it was all centred in her dear horse. Without him her life would have been nothing. Nothing to work for, nothing to grieve over, nothing to thrill. Whatever happened in the next few days, there was not one thing she would regret, afterwards. Even if . . . no . . . one did not think of that . . . it was the ultimate, the unthinkable.

They were driving up the day before. Peter was going up in his car with Myra, Jimmy was driving the lorry and Wisbey was coming as lad for Buffoon – his treat. Poor Sarah had to stay in charge at home. Tessa, pressed to go in the car, elected to go in the lorry, with Buffoon. Of course.

"You'll want all the rest you can get," complained Myra.

"I can rest afterwards," Tessa said.

She had scarcely slept for nights past – what difference would it make? She had lost weight and her face was pale and drawn with blue smudges under her eyes. But the eyes against the pallor burned with more fire than ever.

The April weather was typical: cold and windy, with bright sunshine and fierce, short showers. The going was said to be soft, which suited Buffoon. The softer the better. It was raining when the lorry arrived at Aintree.

They pulled into the horsebox entrance, down the lane to the stables, which were familiar this time. Just like the last time, racing was in progress and the place was humming, horses and people coming and going in all directions. Jimmy went off to find Buffoon's box, and Tessa stayed in the warm cab, wondering what on earth she was doing in the place. She was out of her mind!

Jimmy came back with Buffoon's stable number and they unloaded him and led him into the yards. Lucky shuffled along behind as usual, anxious to explore the new quarters. Tessa busied herself feverishly, making Buffoon comfortable. He was excited (remembering last time?) and kept walking to the door to look out, whinnying every now and then as a horse passed.

"We'll walk him out later, when racing's finished, let him have a bite of grass," Jimmy said. "Peter'll be along, and we'll walk the course. Remember what I said before, it doesn't look so bad from the back of a seventeen-hand horse."

The last race was over. A cold silvery light gleamed on the factories across the great, dun abandonment of the Aintree acres. The crowds streamed out from the stands, the litter blew aimlessly on the cold wind. Most of the horses were going and the yards emptied, leaving tomorrow's runners exploring their new boxes or settling down to their haynets. Buffoon was not disturbed, looking for a feed. Lucky had settled to doze, propped on the manger.

Peter turned up, having left Myra in a hotel. They went out to walk the course, not alone, for streams of spectators and interested parties were out to do the same, mostly laughing and having their photos taken against the thick black hedges.

Tessa didn't laugh. It was true how different they were, these fences, from the ordinary racetrack, so strong and forbidding.

"You can take a bit out of the top, but no more," Peter said to her. "But Buffoon knows his stuff. It's the traffic you've got to look out for, not Buffoon's jumping. Keep safe."

They walked round the once. Tomorrow it was twice round. The biggest jumps were five feet high and had ditches six feet wide on the take-off side. One of these was the third jump and Tessa, looking at it, thought that if she survived this one, and the stampede over the two preceding, she would have something to chalk up whatever might happen thereafter. There were forty runners and some of the jumps were none too wide. To get a clear view would be a bonus, let alone elbow room. The famous Bechers Brook looked unexpectedly innocuous on the approach, but the drop behind wasn't nice at all. Some girls were standing against it having their photographs taken. Even with their arms raised above their heads they did not break the skyline of solid spruce-covered wall. But Jimmy said at speed it would be quite different. Buffoon would ping it.

"It's easier on the outside, remember. The drop is less. But the good horses will be on the inside. Follow Tom if you get a chance."

The next jump, narrow and at an angle, was not inviting. This was the famous Foinavon Fence when the whole field had piled up and the winner was the only horse so far behind that he was able to pick his way through the carnage when he got to it and continue on his way. This side of the course was flanked on the outside by a high embankment and a railway siding. Where the railway crossed a canal at the top end, the racecourse abruptly turned left to avoid going into the water.

"The horses used to fall in quite often. But they've built a fence since."

Drab housing shut off further views.

"The trouble with jumps this high," Peter said, "is that you can't see what's on the other side."

"Bodies, you mean?" asked Wisbey.

"Yes. Unless you're in the lead. Then there aren't any."

Peter was trying to find the best ground.

"We'll walk it again tomorrow, when they've tidied it all up. It helps to know, when your horse is getting tired. And navigation – in case you're in front, Tessa." He laughed. "The courses cross up here."

There was an ordinary course inside the grandstand end of the Grand National course that was used for all the other races.

The races that didn't matter, thought Tessa. They could have entered one of those. Having seen the fences she knew now what everyone said was true: she was mad. Yet she had never mistrusted her talent. She was not afraid of riding the fences. She wasn't *afraid*. But she felt . . . there were no words for what she felt. She said nothing.

"Scared?" jeered Wisbey.

They came round the home turn, up to the Chair, the biggest of all the fences, in front of the stands, jumped only on the first circuit, and then up the long, long run in. The sun was sinking behind them. A factory hooter bleated for knocking-off time.

How strange, thought Tessa. Whatever was going to happen?

They went back to the stables. This time tomorrow it would all be over.

Tessa refused to go out with them, for a meal, in spite of all the persuasion. She wanted to be on her own, to be with Buffoon, eat in the lads' canteen, she didn't want to know anyone.

"Leave her," Jimmy said to Peter.

They went off in Peter's car and Tessa went back to Buffoon. She wasn't going to leave him. Not now. Not ever.

12

The Race

The morning dawned cold and wet. Tessa rode out along with all the others, fed and groomed Buffoon and then was only too grateful to be taken under Peter's wing. He arrived in his car and took her off for breakfast in the smart hotel.

"And a rest, Tessa. You can lie about, have a hot bath, drink coffee. Wind down. You should have come back last night."

"It's better now," Tessa said.

Jimmy and Wisbey were at the stables. She could relax, read the papers. Marimba and Tom were still favourite, Buffoon at fifty-to-one. There were a few pieces on her and her old horse, but nothing that she had not read before. She did not want to read it again. But she enjoyed her morning of leisure, sunk into one of the hotel's deep, plushy armchairs with the central heating purring around her and the coffee-pot at her elbow. At least it was better than sweating it out in a sauna like most of her male companions, to get weight off. She was allotted to carry ten stone and only weighed eight. She could eat as many chocolate biscuits as she liked, and would still have to have lead weights inserted in her saddle-cloth to give Buffoon his proper weight.

Peter kept the panicking Myra out of her hair, treated her to a light lunch and then drove her back to the course.

The traffic was solid, the punters streaming in as the rain gave way to fitful sunshine. The excitement was tangible, the crowd exuding an electricity that sparked in every face, the bookmakers shouting, the loudspeaker voice flaring down the wind. In the stables the activity was as frenzied, the same excitement contained in the faces of the travelling lads and the girls who all recognized that the day was special. It wasn't like an ordinary racing day at all. Tessa was not alone in her shell of amazement. Did Buffoon sense it too, looking out over his door with his ears pricked up, the tips almost touching, as horses for the first races were led past? He knew he was going to race. But did he remember where he was? Did he remember the first time over the great fences, the surprise of Bechers, the sharp turn by the canal? Tessa thought he did. Buffoon wasn't stupid.

"But you've got me with you this time."

For better or for worse. Tessa put her arms round his neck and laid her cheek against his.

"We'll make it, Buffy," she whispered. "I don't care what they say."

Maybe it was wishful thinking, but it buoyed her up while the minutes ticked past. Into the weighing room . . . her colours . . . pushed here and there . . . seeing Tom at one point in just his breeches, laughing with a valet. "This way." They looked after her, the only female, patronizing. She didn't care. It was all a dream, until she was outside again in the queue of lean men and the camera lights were flashing and the television boom pushed in her face. "What was she feeling?" She couldn't answer, there being no words. Oh, to be out there on Buffoon's back!

"Oh my God, I don't know how you feel, but I'm knocked up already," Myra muttered to her. "I don't think I can watch this at all."

"Ma, he's the safest horse in the race!"

What a stupid thing to say, tempting fate! Oh Buffy, why am I doing this to you?

A mad face in the crowd, shouting, "Me darling! Go for it, me darling! I've put me shirt on you, and me trousers too!"

Her idiot, drunken father, with his idiot, drunken friends, all waving. Her heart lurched with the old wild, despairing love. Her *father*! No wonder she was such an idiot too, with those inherited genes. . .

"Dad, save it! You're crazy!" She had to laugh.

They disappeared in the crush.

Greevy came up and gripped her hand.

"Best of luck, Tessa! Stay safe! I'm rooting for you."

And two familiar faces leaning over the paddock rail, shouting at her. Shouting? Her staid schoolteachers, Mrs Alston and the Battleaxe! Their faces red, their smart hats awry, they shouted out good wishes.

Tessa's emotions were shattered in all directions. Everyone had gone mad, not only herself. Then Jimmy's hand on her shoulder, hard and purposeful.

"You're a great girl, Tessa. Enjoy it. It won't happen again, it's your chance."

She looked at him, knowing suddenly that it was his teaching and support that had got her where she was. He had always gone along with her dreams. Dear Jimmy. She loved him! He legged her into the saddle.

"I wouldn't mind being in your place now," she said.

He laughed.

Tessa sat high, perched over the bony mountain of Buffoon's withers, seeing the familiar rabbity ears ahead of her twitching to the excitement. This was her place, whatever the surroundings. She was at home. Her horse. A shiver of pure exaltation went through her. Whatever happened, it was worth it. All the heartache . . . and now . . . jostled, whistled at, exclaimed over, they moved forward into the parade.

Wisbey was on the leading-rein, the official lad, excited at the task, to lead Buffoon down the course in the parade before the start. Peter and Myra and Jimmy departed to try and find a good place in the stands and Tessa rode out with all the others. They milled around, getting into parade order, and Tom went past on Marimba. At close quarters the horse looked magnificent, a big, spare animal with a long, elastic stride, very laid back but interested in all the excitement, looking about him with bold, intelligent eyes. Tessa, who told herself she wasn't thinking about winning, did not see how he could be beaten. But then, anything could, and did, happen in the National. Tom didn't see her. He was pale and serious, not laughing any more.

They went down past the stands, interminably, and then the

first horse turned and was away. One by one they all cantered off down to the start.

"It's all yours, matey," Wisbey said as he unclipped the lead-rope. "Best of luck, Tess."

For once he was serious too.

At last!

It was fantastic to be moving, to let the brakes off, alone at last with her horse. The presence of all those thousands of people seemed distant now, of no account. She had no cares, riding her own horse, no one to let down but herself. No one to blame. Only Buffoon and herself, to do what they could.

Milling around at the start, she saw Tom again. She thought of Maurice watching him, having staked everything – what a burden Marimba carried along with the top weight! She wanted Tom to win, but not Maurice. Impossible. Tom was lining up on the inside next to the rail. Tessa got behind him, knowing the good ones were on the inside. She didn't want to be behind no-hopers at the first fence where usually there were fallers. Not to be brought down, that was the priority. At the back, she could move across wherever there was a gap.

That was the plan, but when the tapes went up, it was all such mayhem that her plans were forgotten. A horse barged into her from behind (Buffoon never being the liveliest horse away) and nearly knocked her out of the saddle, and when she got herself balanced again another horse gave her a bang on the other side. Their stirrups clinked together and the other jockey swore at her. Tessa swore back, enjoying it. Buffoon was running straight as a die, at his own pace, and the other horse went on, came to the first fence and disappeared from sight as if shot.

Tessa had time to see, make up her mind and steer clear, pulling Buffoon across so that he was nicely sighted. He flew over the big fence easily. Tessa saw three horses down, and the rest of the field a great wedge of flying tails and butterfly silks fluttering ahead of her. The speed was crazy. Buffoon was last by the look of it, so she took him back to the inside to save ground. Now she could see nothing of the next jump, only hope and pray. She should have been on the outside but it was too late now.

There was nothing ahead of her but backs and buttocks, a glimpse of the high iron gateways shutting off the Melling road, of giant hoardings. Somewhere ahead five foot of solid thorn hedge was lying in wait – it must be soon!

The horse ahead of them changed shape, launching skywards. Tessa, ready for it, felt Buffoon's momentary check of surprise, the quick, self-preserving extra stride, and then they were airborne, magnificently, Buffoon's powerful quarters catapulting them over the obstacle with startled generosity. The air was filled with the crashing of twigs and expletives and Tessa suddenly saw the whole field ahead of her, charging on like cavalry, the course running like a green river into the far, far distance. Buffoon landed with a surprised grunt, and she drove him on, imbued now with the desire to keep in touch.

"Not too far behind, you old beggar, Buffy. This is important!"

He cocked an ear. The third jump, Tessa remembered, was nasty with a ditch in front like an elephant trap. She saw it coming, sat into Buffoon with all her strength, driving with back and legs, heard the clonking and crashing of the horses in front and saw the backsides flying, white breeches and swirling tails. A jockey rolled under Buffoon's feet but Buffoon sidestepped to miss him, nearly pitching Tessa off over his shoulder. . . She grabbed his unplaited mane, saw the jockey momentarily curled up like a hedgehog beneath her, rolling away under the rail. And then it was on to the next.

Two loose horses now ran alongside, which was not good. She could not move out now if she wanted, and was afraid they might cross in front of her. She waved her whip and shouted at the nearest, and it veered away, saw the jump ahead and pricked its ears. It sailed over and Buffoon went with it, stride for stride. Who needs a rider? Tessa wondered.

Buffoon had got the measure of the big fences now. There were a lot of horses ahead of them but quite a lot of disaster behind, and still the loose horses alongside. Shut in, Tessa knew she was going to have to ride Bechers on the inside, whether she liked it or not. But her confidence was growing with every stride, and when the famous jump came Buffoon met it on a perfect stride and soared over. Landing seemed to last for ever with the big drop, but Buffoon got it right, landed safely and gathered his legs together neatly with just a snort of surprise to show his feelings. The cold wind knifed through Tessa's sweaty silks and for a moment in the air she felt as if she was out of the race, in another world altogether, on wings. Her heart was flying. The feeling of bliss laced with genuine fear was a cocktail she had never experienced – she could think of no other circumstances that could induce it.

"Oh Buffy!" she shouted at him. "You are wonderful."

Flecks of foam from his mouth and dollops of wet mud sprayed her face. She had to wipe her goggles on her sleeve to see the next jump, the narrow one before the Canal turn. It was at an angle, nasty, but luckily her loose horse companions went veering out to the right, straight on and jumped on the far side, so she was able to steer nicely round on the inside and keep in tight for the Canal turn. By her inside tactics she was keeping quite well up, and when the first horses went into the Canal turn she got a good view of Tom in the lead, jumping and turning at the same time so that his great horse made two lengths on the ones beside him, making almost a right-angle in mid-air. Strength and balance . . . Tom was a great rider. When Tessa came to the same spot Buffoon jumped on the inside but went much wider than Marimba, galloping out into wide open spaces but, fortunately, not taking anyone with him.

Tessa heaved him round, swearing at her incompetence. Buffoon went charging off on the new course, seeing his companions ahead of him, and went into Valentines in a smother of flying spruce, through one of the kicked-out gaps. There was a strong smell of resinous pine joined with the smell of steaming horse and wet grass, and more mud spattered her goggles. Tessa felt as if her arms were being pulled out, dishevelled and not much in control. The jumps were coming up fast and all she could do was steer and hope for the best, tired already and disillusioned as to her talent. It all seemed a great muddle with herself surviving more than dictating. But at least she was still there! Greater jockeys than herself had come to grief. But Tom on Marimba was miles ahead.

Buffoon seemed happy enough, loping along in his usual not very assertive way, no doubt wondering when the winning post was coming up. In the lull after the twelfth jump, when there was a long way to go without obstacles, Tessa tried to gather herself together and take a breather. They weren't even halfway yet and she felt she had had a hard day. And the next jump was the enormous Chair in front of the stands where Jimmy and Peter would be watching along with thousands of other people. In the flesh.

But she was still there, and there were horses behind her, and loose horses both behind and in front, and Buffoon felt full of running. And interested. He could hear the start of the cheering from the stands as the first horses rounded the long bend and came into the straight, and his big ears pricked up and Tessa told him he was a good boy and there were miles to go yet. And as he settled into his long stride into the straight she felt that they were catching up, although she had been sitting quite still on him. The ground was certainly heavy and no doubt the pace was not really fast, but it suited Buffoon more than some of the more skittish competitors. She could see the Chair now and hear the roar of the crowd. The big jump was narrow but by the time she got to it the leading horses were over and heading for the water jump. She had all the room in the world. Buffoon judged his stride, lengthened without her help and flew over as if it were a mere hurdle, so big that she was almost dislodged. But no, the landing was balanced and smooth. With the great roar of the crowd in her ears she went as if on wings to the lovely easy water jump, soared over it and was away round the turn and out into the country again. She could feel Buffoon's surprise, looking for the stable, but she legged him sharply towards the inside rail. The ant-like figures of the lads whose horses were galloping loose were bobbing about the side of the course in an effort to catch them. But not Wisbey! She would make Wisbey eat his scornful words! Perhaps even now he was cheering her on.

He was. Tears streamed down his cheeks.

"Keep it up, Tess! You're going a bomb! Buffoon, you old beggar! Come on, Tess, come on, you old sod!"

Amongst the other lads he bobbed about like a jerking puppet. Some of the others were shouting with him, others were blaspheming, a girl was crying. Several had run out to try and catch their loose horses.

Down on the rails Declan and his friends were shouting hoarsely. Declan was telling everyone within a ten-metre radius that it was his girl, his horse, the horse he had bred out of his old blind mare Shiner, God rest her soul, and his own little girl on top – no, not Shiner – on top of Buffoon that great leggy chestnut that looked like a cross between a giraffe and an elephant . . . the trouble I had to raise him and the mare wouldn't suckle him . . . and the wife left me and took my little girl with her and they left me all alone and the horses to raise. . . "Poor Declan!" his friends declared. "And all me savings is on me little girl, me last hundred pounds, and she's going for Bechers a second time, God bless her. . . !" He swayed and wept and the crowd told him he was a daft old codger and yelled for Buffoon.

In the stands Mrs Alston said to the Battleaxe, "Is that our Tessa, still there? All those horses look the same to me, but her horse is red, and it looks like a girl, the one at the back. . . ?"

"Yes, I think so. The big horse and the little jockey. In yellow."

"It's not a girl's thing! So rough!"

"Yes, but isn't it exciting!" The Battleaxe's nose gleamed red in a weak burst of sunshine. "Such a change from the academic life!"

"Yes, you could say that. Amazing. I find it quite amazing."

Several rows higher up Myra was sobbing too hard to see anything through her shaking binoculars. Peter was trying to fend her off, keeping his gaze steady on the large TV screen of the front runners. But Tessa wasn't there and he resorted to the binoculars again.

"She's not out of touch," Jimmy said. "Not with Buffoon. He'll plug on – unless the age tells."

"There's no knowing."

He spoke calmly, but he was trembling. He had never thought to have a horse in this race again, ever. And now he had one, against his better instincts, it was going better than he had ever supposed possible. It was terrible what it did to the nerves. Even Jimmy, desperate for a cigarette but unable to roll one, was shivering beside him.

And Maurice, seeing the strength of his horse up in front, running strongly, felt all the old optimism of his early days swelling triumphantly in his breast. This was what it was all about, to have the best, to be on a winner, the credit account about to leap once more into the black, the accolades to fall about his shoulders. People respected winners. His good horses gave him respect, admiration, the access to important people. He paid good money for them. He expected them to return the favour. He breathed heavily, willing his winner on.

His trainer fidgeted uncertainly at his side, full of hope, mixed with dread. Morrison was a terrible man to train for, he had never met the like. But to have a horse like that in his stables – Marimba! It was an opportunity that only came once in a lifetime, not to be turned down by a struggling optimist like himself. Marimba could put him on the map. It was worth putting up with a little unpleasantness at times for that. It was an honour to have to do with a horse like Marimba. And the luck of the gods that Bryant had agreed to stay with him. The little man, full of clashing uncertainties, sighed with joy to see how his horse jumped, so bold and fluent! What a horse! A

345

worthy favourite. If he lasted out he was a sure winner. And with Bryant on top everything was in his favour.

The trainer was white as a sheet, and beads of sweat stood out on his forehead.

It was all different now, somehow, on the second circuit. All the no-hopers had gone. Tessa was in with the cream, the horses which won races. Would win this one. Her sense of panic had settled now to grim determination. To make a mistake now would be far more painful than it might have been earlier. It all mattered now, when it had started as a wild and unlikely adventure. To have lasted so far . . . it wasn't just a fun ride out, how she had pretended. Now she was in with a chance to prove herself and the horse felt great beneath her, as well as he had ever felt, even with those big exhausting jumps behind him. If only she was going to last as long as him! Her muscles were aching already and she was out of breath, not with panic but with the beginnings of exhaustion. All the nights without sleeping were catching up on her. But I *am* strong, she told herself. I will do it. She wanted to do it for Tom.

Marimba was still in front. The front runners had strung out and by the time they came to Bechers again she was definitely catching up. There were only about a dozen horses ahead and of these, two refused and one fell. The nearest refuser turned in Tessa's direction to run across, saw her coming and hesitated in its stride. Tessa had a glimpse of its glazed eye and blood-filled nostril and its jockey's face buried right up in its mane between its ears. Her foot caught the horse's shoulder as she took off, knocking Buffoon slightly off balance, so this time as she flew through the air she had a heart-stopping doubt as to whether she would still be poised over the saddle at the bottom of the long plunge down, or over Buffoon's ears instead. The view down was not comforting either, heads rolling below and the flash of upturned hooves flailing just where they wanted to go. Buffoon gave a convulsive paddle behind and landed a couple of inches clear of the faller. It was touch and go for Tessa, staying aboard, but sheer willpower prevailed. Buffoon staggered up the drop and grunted indignantly as he gathered himself together.

Two Bechers behind her! Tessa felt the excitement knotting in her stomach as two more horses in front ran wide at the Canal turn. This time she was ready for the sharp angle and Buffoon obeyed her strong pressure to go left – or perhaps he remembered it from last time, for they made up two or three lengths on the horses in front. As they headed for Valentines a grey horse came alongside her and its jockey said, "You're going great guns, lady. Keep it up."

The grey horse refused and its rider flew over Valentines alone. Tessa steered for a gap as the fence was much dishevelled and when she looked up she found that she was on the tail now of the only horses in the race, six of them led by Marimba. Marimba was swinging along, but Tessa remembered that he had top weight, nearly two stone more than Buffoon. It was a good horse that could carry that and find the strength to win if it came to a battle after the last. The excitement of the way things were turning out made Tessa's head reel. Her progress was incredible. She was light-headed and felt like a drunk with her achievement – the Chair and two Bechers behind her, and now only easy jumps ahead and the company of fast-tiring horses. She knew Buffoon's stamina was his forte, not his speed, but the deep going had carved up most of the brave horses while Buffoon was plugging away in his element. He was probably wondering if he could get his tea the next time round.

But he was *old*, they said. He was fourteen. It was impossible for a horse as old as Buffoon to win. It never happened. Nor a girl. No, I'm not going to win, she told herself. Keep calm. Sit still. Conserve your strength.

They were going round the long, long jumpless bend into the straight. Two more jumps and then, after that, the merciless run-in where fortunes often changed, right up to the winning post. She was only some five or so lengths off Marimba, and alongside three others. Their jockeys were looking at her and saying, "God almighty, what are you doing here?"

She grinned. She laughed. She prayed. It wasn't her. It was Buffoon. She only had to sit there. Tom looked round, saw her, and nearly fell off. He looked round a second time to make sure.

"Go on, gel. Make history," said one of the jockeys.

Now she was legging Buffoon along, working with all the

348

shreds of her remaining strength to hold him together, make him know it mattered. He pulled out some more and went up to Marimba. There were just the two of them now, going to the last jump. I've got to beat him, Tessa thought, beat Tom and beat Maurice. *Beat Maurice!* But Tom's riding could get his horse there, even with his weight. She was just a mess on poor Buffoon, arms and legs pumping to little avail. As if it mattered, when he swung along doing his own thing . . . he did not seem in any way distressed, his ungainly stride reaching over the soaked turf, his mothy tail floating out behind. He went to reach long for the last jump, thought better of it and put a quick one in, and jumped neatly. Marimba hit it hard and rolled in his stride, losing a couple of lengths. The roar of the crowd was like the sea closing over her.

The commentator's voice was hysterical:

"This is the most amazing race! It's Crisp and Red Rum all over again! The top weight and the outsider! Brave, brave Marimba! And *fourteen-year-old* Buffoon! Unbelievable! And a girl – a *girl* —"

As if the rider were an ostrich, or a monkey. A *girl*!

Tessa felt that she was going down, drowning, as Buffoon plugged on to the post. He was doing it all without her help now for all her bones had turned to jelly. Marimba, one of the bravest, was making a renewed challenge, with a rider who was the best on the field – a rider who had completely forgotten any sympathy for the girl ahead of him. Tom wanted the Grand National as badly as Tessa. Didn't every jockey? At the end it was the only thing, to ride one's heart out for the unforgiving red disc that marked the winning post so far, far away. The horse reeled, the jockey's lungs were bursting, the crowd screamed. Inch by inch Marimba crept back to Buffoon, Tom holding him together, asking him, but never using his whip because he knew the horse was giving his all. The horse was a marvel. The crowd adored his courage.

But Buffoon, the great ugly *old* horse, was more than a marvel – he was a miracle. His ungainly legs, looking twice as long as neat Marimba's, gangled past the elbow-bend of the notorious run-in and his rabbit's ears twitched up to the amazing noise that filled the sky. He ran straight as a die. "Looking for Lucky. Looking for his tea," Wisbey said afterwards. "What is this?" he was asking Tessa. "What do you want of me? Isn't this enough?" But the girl's will was boring through his fame, asking, *asking* . . . he was aware of it, the crazy demand that emanated from the rolling body on top: "*Go on! Go on!*" That constant in his life, the flimsy girl, wanted it more than she had ever wanted anything, he knew it. He obliged. He kept on, as asked, and Marimba came to his girth, to his neck . . . the crowd was in hysterics, shrieking, shrieking, and the two horses went past the post locked together. Save that Buffoon's long ugly nose was in front by a head and everybody knew it.

Tom knew it.

Tessa didn't.

As the horses felt the messages from above fade and dropped into an exhausted canter side by side, Tom put his arm out and hugged Tessa, all but bringing her off.

"You've done it. You won!"

"*You* won!"

"No. It's a photo, but you got it!"

Tessa didn't believe it. But she was past thinking anything, just a blob of exhaustion, trying not to fall off. They pulled up and were almost alone for a few seconds. Tessa looked at Tom and an amazing feeling came over her, not about Buffoon at all, but about Tom. She still didn't recognize it.

"Tom—"

But the people were converging, people as hysterical as herself, thousands of them. First she saw Wisbey, weeping copious tears of joy, then Peter, white as a sheet (her mother had fainted in the stands and Jimmy had nobly stayed to take care of her), the hulk of Mr Raleigh wreathed in smiles, her two schoolteachers waving madly, and thousands of men she had never seen reaching up to touch her, pat Buffoon, congratulate her. Tom kept by her side. He held her hand as the two horses walked back together, and the police horses closed round them both because Tom wouldn't let go. Two winners. But when they got to the winner's enclosure, then Tom let go and pulled Marimba up outside. Tessa stopped too.

But Tom said, "It's yours. Go on."

And Wisbey led Buffoon in, because Tessa wouldn't go.

When she had moved, Tom followed and pulled up in second place.

And when she slid and down and collapsed in Peter's arms, she had a strange vision of faces: besides Peter, and now her swooning mother held up by a grinning Jimmy, she saw her father Declan and her stepfather Maurice, not to mention all the well-known faces of the television people. And there was Buffoon, and – because it was her father who had made him – it was to her father she turned and held out her arms. He lifted her up and kissed her wildly. He smelled of whisky and sweat and manure, just like old times, and he laughed as she always remembered him laughing when she was three years old. Then he dropped her and kissed her mother, and her mother kissed him back and then kissed Peter, to be fair, and Jimmy kissed Tessa. And Tessa turned and buried her face into Buffoon's sweat-slimy neck – it was all too much for her to show the world. The television people couldn't, for once, get anyone's attention at all, until Peter remembered his profession and gave them a mumble.

Beside her in the enclosure Marimba stood head down, flanks heaving, the beaten favourite. Tom had his arm round his neck, grinning, and the little trainer was embracing them both, thrilled out of his wits by the horse's courage. The owner had no place in this picture, as he did not wish to join in the celebration of what he could only regard as defeat. His world had broken apart, after the certainty that he had won. He was finished.

Recognizing drama, part of their job, the television

interviewer turned to him, standing beside Marimba, and slyly asked, "How does it feel to be beaten by your stepdaughter?"

And, large on the television screen, across all the world, a close-up of Maurice showed what he thought. He didn't have to say it. He showed no joy at the fantastic courage of his own horse, no admiration for the skill of his jockey at getting so close, no warmth for the amazing scenes around him. He just showed, in close-up, all the bitterness of the bad loser. He showed consuming rage and hatred, and devastating humiliation. (Afterwards, on the video, Tessa played it over and over, more than the bit of her passing the winning post.)

He said, grinding it out, "She did well."

What else could he say?

With such an embarrassing response they turned to Myra. With her bright cheeks and blowing hair she chattered nineteen to the dozen to the bemused interviewer. She was their star. Peter was beyond words, and Jimmy never had many at the best of times. And Tessa . . . all she could do was hug her horse and cry.

"You've got to weigh in," Peter told her, smiling. "Don't lose it all by forgetting. You're a pro, remember."

Tessa pulled herself together.

Inside the door to the weighing room the press missed their picture of the day. Tom followed her in, caught her round the shoulders and kissed her on the lips. Mud, sweat and tears mingled like blood in a tryst. Tessa kissed him back, forgetting Buffoon.

"There's a saying," Tom said, "if you can't beat 'em, join 'em. Think about it."

"I love you, Tom."

"You love everyone, this minute. Say it tomorrow. And then I'll know."

"Yes, tomorrow too."

He laughed. The returning jockeys all jeered and cheered and they went to the scales and the loudspeaker announced to the world, "Weighed in."

It was over. Done.

And Buffoon?

Did he know he had won the Grand National?

He was tired beyond anything he had known before, having been asked for more when he had thought he had given his all. Yet, being asked, he had responded. He had found more, right at the end. He would have responded until death. It was in his nature. He had raced enough to know what they wanted, after all. To beat the others. Sometimes the others were impossibly far away and sometimes, on good days, they could be caught. But this time . . . it was so *far*, different. Even when he thought he had won a horse was still coming back at him and Tessa was still willing him on. Her spirit and intention he had understood only too clearly, even if her body was a hopeless floppy thing of little use to him. He would do it for Tessa, would do it for anybody, really, if that was what they wanted. They asked him. He obliged. He enjoyed it. But this time it had been painful, beyond the call of duty. There must be something special about this day, the excitement and the enormous crowd, the noise so intense, and now the attention, hugs and kisses more than anything he had known before. He knew he had been here before, he remembered how big the jumps were. This time he had been ready for them. He hadn't enjoyed it before, there had been something wrong, but today had been fine. Only the last stretch . . . that had been hard.

He wanted Lucky, and his stable. He wanted quiet, and his tea. He knew he would get all these things. He was secure, with the people he was used to. They asked him strange things sometimes, but they gave him everything he needed. He was not afraid.

Late the next day – she had lost all count of time – Tessa was in Sarah's caravan, telling her how it had been.

"My dad was there, Declan, yelling his head off. He's crazy, that man. I can see now why my mother left him."

"Yes. Not husband material, Declan Blackthorn."

"And Greevy, can you believe, wishing me luck. So civilized!"

"Working for Raleigh has done wonders for him. Getting away from his father, it gave him his chance. Mixing with nice people, it rubs off. I'm getting nicer by the day, have you noticed? Since I came here."

"And me!"

"It's the love of a good horse made something out of you,

Tessa. Loving Buffoon. It's what I need, the love of something, but God knows what, or who."

"Sarah!"

Sarah – Tessa's strength, her mother-figure, her shoulder to cry on – suddenly looked stricken. If Tessa didn't know her so well, she would have said she was suddenly close to tears.

Perhaps the shock showed in her face, for Sarah then laughed, harshly, and said, "I'm going away now summer's coming, and I shan't come back. I shall look for pastures new."

"Sarah! No!"

"There are reasons, Tessa. Use your loaf. You've found what you're looking for, but—" She shrugged. "I thought I had, but—" She shrugged again. Then laughed. "I'm not going to spell it out. You've eyes in your head and – at last – a heart. You'll understand, sooner or later."

With these engimatic words she closed the conversation by asking what they should cook for supper.

Later – a long time later – Tessa realized what she was talking about. Sarah loved Jimmy. And Jimmy? Jimmy was his own person. He only loved Walter, his lurcher.

After the supper – egg and chips – Tessa crept out to Buffoon's box. It was a clear spring night with stars crisp and glittering in the sky, cold, awash with the smells of spring and promise. Tessa, who had thought it was over, knew it was only just starting.

"Buffy?"

She slid the bolts back, and the horse turned round to her, knuckering softly. The journey home had passed in a dream, and only now she was back were Tessa's feet beginning to touch the ground. She hadn't been able to sleep, even now. She felt she could never sleep again, not while there was so much glory in her head. She wanted to be back, solid, on the ground. With Buffy. The smell of his warm rugs and Lucky's old-pony breath, the sound of horses munching hay in the night . . . she was soothed. She lay in the straw and stared at the starlit outline of Buffoon's back against the open half-door, and the patrician curve of his brave nose, the nose whereby the great race had been won. He had made it, against all the odds, made history, like the jockey said. She would never ask him for anything again, only make him happy, riding across the downs. He could retire, and she would go on, with Tom, wherever the path led.

And, at last, snuggled into the straw, she slept.

K. M. Peyton was born in 1929 and wrote her first book at the age of nine. It was called *Grey Star, the Story of a Racehorse*. Several books later, her first was published when she was fifteen. *Sabre, the Horse From the Sea* was followed by two more pony books written under her maiden name of Kathleen Herald. At first Kathleen only wrote pony books as, growing up in a London suburb, she could not have a horse of her own so put her pony-obsessed daydreams down on paper.

Winner of the prestigious Carnegie Medal and the Guardian Award, K. M. Peyton is the author of over fifty well-loved novels for young readers including the bestselling Flambards series.

K. M. Peyton lives in Essex with her husband Mike and her horses.

www.kmpeyton.co.uk

If you enjoyed

Blind Beauty

you'll love. . .

K. M. Peyton
Paradise House

"I have yet to meet a pony-lover who could resist K. M. Peyton's glorious books"

MEG ROSOFF

When Alice's pony bolts and crashes into a family of strangers, her life is changed forever.

Befriended by the family, her dreams come true when she is allowed to wander freely in their stable of racehorses. There she forms a special bond with one stallion – the beautiful, but dangerous, Snatchcorn.

But she soon learns that Snatchcorn's life is in danger. Can she find a way to save him before it's too late?